The Melted Pineapple

The Mason Braithwaite Paranormal Mystery Series, book 11

In this series:

Signs Point to Yes

The Desert Rats

Reach for the Sky

Billy Blood

Rubber-Band Ball

The Invisible Arrow

Penstock Canyon

The Man from Grapalia

The Mythical Blond

Stealth Glasses

The Melted Pineapple

Night on the Water

The Landers Mystique

DAGMARMIURA.COM

Praise for the series:

Mason is a hero like none who have come before him: a sensitive, queer P.I. whose only weapon is his intuition. This book turns the detective genre on its head and makes you think about the ninety percent of your brain you're not using.
—Teja Watson, author of *Attic.doc*

Every foray by Church's wonderful psychic detective Mason Braithwaite is a truly suspenseful page-turner in the most unusual crime series ever, and certainly one that no aficionado of crime fiction should miss.
—David Osborn, author of the best-selling thrillers *The French Decision* and *Love and Treason*

Thanks to Christopher Church for giving us another exciting and well written adventure with one of my new heroes.
—Amos Lassen

Another fast-paced ride through Los Angeles by Church, who continues to reinvent and reinvigorate Mason Braithwaite. Church's writing is vivid, the worlds he creates believable, and his characters have a breadth of humanity, strength, and vulnerability that makes the series a fun-filled, page-turning adventure.
—Jeremy Randolph, author of *The Mural*

The Melted Pineapple

The
Melted
Pineapple

Christopher Church

DAGMAR
MIURA
LOS ANGELES

Published by Dagmar Miura
Los Angeles
www.dagmarmiura.com

The Melted Pineapple

First published 2020

ISBN: 978-1-951130-19-0

He was too new in this place even to get mail, Mason thought, opening his mailbox in the little postal alcove only to find it empty. His office upstairs was starting to shape up, now that he'd moved in his desk and his bookcases, but there was still a lot of open floor in the spare modern space. Someone came in behind him, and he turned to look once he'd twisted the little key to close the box again. It was a woman, in her forties, her dark hair pulled back. She had her keys in hand.

"Hey, 1020," she said cheerfully, gesturing to his mailbox. "I'm in 920, right downstairs from you. Are you new?"

"I just moved my furniture in this week," Mason said. "I love this building."

"Keep the windows closed," she said with a wry smile, pulling a sheaf of paper out of her box and snapping it shut. "The air quality is really bad downtown."

"Good to know," he said, and introduced himself.

"I'm Teresa," she said, tucking her mail into her handbag. "Did you happen to notice the missing space in your office?"

He frowned. "What do you mean, 'missing'?"

"If your office has the same floor plan as mine, the restroom is shorter than the main room. There's some serious missing space behind it."

"Huh," Mason said, eyeing her more closely. She was being serious. "My shrink is one floor above me in the same unit, and her layout is identical to mine. So it's probably the same as yours."

"Come on up, and I'll show you. Are you on your way in?"

"I'm actually on my way out," he said, grinning at her, "but I can spare a minute for a mystery."

He followed her to the elevator, dropping his keys in his pants pocket and standing as far away from her in the car as he could. Besides the fact that he towered over her and most other people, which made him physically intimidating whether he wanted to be or not, there was a good chance he smelled ripe, after working up a sweat arranging his office furniture.

"You look like you've been doing manual labor," Teresa said, as if reading his mind. "You're flushed."

"That's just the red-headed thing," Mason said, absently adjusting his backpack straps in his sweaty armpits. "No pigment to hide the blood flow."

She chuckled. "You said your shrink was in 1120— it's convenient to have her right upstairs. Is that a coincidence, or did you pick her based on proximity?"

"There are no coincidences," Mason said, following her off the elevator. "I've been seeing her for quite a while, and I picked my office because I loved hers so much."

What he didn't explain was that he was able to afford such a glammy office space because his rent was indefinitely set at zero—he'd done a favor for the building's owners, posing as the CEO of their holding company. It probably wasn't fraud, he told himself, feeling the familiar pang of concern at the memory. They'd had Mason use a pseudonym and sign documents on behalf of the company when they'd purchased the building because the pair of them were so young, and they didn't want that to raise suspicion. Mason didn't know all the details of how two teenagers had acquired the funds to buy a whole office building, but he knew it was shady enough that they were wise to avoid attracting attention. Since that day he'd woken up in a cold sweat more than once, feeling panicky at being complicit in the subterfuge, but he was getting used to the idea, and so far there hadn't been any fallout.

Teresa twisted her key in the lock to suite 920 and pushed open the door. Mason could see right away that the floor plan was identical to his. This space was a lot more crowded, though—work tables laden with fabric and stacks of garments in various stages of assembly. A dark-haired woman worked intently at a sewing machine, calling out a greeting but not looking up at them as they came in.

It seemed odd that Teresa was running a factory here, as the fashion district was several blocks south, and the vibe of this building was unequivocally white-collar. But only part of the space was for manufacturing—at the back were a couple of desks, and near the entrance were some stylish lounge chairs and a glass-topped coffee table. Teresa must be using it as her office and her showroom as well.

The way she'd used the tall windows was clueless, he thought—they were ignored, just a thing to walk past. Upstairs in his space those beautiful windows were the focus, with his sofa and lounge chairs right under them, his desk facing them.

"What kind of business do you run here?" he asked.

"It's a fashion line," she said, setting her handbag on a worktable.

"Cool," he said, looking around. "Women's wear?"

"For dogs," she said, meeting his eye. "Urban streetwear and sportswear. Things like hoodies, yoga clothes, even skiwear."

He grinned. "How fun is that? Too bad I don't have a dog."

Teresa walked over to the restroom door. "Look inside and focus on the back wall," she said, "and think about how far it is from the doorway. Then step back into the main room and look in the same direction toward the same wall."

Standing on the threshold of the small room, he clicked on the light. It was the same as his, in real-estate parlance a three-quarter bath, with a sink and toilet and a shower stall. He focused on the distance to the back wall, and then stepped out and stepped sideways to look toward the windows in the larger office, as she'd instructed. She was right—the difference was evident. Why hadn't he noticed that in his own space?

"It's shorter," he said. "A lot."

"I haven't measured it, but it looks like maybe ten feet."

"That sounds right."

"The restroom is ten feet wide, so the missing space behind it is about ten by ten square."

Mason glanced into the restroom again, then stepped out and looked past its door. The far side of it was an exterior wall as well, he realized, because there was a window on that side too, farther along in the suite's storage alcove.

"That's an outside wall," he said, and gestured to the window. "That means the missing space isn't part of another unit. Two sides are in your unit, and the other two sides are air."

She nodded emphatically. "A hundred feet above the street."

"I wonder what it looks like from outside?"

"I thought of that too. When you look at the building from across the street, it's just blank terra-cotta tile. There aren't any windows or anything near the corner, just the ones you can see from inside."

Moving back toward her desk, he stopped when he could see into the restroom and see the tall windows in the adjacent wall at the same time. It was unmistakable from this vantage point—a whole corner of the suite was walled off, and the placement of the restroom effectively concealed it.

He grinned at her. "That's quite a mystery."

"I wondered if it was maybe a stairwell, or a private elevator for the penthouse, or even a 1930s dumbwaiter that no one uses anymore."

"I know the landlords," Mason said. "They live on the top floor. I can ask them."

"Nice," she said, raising her eyebrows. "I've only ever dealt with that woman in the management office, and she's clueless. Do you have a phone number? Maybe we could ask now."

"Sure." Pulling out his cell phone, Mason found Owen's number and waited while it rang.

"Hey, bud," Owen answered. "I'm on my way to class—what can I do for you?"

"I have some questions about the building, but only if you've got a minute."

"Tomorrow's Saturday, so I'll be home," he said. "Can we meet then?"

Mason ended the call and said to Teresa, "He's busy. I'll get into it with him on the weekend."

Teresa stepped over to her desk and grabbed a business card out of a little tray, handing it to Mason. It was embossed with her name and number, a paw-print logo, and CANINE HAUTE COUTURE. "Let me know what you find out."

"Thanks," he said, slipping it into his pocket. "I will." Slipping his backpack off one shoulder, he pulled out one of his own business cards and handed it to her.

"Psychic investigator," she said, glancing at it, then laughed. "How wacky is that? You have to love LA."

Mason could feel his face redden, but said goodbye affably and headed for the door. What he did for a living was certainly no wackier than skiwear for dogs. One thing she was right about, though, was that neither one of them was bucking the popular stereotypes of Los Angeles's ethereal culture.

Walking through the lobby, he said good night to the security guard at the desk and made his way across the street to the metro, trotting down the stairs into the earth. He was tired, and his muscles were aching from shoving furniture around, so he was happy to find a place to sit even though it was rush hour. At the station near home he reemerged into the fading daylight and unlocked his bicycle, pedaling up into his hilly neighborhood. The last few blocks were up a sharp incline, and even in the chilly fall air he had worked up a sweat by the time he got to the house he shared with Ned and Peggy.

When he heard Mason come in, Ned came up the hallway from his office to kiss him hello. Mason was always happy to come home to this guy, so effortlessly suave and polished, even when he didn't have to be, his jet-black hair natty no matter what he did to it. He was dressed for a day working at home, in a dark polo shirt and jeans.

"You look wiped out," Ned said, stepping back.

"I've been moving furniture. Things are shaping up."

"Great news," Ned said. "So I'm thinking couscous and veggies for dinner. It's kind of boring."

"Not to me. I can't wait," Mason said, pulling off his backpack.

"It'll be an hour or so," Ned said, and headed for the kitchen.

Mason went down the hall to their bedroom and heard the voice of their roommate, Peggy, as he passed her door. She must be on a phone call. After he stripped off his sweaty clothes, he got in the shower, then put on clean pants and a T-shirt and stretched out on the bed.

Ned woke him sometime later. "Ready for couscous? Peggy made a killer salad too."

"I wouldn't want to miss that," Mason said, and sat up, willing himself into lucidity. He knew he had it good—between Ned and Peggy, both enthusiastic vegan cooks, he ate well.

When he came down the hall, Ned was passing bowls across the counter that separated the kitchen from the main room, and Peggy was lifting them over to the dining table. He sat with them and tucked in, and as always, it was delicious.

"I love the way you spiced this," Peggy said, sampling the veggies. "You'll have to explain the process for me."

She'd recently taken a teaching job, and it agreed with her a lot more than her previous days of toil in a stuffy law office. Teaching music meant she was engaging with her true passion. Mason could see it in her now, her expression content, her wiry frame relaxed, her long hair tied casually behind her head.

"How's the decorating going?" she asked him.

"My little desk and bookcases are dwarfed in all that space. I bought a sofa and chairs at the thrift store to help, but I still need more furniture. The sofa is plaid, and I thought it might make it look like a suburban rec room, but it's fine—I put it under the windows."

"I like the rec room theme," Peggy said. "You should get a pool table."

He scoffed. "That wouldn't really project an appropriate degree of professionalism."

"Do psychics really have professional standards?" Ned asked, waving his fork.

Mason shot him a look. "Wait till I get that place

whipped into shape. It's going to blow your mind."

Ned chuckled as he reached for his salad.

"I met my downstairs neighbor today," Mason said. "She pointed out something weird. The corner of our offices is missing."

"Missing how?" Peggy asked, frowning.

He explained what Teresa had shown him, the walled-off square in the corner.

"Ten by ten is too big to be a support column, or even a utility shaft," Ned said. "There's something else in there."

"Teresa thought maybe a disused dumbwaiter."

Ned shook his head. "The whole building was renovated recently, right? They would have taken out stuff like that."

"Well, hopefully Owen will know," Mason said. "I'm meeting him tomorrow."

"I had him in a class today," Peggy said. "He's getting really good on guitar. He must be practicing a lot."

She and Owen had both wound up at the same creative arts high school through a client of Mason's and a couple of convoluted twists.

"I love that you're teaching," Mason said. "You're so much lighter these days."

"It's true," Ned agreed, looking at her. "Lighter and brighter and happier."

Peggy laughed. "I'm glad you can see it, because I'm definitely feeling it."

After they'd eaten, Mason helped clean up and then sat cross-legged on the sofa with his computer. He'd never really read anything about the Primavera Building, where his office was, although he knew it had been completed in the late 1920s. Every time he came up out of the metro and walked toward it, he admired the soaring art deco design and the orange-tinted tile. From working with Owen and Sweet Marie when they bought it, he knew it had been commissioned by the long-defunct Cudahy Mutual Insurance Company.

Someone had created a page with an outline of the company's history, but it focused on the founders and the executives, only briefly mentioning the building. An architectural conservancy group had a brief write-up that outlined the history of the structure, and he scrolled through it, reading about its inception and its completion on the eve of the Great Depression. The architect, Augustus Hawley, wasn't a big name, but he had designed a slew of houses and lesser commercial structures, including another deco tower in Chicago. He was described as "eccentric," but nothing Mason could see in the images of his work reflected that—the buildings were elegant, timeless, pleasing to look at.

There were a couple of black-and-white photos from the Primavera Building's opening in 1929, and several in garish color from the 1970s, when a bank took over the space for its offices. It was an unfortunate time for interior design, he thought, scrolling through images depicting boxy fluorescent lighting, busy burnt-orange patterned carpets, and furniture upholstered in shades of brown and avocado. His new thrift-store sofa wouldn't look out of place in this landscape, he realized. That was a depressing thought.

Most intriguing were the before-and-after photos of

several of the offices taken just a few years ago when the building had been extensively renovated. The lobby and the facades had been restored to their art deco glamour, but the aging interiors had been gutted and extensively reworked into modern and spare open spaces, with exposed concrete and few modern additions apart from the lighting, the restrooms, and based on these photos, kitchen appliances in some of the other suites.

None of the photos were of the offices in Mason's and Teresa's corner of the building, and no mention was made of the missing space. After he dug around on the Web a little longer, finding only tangential references to the building and no substance, he folded his laptop closed, and arched his back in a long stretch.

Ned was already in bed, reading a novel by the light of his bedside lamp. Mason undressed and climbed in beside him, snuggling up close and enjoying Ned's body heat. Ned shifted position, leaning into him, and they stayed that way as Mason drifted into the hypnagogic state.

He found himself at the edge of a cliff, and he inhaled sharply when he looked down into the abyss. It was daytime, at least. Maybe he was in the Rockies, based on the blue-gray light; it definitely wasn't the Sierras. There were steps here, hewn from the rocky gray face of the cliff. He knew he had to head down, and took a first tentative step. As he descended he saw that the stairs zigzagged farther downward, disappearing from view. Eventually he lost the scene, drifter deeper into sleep, not bothering to stir himself awake to write it down.

❧

Waking early, at least for him, Mason slapped off the alarm on his phone and forced himself to sit up, blinking sleep out of his eyes. When he went out to the living room Ned was sitting on one of the stools at the kitchen counter with his phone.

"Did you have breakfast?" Mason asked him.

Ned grinned. "Hours ago."

"Peggy's out?"

"Also hours ago."

"Morning people," Mason muttered, and got the espresso machine working, dumping the whole little pot into a mug, then sat at the counter with Ned, sipping the life-giving nectar and munching on muesli.

Eventually enough caffeine was flowing for him to function in the world, and he pulled on his backpack, kissed Ned good-bye, and cycled down the hill in the brisk air. He locked up his bike at the station and rode the train downtown.

In his office he assessed the space with fresh eyes and decided the bookcases were indeed in the right place, back against the far wall, and so was the desk. Walking over to the restroom, he stood at the doorway and looked to the back. The room was exactly the same as Teresa's, right down to the subway tile around the sink, the back wall hiding an equal volume of missing space. He checked the time on his phone and then went out again, locking his office door and walking out to the stairwell next to the elevators. Climbing up two stairs at a time, he was quickly at Miss Cassie's door, where the sign read COME IN. He slid it across to read PLEASE KNOCK, and then twisted the handle and went in.

"Mason," she said, looking up from her desk. "Right on time."

He greeted her and took his usual chair over by the tall windows, and she joined him, sitting on the adjacent sofa. Miss Cassie had some weight on her frame, which wasn't unusual for her age, probably pushing sixty. She kept her African hair ironed flat and styled upscale, and always wore sharply tailored suits, today in burgundy with a floral scarf accenting it. Mason had met her when he'd done some work at her church in South LA, where he'd built a rapport with Miss Cassie, and afterward she'd cajoled him into becoming her client.

"How are things going?" she asked, folding open her tablet and swiping through her notes.

"I have to say life's pretty good. I moved into a new office."

She looked up at him, not masking her surprise. "I'm glad you're doing well enough financially to rent commercial space. Are you going to use it for meeting clients?"

"I don't really need it for that, or for any reason, really. After you let me use this office when you were away, I wanted something similar, a place just for work."

Miss Cassie glanced around the room. "This is a lovely space. I'm glad you enjoyed it."

"Mine is almost the same, but with crummier furniture. I'm in the suite right below this."

"What?" she demanded, her voice rising. "In this building? You're going to be my neighbor?"

"When I was using your office I met the new landlord, and some of the units were empty. We struck a deal."

"I thought the new owner was a corporation," she said. "I met one of their employees, a young man named Sweet Marie."

"I know him. He's a nice kid." Mason smiled. "I won't have far to commute for our sessions."

"I'll say," she said, her tone still sharp, concern in her eyes. "Have we ever talked about boundaries?"

"I don't remember." Mason sat up, leaning toward her. "Listen, did you ever notice the missing space behind the restroom?"

"What are you talking about?"

"I'll show you," he said, and jumped to his feet.

Miss Cassie followed him over to the restroom doorway, and he pointed out the discrepancy in the depth of the room.

"I never noticed that," she said, stepping between the two vantage points for another look. She pursed her lips. "You certainly have an eye for detail."

"Actually I totally missed it too," he said as they sat down again. "The woman in 920 with the dog-wear company pointed it out. Strange, right?"

Calmer now, Miss Cassie looked at him thoughtfully. "It must be for water pipes and electricity."

"It's at least ten feet square—doesn't that seem like too much space for utilities? I'm going to look into it, though."

"I'm sure it's more straightforward than your paranormal mysteries," she said, and shifted the conversation to his regular shrink work. Halfway through their fifty-minute hour, Mason pulled his notepad out of his backpack to make some notes, and soon enough Miss Cassie glanced pointedly at the clock to wrap things up.

"Always a pleasure, Mason," she said, rising and walking him to the door. "See you next time."

"You might see me before that, since we share the building," he said as he left.

Downstairs, he found a guy squatting in front of his office door, stirring a little paint can with a stick. Newspaper was laid out to cover the floor, and a toolbox sat open against the wall. As he approached, Mason got a whiff of strong chemicals, solvent or adhesive or both. On the door were the beginnings of his name, just MASON so far, in mustard-yellow raised lettering.

"It looks great," Mason said, admiring it. "It really pops against the black."

Glancing at the keys in Mason's hand, the guy nodded at the door. "You must be Mason."

"Rodrigo, right?" Mason said. "Thanks for coming. I love the color, but is there any chance the letters will fall off?"

"Not unless you hit them with a hammer," he said, still stirring the redolent contents of the little can. "This glue will still be here after the sun goes nova."

"I'll make a point of not hammering on them, then. Listen, I might have to leave again soon, but can you invoice me for what I owe you once you're finished?"

Rodrigo grinned. "I'll glue it to your door."

Mason twisted his key in the lock and pushed inside, letting Rodrigo close the door again, then dropped his backpack on the sofa, looking to the corner with the missing space. It was hard not to focus on it, now that he knew it was there. His desk was definitely positioned better than Miss Cassie's, facing the windows rather than the door. He dropped into his desk chair and eyed the empty floor space. On the other hand, her stylish setup probably cost ten times what his furniture had.

He indulged himself a moment of gazing out at the towers of the Financial District, then fished in his pants pocket for his phone, thumb-typing a text to Owen:

I'm in my office. Can you drop by?

His reply came just a moment later:

Headed down now.

Another message popped up before he could put his phone away, from Peggy:

Driving past your office very soon. Are you there?

He wrote back,

Come on up.

A knock on the door roused Mason from his thoughts, and he got up to open it for Owen, who stepped past Rodrigo, mumbling an apology. Mason had to smile at the sight of him—the kid looked great compared to when they had first met, when Owen had been on the verge of homelessness, holed up in a friend's seedy apartment. Today dressed in trendy green jeans and a raucous band T-shirt, his thick African hair was pulled back, unkempt but chic. Clearly he'd spent some money on it.

Owen gave Mason a little hug and said, "I love your name on the door—it's so bold."

"Fun, right?" Mason said. "So how's life in the penthouse?"

"Sweet—I wish I had more time to hang out there. I'm at school a lot."

"That seems appropriate," Mason said flatly, "seeing as you're sixteen."

There was a knock at the door, and Mason stepped over to open it for Peggy.

"So many visitors for a Saturday," Rodrigo said pointedly.

"Excuse me," Peggy said, stepping past him. She was wearing jeans and a gray sweater, and her comfortable tennis shoes.

"Hey, teacher," Owen said.

"You do not get to call me that after hours."

Owen grinned and raised his hands in mock surrender.

"I thought I'd check out how your decorating was going," she said, looking around at the office. "You're right—you need more furniture."

"I'm going to get an espresso machine," Mason said, "so I don't have to keep running downstairs to the coffee joint, and a portable bar, because that's just cool. But neither one is going to take up much space."

"Recently," Peggy said, looking at Owen and taking on the authoritative tone of the teacher, "Ned and I have characterized Mason's life with a phrase that sums it up succinctly: the perpetual whirl of confusion." She looked to Mason. "In that vein, perhaps this place needs a merry-go-round. There's definitely enough room."

"What a brilliant idea," Mason said, with mock amazement. "Thanks for that."

"You'll figure it out," Owen said. "I can give you my decorator's number if you need help."

Peggy grinned. "You're the only teenager I've ever met who has his own decorator."

"A friend once told me not to be afraid to ask for help," he said, eyeing Mason. "Our pad definitely needed a professional."

"I was just about to show Owen something odd," Mason said, clapping his hands. "Did you notice the missing space in these offices? It's the same in mine, and in Miss Cassie's on 11, and the couture woman downstairs."

"What are you talking about?" Owen said.

Mason led them to the restroom door. "Look at the back wall, and then look into the main room toward the windows."

Owen and Peggy both did, taking turns.

"Do you see it?" Mason asked.

"That's so strange," Peggy said. She stepped sideways to look into the restroom again, and put her hands on her hips.

Owen stared at the windows, lost in thought. "That's an outside wall," he said finally, and turned, looking past the restroom. "So is that one. Your unit completely surrounds that corner. It's a huge amount of space."

"Ten by ten, at least," Mason said.

"So what's in there?" Owen asked.

Mason threw up his hands. "As the owner of the building, I thought you might know."

"It's not just your unit," Owen said, stepping back to the restroom door to look again. "Floors 2 through 11 are all identical."

"Do you have blueprints for the building?" Peggy asked.

"You mean floor plans," Owen said, his tone brightening. "The last owners did a gut renovation a few years ago, and there are big sheets with a layout for each floor. They're in the management office."

She waved an arm. "Let's go look."

Mason led them to the door, knocking on it before gingerly pulling it open. "Coming out," he said.

"Excuse us," Owen said as they slipped by.

Rodrigo responded with a resigned "It's OK."

They rode the elevator to the second floor and followed Owen to the management office. The door was closed, probably because it was Saturday; Mason had always found it propped open during office hours. Owen dug in his pants pocket for his keys, then unlocked it, and they followed him inside, waiting as he pulled open the high cupboards at the back, one by one, until he found a thick poster tube. Pulling out the roll of oversize sheets, Mason and Peggy helped spread them out on one of the desks in the crowded space.

They weren't blue, despite the name Peggy had used, just plain black ink on white paper. Mason put a stapler on one corner of the top sheet to keep it from rolling up on itself, and held the other side down with his palm. The sheet was marked 9TH, and the three of them stared at the jumble of lines.

"This is the dog-clothes woman's floor," Owen said, "but where exactly is her office? There are nine suites on those floors."

"Dog clothes?" Peggy asked, raising an eyebrow.

"Her name is Teresa," Mason said. "She's the one who pointed out the discrepancy in the restroom wall. Her company makes couture for dogs."

"Such a great idea," Peggy said. "Dogs are all different sizes. There's way more variation than with people, so couture is a perfect solution."

"Here," Mason said, pointing to the drawing. He cocked his head. "Those are the elevators, don't you think? Three heavy boxes right beside the stairwell. So 920 is down the hall and right." He traced the familiar route with his finger, and the drawing started to make sense. "Here's her office door …"

"That's right," Owen exclaimed, and pointed to a crowded part of the image. "And here's her restroom—sink, toilet, shower stall, they're all there."

When Owen pulled his finger away, Mason saw it—and he knew Peggy and Owen did too, as they stood there in silence, staring at it the same way he was. Behind the restroom, in the corner of the building, was a perfectly square space, blank white paper, with nothing drawn inside it.

Mason finally spoke. "It looks like it has solid walls on all four sides."

"How can you tell?" Peggy asked.

"These are the windows in the office. See how they're shown as thinner sections of the wall? And the office door is just a blank space. The missing void has nothing like that, just four solid walls."

"Is it the same on every floor?" she asked.

Owen rolled the top sheet aside, revealing the one below. It looked identical, as did all the others, until they got to the ground floor.

"This is the coffeehouse," Owen said, pointing out the long open space at the side of the drawing.

"But the void is the same," Peggy said. "Solid walls, and nothing inside it."

"There's nothing drawn on the floor plan," Mason said, meeting her eye, "but that doesn't mean there's nothing in there."

"So what the hell is it?" Peggy demanded.

Mason laughed. "Can I take some photos?"

"Fine by me," Owen said, and set a coffee cup on the corner of the drawing he'd been holding, then stepped back.

Mason pulled out his phone and snapped a photo of the relevant corner of the ground floor, and the legend at the side of the page, then rolled out the sheet labeled 3RD and photographed it too.

"What about the top floor?" Mason said. "We didn't see a sheet for that."

"Huh," Owen said, and stepped back to the table, thumbing through the sheets and peeling them aside. "Here," he said finally, and pulled it out, with Peggy's help awkwardly setting it on top of the others.

Peggy smoothed out the paper, and Mason saw it was labeled 12TH. There were far fewer boxes and lines on this sheet, just the outer walls and a few interior rooms near the elevators, but most of the space was open, dotted only with little black squares.

"What are those?" Peggy asked, pointing to one.

"They must be the columns," Owen said. "I guess that's what holds the roof up."

In the corner the void was drawn the same way, a square empty space with solid walls around it.

"There's no restroom," Peggy said. Where the plumbing had been depicted on the lower floors was empty space on this sheet.

"The penthouse has a full bathroom, over here," Owen said, pointing to the other side of the building. "It's bigger, right, because it's residential."

It was much bigger, Mason thought, looking at the drawing, and there was also a smaller half bath closer to the elevators.

"But what's this?" Mason asked, frowning and pointing to an empty box adjacent to the void, on the other side of it from where the restrooms were on the lower floors. It was a long room, with an opening for a door indicated at the end.

"It's bigger than the restroom on Mason's floor," Peggy said.

"There's no plumbing, though," Mason said. "On the other floors you could see the sink and all that."

"I know what it is," Owen said quietly.

"You mean the missing space?" Mason said, feeling his heart start to pound.

"No—the room next to it."

Peggy stared at him, and gestured impatiently.

"You should come up and see."

Owen quickly rolled up the floor plans and slid them back into their tube, putting it back into the cabinet and then locking the office door as they left. In the elevator Mason pressed the button labeled 12, positioned on its own above the double row of numbers for the other floors. When the doors opened, the lobby looked different than the ones below, and it took Mason a second to figure out why: there was no hallway, just a foyer with several doors spaced far apart. A little table opposite the elevators sat below a framed mirror and bore a potted fern, giving the space a bland innocuous vibe, like a hotel.

Owen unlocked the door closest to the elevators and pushed inside, and when Mason stepped in he couldn't help but exclaim "Wow." The penthouse occupied the entire floor, one vast room with windows on three sides, the view broken only by the structural columns.

"This is stunning, Owen," Peggy said, taking it in.

"Thanks."

"It really is," Mason said. "I can see why you hired a decorator."

"We had to. It would have taken us a year to figure out the furniture by ourselves."

"There's so much space," Peggy said. "You almost want to put up walls."

"We talked about that. Right now we have a bunch of zones. This is the living zone," he said, gesturing to a pair of sofas positioned to face each other across a rug and a low table, with armchairs at either end, "and the work zone," which had a couple of desks. Gesturing to the distant bed, he said, "and that's the action center."

Peggy scoffed.

"Where is Sweet Marie?" Mason asked.

"With his family in Santa Barbara. I'm driving up there later today."

Mason suppressed the urge to ask, "You can drive?" and said instead, "I'm glad he's reconnecting with them."

"This is the same view as from Mason's office," Peggy said, moving toward the windows.

Owen followed her, and gestured to a foosball table in the corner. "And this is where the restroom would be in your unit."

"So this is the room we saw in the blueprint," Mason said, facing a set of louvered folding doors.

Owen pulled them open, clicked on the lights, and stood aside. "Our closet."

"Appropriately huge, like everything up here," Peggy said, folding her arms.

Mason looked into the closet, then stepped aside to look toward the foosball table. "It's the same thing as with the restrooms on the lower floors. The back wall is way too close."

"The blueprint showed the same void in the corner," Peggy said. "It's just configured differently."

"There's more," Owen said, grinning at them. "You're going to love this."

He stepped into the closet and went to the back. Peggy followed him in, then Mason.

"There certainly are a lot of girl clothes in here," Peggy said.

"Sweet Marie does drag," Owen said, and picked up the Japanese paper screen that covered the middle of the back wall, folding it closed and setting it aside. In the wall was a midnight-blue door in a heavy frame, with an arching banner across the top in gold lettering that read MONTCLAIR SECURITY. It was a safe, and judging by the timeworn handle and the numbered dial, it was as old as the building itself.

"It's huge," Peggy said.

Indeed, Mason thought, he would barely have to duck to step inside.

"I was told it was too heavy to remove, so during the renovation they just drywalled around it," Owen said.

"I'm glad they didn't board it over," Mason said. "It's beautiful. Look at this." He ran his fingers over a lattice decoration at eye level, random curves and lines in the same gold paint as the manufacturer's banner above it. The door was cool to the touch, metallic and glossy.

"Can we get into it?" Peggy asked impatiently.

"In the paperwork they said the combination had been lost."

Mason stepped back, folding his arms. "I don't think it's real."

"It seems pretty real to me," Owen said, and twisted the numbered dial. It clicked softly as it spun, clearly connected to an internal mechanism. He heaved on the heavy brass handle. It didn't budge, but from deep inside the door came the muted sound of steel banging up against steel.

"Sure," Mason said, "but it has no depth. The distance to the outside wall doesn't look any deeper than in the other units. Look at the floor plan."

He pulled out his phone and found the right photo, handing it to Owen. Peggy crowded next to him, looking at the screen over his shoulder.

"This shows the back of the closet sharing a wall with the void," Peggy said. "There's no room for a safe between them."

"Maybe it's a really shallow safe," Owen said, handing the phone back to Mason.

"Do you have a measuring tape?" Peggy asked him. Owen shook his head. "Not here. Maybe the valet?"

"There's one in my office," Mason said.

"I'll go—I have to pee anyway, and it's more polite to use yours. Keys," she said, and waggled her fingers, and once he'd handed them over, walked toward the front door.

"It's in my bottom desk drawer," he called after her.

Owen followed her out of the closet.

"So how is life with Sweet Marie?" Mason asked, gazing around the vast penthouse again.

"He's flourishing with the breathing room that our trust fund allows."

"I remember where you were living before," Mason said. "Things have changed dramatically."

"He finished his college courses this summer, and now he's spending a lot of time with the manager, helping her run the building."

"What's the couple part like? It seems like you're pretty committed. Do you fight, or is it all roses and sunshine?"

Owen grinned. "Things get shouty once in a while, but mostly it's pretty great. I think sharing this whole experience of sudden wealth has made us closer."

"What about work? Is there a career path in the future for either of you?"

"I think we're just going to be landlords, and pursue our interests—my music, and his performance. So far, running the building hasn't been that difficult." He nodded to the windows on the other side of the apartment, beyond another island of living room furniture corralled in a clump. "You should check out the patio."

They walked over to the glass and out through a set of French doors. The wide space was sheltered from the wind and had a couple of chaise longues and a table, but most compelling was the height, made more dramatic because the floor ended with no interruption, a precipice protected only by a metal railing atop a clear glass barrier. That had to be part of the renovation, Mason realized, as it was made of shiny modern chrome and glass panels. In the 1920s they would have built a sturdy stone wall for a space like this, which would have made it a lot less breathtaking. Different from Mason's windows, the view here was out over the Historic Core and its comparatively low-rise skyscrapers.

"You have to have a party out here," Mason said, leaning gingerly on the railing, "and you have to invite me."

Peggy's voice echoed faintly inside, calling their names, and they went back in to find her at the closet.

"I measured the back wall of Mason's restroom," she said. "It's exactly ten feet wide. That means the void on the blueprints has to be ten feet square."

"Good thinking," Owen said.

"Let's measure the safe," Mason said.

He followed Peggy into the closet and held the end of the tape while she stretched it along the back wall, draping it across the safe door and shoving a rack of shirts out of the way to reach the side wall.

"About ten feet," Peggy announced, "just as we

expected. Now how do we measure the depth of the safe?"

"Measure from the closet door to the safe door, and then measure from the closet door to the outside wall," Mason said. "The difference between them is the size of the safe and the void together."

The pair of them measured the depth of the closet, with Owen watching from the doorway. On the outside, Mason carried the end of the tape past the foosball table to the outside wall, and Peggy pulled it taut, studying her end.

"Twenty-eight feet, seven inches," she said.

Owen frowned. "You said the closet was exactly eighteen feet long. That means if the void is ten feet, the safe is only seven inches deep."

"Should we measure again?" Peggy asked.

"It's not a mistake," Mason said, walking back to them with the end of the tape. "It's not really a safe."

"So what is it?" Peggy said, eyeing him and letting the metal ribbon wind itself into its case.

"I think maybe it's a door into the void."

"Maybe the void is a safe," Owen said. "A walk-in safe, like in a bank."

"A vault," Peggy offered.

"Exactly," he said. "Maybe in the beginning every floor had a vault."

Mason shook his head. "I don't think so. I did some reading about this building, and it was commissioned to be an insurance company's offices. They wouldn't have anything of value except paperwork. There wouldn't have been any need for a massive walk-in vault on every floor—just one for the boss, or maybe for the people who handled the money."

"Are there vault doors on any of the other floors?" Peggy asked.

"No," Owen said, "but maybe they got walled up in the renovation."

"It's an interesting idea," Peggy said. "A vault on every floor would explain why there's a void on every floor. I wish we could look. I know I saw the blueprints, but I kind of want to see the other floors for myself."

"We can," Owen said. "I have keys to everything, and most of the tenants won't be around—it's Saturday."

"That seems kind of unscrupulous," Mason said.

"Dude, we're not going to touch their stuff," Owen said. "We're just going to look at their walls."

"May I cast the deciding vote?" Peggy said. "I say we do it."

They both looked at Mason. He laughed and said, "Lead on."

Owen headed out to the elevators, pausing to lock his front door.

On the ride down, Mason said, "We can probably skip my office, as you've both seen it, and I was in Miss Cassie's this morning. I saw Teresa's on 9 yesterday too, and all three are identical."

"We can start on 2," Owen said, and they followed him off the elevator. He went into the management office again, and said to Peggy and Mason, "I'll be right back." He reemerged a moment later with a big ring of keys, and headed down the hall toward the office that corresponded to Mason's.

"I think these guys do some kind of IT thing," he said, rapping sharply on the door beside the plaque labeled 220. He knocked again and said, "Management," then waited for a moment, listening, before he found the right key and opened the door.

The interior was flashy, with matching black furniture in discrete carpeted areas, a long conference table, and desks laden with multiple video screens.

"They have art on the walls," Mason said quietly, even though there was no one to overhear them. "I never thought of that."

"It's a big room. You need big art," Peggy said, then added emphatically, "and you can't buy it at the thrift store."

Mason followed Owen to the doorway into the restroom.

"The layout is identical to yours, wouldn't you say?" Owen said.

"The size looks the same," Mason said. "I don't have a wicker tray with individual hand towels, though. That's so fancy."

Owen locked the door after them and pulled his phone out of his pants. "I have a phone number for 320," he said. "I'll see whether they're around."

They waited in the elevator lobby, the sound of ringing faintly audible from Owen's phone, but no one picked up. He led them up the stairs to the office door and knocked again, listing for movement within, and then unlocked it and pushed in.

"It's so interesting how everyone treats the same space so differently," Peggy said. Here there were four desks shoved up against the windowsill, facing outward, with a row of cabinets a few feet behind.

Again the restroom looked the same, although it

could use a cleaning, Mason thought.

"420 is vacant," Owen said as they trooped up the stairs, and he unlocked the door to the suite.

"It looks like your office did a week ago," Peggy said.

She was right, Mason thought, looking around the space. It seemed larger without any furniture in it. The restroom and the walls were exactly the same as in all the others, and once they were in the elevator lobby again, Owen phoned the tenant in 520.

"Hey," he said, sounding surprised that someone had answered. "Can I come in and have a quick look at your plumbing? I just need to check on something."

Peggy and Mason followed Owen up the stairs but waited in the elevator lobby while he went into the office.

When he returned a minute later, he shrugged and said, "Same damn thing."

The last three were no different, and by the time they walked out of 820, Mason was dizzy.

"That's all of them," Mason said. "Nothing different on any floor."

"We're not going into the dog couture office?" Peggy frowned. "I wanted to see what dog couture looks like."

"Her missing space is the same as mine," Mason said.

"What about the coffee place on the ground floor?" she said. "We should look at that too."

"That's easy," Owen said. "You don't even need a key to get in."

They took the elevator to the lobby and went out to the street. Owen greeted the security guard by name as they walked by her desk. The shop was quiet, with only a few tables occupied, which wasn't surprising in an office district on the weekend, and the three of them stood inside the doorway. It took Mason a moment to get oriented.

"That's the side my windows are on," he said, "so my restroom would be right about there." He pointed to the kitchen, visible behind the service counter.

"That's where they do the dishes, so the plumbing is consistent with the higher floors," Owen said.

"But the void is the same," Peggy said, stepping closer to the counter. "Two solid walls around the missing space."

Mason stepped outside to look at the outer walls. One side had the coffee house's logo mounted on it, and the other had a display case for advertising posters, but they were also solid walls. He looked up, stepping back toward the street and craning his neck to follow the orange-tiled line of the building toward the sky. It was consistently blank, as Teresa had said, with no windows near this corner on any floor.

"The way the shop is configured really disguises the missing space," Owen said. "You wouldn't notice it unless you knew it was there."

"Almost like it was intentional," Mason said. "I wonder if that was part of the renovation design?"

"Or maybe it just deemphasizes it," Peggy said. "If you had a big chunk of unusable space, you wouldn't want it to stand out."

Owen threw up his hands. "So now we've seen every floor. Do either of you want an espresso while we're here?"

"I was just thinking that," Mason said.

"I'll get them. You want a triple?"

"That seems like the most sensible thing," Mason said.

"Peggy?"

"Black coffee," she said. "And I only need one."

They sat near the window while Owen ordered. Mason did a neck roll, working to release the stress of the day. Peggy looked tired too, he thought. Owen set cups down on the table for them and slid onto a seat.

"We need to get into that safe," Mason said.

"Agreed." Owen nodded and sipped at his espresso. "Any ideas?"

"It's so historic, and it's inside your closet, so I'm sure you don't want to try to cut into it or blow it up. I'll read up on whether there are any nondestructive techniques."

Peggy wrapped her hands around her cup. "When are you leaving for Santa Barbara?"

"Soon," Owen said, and pulled out his phone to glance at the screen. "It's getting late—I should probably go." He grinned. "This has been fun—and pretty weird."

"What did you expect, letting a psychic detective move into your building?" Peggy said.

"It's not like he caused it," Owen said.

"Weirdness swirls around Mason like a vortex, remember? The perpetual whirl of confusion." She mimed a whirlwind, twisting her finger in the air.

Owen chuckled, rising from his chair, and said good-bye.

Once he was gone, Peggy said, "Do you need a ride home?"

"Thanks, but I'll see you there later," Mason said,

and slammed the rest of his espresso.

"Furniture work?" she asked, rising with him. "Seeing all those duplicate offices decorated differently should provide some inspiration."

"More important right now is safe-cracking," he said, and waved good-bye as he headed upstairs to his office. Rodrigo was gone, and even though it was partially obscured by a sheet of paper folded in thirds and taped over it, as he approached his door he broke into a broad smile. He pulled off Rodrigo's invoice and admired his handiwork:

MASON BRAITHWAITE
PSYCHIC INVESTIGATIONS

The yellow really stood out, and the 3-D effect of the letters was absolutely perfect. Rodrigo had done a great job.

Once he was at his desk he pulled his computer out of his backpack and did some research on safes. There wasn't a lot of enlightening information, except that the idea of listening to the tumblers with a stethoscope to determine the combination was a fiction that only worked in old movies. With most combination locks, even old ones, it was impossible to hear the mechanism, according to a local locksmith's website, which also offered to transport problematic safes to their facility in the high desert, where they could open it using "cutting-edge cutting technology or percussive methods." That definitely wasn't going to be the first approach, Mason thought.

Maybe psychic insight would tell him more. He folded his laptop closed and moved to the sofa, closing his eyes and enjoying the warm sun through the windows. The hidden space was just over there, not far away, and he focused on it, projecting his mind through the wall, into the void behind the restroom. He focused on slowing his breathing, and it took a while to get into the empty state of mind where information sometimes started to drift in.

The missing space was dark and blank, emptiness, and nothing meaningful came to mind. He struggled not to let his mind wander, and had a sudden image of the floor plans, a scrawled signature at the bottom of the drawing. It had been in a little box with the name of the building and the company that had owned it, reproduced identically on each sheet.

Opening his eyes, he sat there thinking about it, not sure if it was a random memory or a valid psychic insight. It was easy enough to check. He pulled out his phone and found the photos he'd taken of the plans. The signature was above the name of the architect, Astrid Luna. Of course, he thought—he should talk to her. She'd designed the restoration and renovation of every part of the building, so she'd know something about the missing space. He'd seen the photos online of the old drywall and drop ceilings being torn out. Why hadn't he thought of this earlier?

Back at his desk, he looked up Astrid Luna, architect, and found a lot of information about her other projects, along with a brief bio that described her as "eccentric in her personal life." There were no other details, but this was the second time he'd encountered that word, *eccentric*—it had been used to describe the original architect, Augustus Hawley. Maybe it was appropriate that she'd been the one to update his work.

Astrid's website had a photo of her. She was probably in her fifties, her dark hair tucked behind her ears, wearing a gentle smile, and posing with her fingers tented. Why did they always photograph artists with their hands? Clicking through the site, he found a list of her professional affiliations, predictably mundane building and design societies, but there was one Mason didn't recognize: Soroptimist International. When he looked it up, it seemed to be an innocuous women's service organization. More interesting was a reference to a photo book of her work that had been published in Argentina. After he checked the catalog to make sure they had it, he slid his computer into his backpack and headed out, walking the few blocks to the central library.

It took him a minute to find the section where the art and design books were, and then to locate the volume in the stacks. Titled simply *Astrid Luna,* it was a heavy oversize tome, and he carried it to a desk with a view of the atrium. The text was in Spanish, which meant Mason couldn't understand much, but the images of her projects were informative—an apartment tower in Buenos Aires, an office building in Houston, a public plaza in Guadalajara. The book's publication predated her work on the Primavera Building's renovation, so there was nothing about it or any other work in California.

Flipping through the wide pages, he decided he liked her style. It felt modern without being fleetingly trendy, and it had the warmth and energy of other Latin American art that he'd seen, with bold rusty reds and saturated yellows, far from being timid or conformist.

Bold design didn't always work, but hers seemed to. Mason's personal standard for assessing the value of architecture was how long it would be until he got sick of looking at it, and with Astrid's work it didn't feel like that would happen quickly.

Setting the book aside, he pulled out his computer and got connected to the library's newspaper index, where he searched for mention of her name. A long list of articles covered the projects she'd worked on, and digging through them by date, he read through several written around the time of the renovation of the Primavera Building. One of them said that during the project, she had relocated to Los Angeles, working out of a studio in La Cañada. This could be great news—if she was still in town, he could go talk to her.

Looking at her website again, there was no indication of where she lived, but there was an email link. Owen would probably have records about the renovation project with a way to contact her, but if he wrote to her directly, he wouldn't have to wait until the kid got back from Santa Barbara. He spent a minute typing out a missive:

> I'm working for the new owners of the Primavera Building. They love your work as well as Augustus Hawley's original. I had some questions about your design choices, and I'd love to meet briefly if you have a few minutes to share your inspirations.

Flattery was the best chance of getting an answer, he thought, rereading it quickly before pressing SEND. Pulling out his pad, he spent a few minutes making notes about Astrid, then shifted gears and searched the library catalog for safes and safe-cracking. Surprisingly there were several books about the technology of safes and vault doors, including two from the 1930s. They were shelved on another floor, so he packed up and walked down the escalator, pulling out the two period books and sitting with them at another desk, appreciating the smell of the ancient paper as he cracked them open. By the time he'd scanned through both sources, he was no wiser about how to get into a safe without the combination.

It was getting late, he saw when he checked the time. Packing up his laptop and notes, he slung his backpack over his shoulder and headed out to the street. On the metro he sat dozing, eyes closed, until his phone buzzed softly in his pocket. He pulled it out to check. It was a response from Astrid Luna. Sitting up quickly, he shook off his drowsiness.

> I'm not surprised those idiots from Texas sold that beautiful building already—they were Philistines. I'd be happy to talk to you about the project. You're welcome to come to my studio. It's not possible this evening, but I'll be here tomorrow evening.

Success, Mason thought, grinning to himself. The plaudits had worked—the ego of the artist liked nothing better than to be massaged. He thumb-typed a quick reply:

> Thanks for being open to meeting. I may bring two colleagues with me from the new ownership.

He waited until he'd climbed up out of the station in his neighborhood and unlocked his bicycle before he made a phone call.

"Sorry to bug you on your trip," he said when

Owen picked up. "I set up a meeting with Astrid Luna, the architect who did the renovation of your building. Is there any chance you want to go with? I'm seeing her tomorrow evening."

"Damn, you work fast. You think she might know about the safe?"

"That and the missing space. She has to know—she redid every inch of that place."

"Well, we're definitely not going to be back till Monday."

"I could postpone," Mason said.

"I feel like that would interrupt your momentum. You can fill us in later."

"I'm also posing as an officer of your holding company to make it more legit. I figured you wouldn't mind, since I was technically your CEO for a couple of hours."

"No worries, man," Owen said. "Take a selfie with her and send it to us."

Mason chuckled. "That's a great idea."

Owen was still such a teenager, he thought, ending the call and climbing on his wheels to ride up the hill. Before he got halfway there, his phone rang, and he stopped at the curb to pull it out. It was Owen again.

"Sweet Marie says we should offer to pay you for doing the research," he said.

"That's very generous. I hadn't thought of that, but I'd love to get paid."

"What do you charge?"

"Usually five hundred a day, but I can give you a friends-and-family discount."

"Don't worry about that," Owen said. "Five bucks

sounds totally reasonable. Plus it flows back to us in your rent."

"I don't pay rent."

"Oh, yeah—I forgot. Anyway, we'll pay you for your time, just so you know."

Mason hung up and stood on his pedals to climb the hill. How much money had the kid acquired if he could drop two zeroes when he talked about it? Owen had assured him it was the kind of money that wouldn't be reported as a loss, and the source could afford to lose it. He didn't want to know any more than that, not really, even though he was so close to it, and was actually benefitting from it. As he rolled up to the garage he pushed the queasiness he felt out of his mind.

"Something smells good," he said as he went in, dropping his backpack by the front door. He could see Peggy in the kitchen, wearing her apron, and he went to the counter to say hello.

"Tamales," she said, looking up from a mixing bowl where she was kneading dough. "I hope they're as good as Ned's mom's."

"I won't be sharing an opinion on that. No matter what I said, it would be a minefield. Ned's out?"

"He had some errands."

"Do you need any help?"

"Nope. You look tired—I'll let you know when it's dinnertime."

"Thanks," he said, grateful to be excused.

Just for a minute, he told himself, he'd stretch out on the bed, and he got comfortable, drifting into the hypnagogic state. He woke to Ned's voice at the foot of the bed, rousing him, and knew it was much later.

Following Ned up the hall, he rolled his neck to help get to full wakefulness, and joined them at the table. The tamales were still hot from the steamer, and he took one and carefully started to peel off the leaf.

"I heard about your prowling adventures," Ned said, looking up from his own leaf manipulations.

"It's not prowling if you're with the landlord," Peggy said.

"After you left I wrote to the architect who did the renovation," Mason said. "She's willing to meet with me. I'm hoping she'll be able to explain what's in the missing spaces."

"She lives around here?" Peggy asked.

"In La Cañada."

"What's her name?" Ned asked.

"Astrid Luna. She's big news in Latin America."

"I don't know her," Ned said, "but I love what she did in your building."

Mason nodded, finally getting the leaf off and digging into his tamale. "She's a Soroptimist."

"I know some Soroptimists," Peggy said. "Those gals really know how to party."

"Owen and Sweet Marie decided to pay me for the research too. I thought maybe they'd want to come along to meet Astrid, but they're out of town."

"When are you going?" Peggy asked, gesturing with her fork.

"Tomorrow night."

"I'll come with you. I'd love to hear about the missing space firsthand."

"Great," Mason said, "but you'll have to pose as staff of the holding company."

Ned glanced up from his phone, his barely nibbled tamale seemingly forgotten. "Is there even a holding company? I thought the whole thing was a sham."

"It's real," Mason said, "but there's just the two boys running it, and their shady lawyer. The sham was me pretending to be their CEO for a day."

"You said La Cañada," Peggy said. "That's awfully far in a Prius."

"I'll buy gas, if that's what you're angling at."

Peggy scowled and nodded toward Ned.

Mason suddenly understood. "It would be far more comfortable to go out there in the Crown Vic," he said, looking pointedly at Ned.

"Mm-hmm." Ned was gazing intently at his phone.

"Hey, mister," Mason said. "You want to meet the architect?"

"I'm just looking at her work," Ned said, finally looking up. "I kind of love it. Can I come with? We can take the Crown Vic."

Mason threw up his hands. "What a brilliant idea."

After dinner Peggy went off to her room, and Mason helped Ned clean up.

"Want to watch *Pica Confessions*?" Ned asked when they'd finished.

"As long as it's not one with bodily fluids."

"Nope—I read about it. This guy drinks perfume. He's subject to a nationwide ban at cosmetics retailers. They keep his photo on the bulletin board in the employee lounge."

"That sounds palatable," Mason said, and after a

forty-minute hour of watching the cringe-inducing madness, he followed Ned to bed.

In the dream world he found himself cycling around the neighborhood, up the hill past their house and down and around again on the familiar streets, but his bicycle was different—bright yellow—and he had a banjo slung over his shoulder instead of his backpack. He couldn't see it, but he knew it was there, knew it was a banjo. He felt light, and happy, even though he had no idea how to play it, in fact had never picked up a banjo in his life, and rode around enjoying the sunshine.

Three

One of the greatest luxuries of working for himself was that more often than not Mason could wake up when his body told him to, rather than to an alarm on someone else's schedule. It felt decadent, even though lots of people slept in on Sunday, and he rolled out of bed in a good mood. Ned was out somewhere, and so was Peggy, probably with her boyfriend, Matt. Mason sat at the counter and ate a leisurely breakfast, and after his second pot of espresso he grabbed his computer and moved to the sofa. Sometimes he regretted not having a desk in the house anymore, but Ned had happily taken over the whole room for his home office. It was completely reasonable, he decided. Ned worked in there every day; he deserved the space.

Online he researched companies that serviced safes, reading about their capabilities, and saved the phone numbers of a couple of possibilities that hinted at being able to open one without destroying it. None of them would be open on Sunday. He'd call tomorrow.

Eventually he tired of looking at the screen and went for a walk, farther up the hill from their house. Last night he'd dreamed about exploring the neighborhood, and had an inkling that it might be significant. Doing it on foot meant that he'd have the time to ponder what he was seeing and perhaps get some insight. His dreams didn't usually contain anything so straightforward, burying their insights under layers of symbolism and innuendo. Nothing meaningful came to mind as he strolled the quiet streets, but even so, it was far from unpleasant.

Ned was home when he got in, puttering in the kitchen, and he spent part of the afternoon cooking and marinating jackfruit. Peggy got home later and made a caesar, a balancing complement to the almost disconcerting texture of the savory fruit.

They sat down for dinner early, and after they'd eaten, Ned asked, "What's Astrid's address?"

Mason found it in his email and recited it.

"It says it's only twenty minutes from here. Right up the 2."

"Do we have to dress up like corporate zombies?" Peggy asked.

"It's the weekend," Mason said. "Logically you wouldn't be dressed for the office. Wear whatever you want."

"You should put on a collared shirt," Ned said, looking askance at Mason's T-shirt as he picked up their plates. "It's still a business meeting."

Ned was right, Mason knew, and he put on a dark green dress shirt, tucking it into a pair of chinos, even though he knew that was futile. The moment he looked away he'd be rumpled and wrinkled and untucked, with a mystery stain of some description on one or both sleeves. Going anywhere with Ned made it worse—Ned was effortlessly flawless, and when he dressed up, his clothes looked like he'd been ironed into them.

"You look good," Peggy said when he came out to the living room.

Mason scoffed. "Not for long. Where's Nedly?"

"Getting the car."

Mason followed her out to the driveway in front of the garage, locking the front door behind them.

"You sit in front," he called to her, and she got in the passenger's side of the roomy old Crown Vic.

Mason climbed in the back and stretched out, gazing at the city and the sky as they went, watching the daylight fade to dusk. Ned drove fast in the light traffic, through their neighborhood to the freeway, gunning it up the ramp. Minutes later his phone showed him where to exit, onto a boulevard and then side streets, leading them up a winding route into the hills.

"The driveways here are far apart," Peggy said. "That always means money."

"It's also her studio," Mason said, "so it makes sense she'd need lots of room."

"Whoa," Ned said, rounding a curve and suddenly braking, then deftly pulling over to the far right.

Bright headlights came slowly around the curve and past the Crown Vic—a highway bus, Mason saw, looking up at it once the glare had passed. It looked old, with swooping aluminum curves rather than boxy modern plastic. The window behind the driver was brightly lit, and in it sat a man reading a newspaper, his face buried in the rustling pages, only the back of his head and his old-timey fedora visible. Mason grinned at the oddness of that, but he inhaled sharply as the next window rolled by. Seated there was a man with the same kind of fedora, also reading a newspaper that obscured his face. Shifting position to get a better look, Mason watched for the third window, knowing what he'd see—the same guy, the same fedora, the same newspaper. And the same again in each window, a whole busload, until he lost count.

"Did you see that?" Mason demanded, craning to look at the back of the lumbering vehicle once it was past. It had New Mexico plates, but he wasn't thinking clearly enough to memorize the number.

"That's why I pulled over," Ned said flatly, nosing back onto the street.

"Did you see the people in the windows?" Mason insisted.

"I just saw the headlights," Peggy said. "What about them?"

"They were all identical, like eight people in a row."

"Maybe it was a church group," Ned said. "They're totally conformist. They always look like clones."

"They were all reading the same newspaper, holding it at exactly the same angle."

"OK," Ned said neutrally, glancing at him in the rearview mirror.

Mason took a deep breath, trying to assuage the surge of adrenaline still coursing in his veins. "I'm telling you, there was something paranormal about that bus."

"That's freaky," Peggy said, turning to look at him, concern in her eyes.

"Extremely freaky—eight identical guys in a row, their newspapers all exactly the same. Who reads newspapers on paper anymore?"

"That reminds me of the blueprints for Owen's building," she said. "Every floor was exactly the same."

"The bus had New Mexico plates," Mason said, leaning ahead between the seats. "What do you suppose that means? Why would it be driving around up in the hills in the middle of nowhere, in the middle of the night?"

"See, this is the problem I have with the whole paranormal thing," Ned said, maneuvering the massive car on the ever narrower roads. "You're making all these assumptions, and you're making it all about you."

"What assumptions?" Mason demanded.

"It's not meaningful that there's a bus with New Mexico plates. All it means is that the bus is from New Mexico. There's probably a church camp farther up the canyon that attracts religious nuts from all over the Southwest."

Mason scoffed and slumped back. "I know paranormal when I see it. I can feel it. Inside the bus was all lit up, way too bright, and all blue, like a jewelry store or something. Who does that on a bus? It was for my benefit."

"I forgot that the world revolves around you," Ned said.

"Dude, chill," Peggy said to him, raising her voice.

She turned to Mason and spoke more gently. "He does kind of have a point."

Mason sighed, and willed himself to calm down. This was emblematic of the psychic's dilemma: how could he relate metaphysical experiences back to the regular world? It wasn't Ned's fault that he just couldn't see it.

"Think what you want," he said, as calmly as he could. "That was a paranormal bus."

They rode in silence for a minute, until Ned slowed the car.

"We're here," he said, and pulled into the gravel driveway, and followed it up toward the house. From what was visible in the headlights, the structure was a long and low ranch house, set amid open lawns.

"It looks like a golf course," Peggy said.

The driveway made a loop in front of the building, and Ned pulled up behind an SUV parked at one side, just beyond the pool of light cast by the fixture over the front door. He killed the engine, and the three of them climbed out.

"Ready?" Mason asked quietly.

Ned nodded confidently, and Peggy said, "Let's rock and roll."

Mason walked up to the door and rang the bell. Inside he could hear footsteps, moving alarmingly fast—someone was running. The door flew open, and there stood Astrid, not much older than in her photo but wearing a bright-red print dress, her dark hair struggling to stay bundled in a chignon, her eyes wild. In one hand she held a stick with a loop of mesh at the end—a net for scooping up fish, or butterflies.

"Help me catch them," she demanded, her words Spanish-accented.

Mason stepped over the threshold as she turned to dash away. "Catch what?"

"Bats," she shouted, and hustled back to him, thrusting the net into his hands. She ran down the hall and disappeared through a wide doorway.

Mason turned to Peggy and Ned, still behind him on the doorstep. Both of them looked startled, but they stepped inside when Mason grinned and trotted after Astrid, brandishing the net.

"Don't hurt them," Ned called after him.

Holding the net aloft and ducking through the doorway she had entered, Mason found himself in what he took to be her work space, with a wide desk, a couple of drafting tables, and deep cabinets with shallow drawers, the kind they used at the library to store maps and oversize drawings. It was a beautiful room—lots of blond wood and a wall of windows to the outside, completely black at this hour. Astrid stood in the middle of the floor, looking up at the ceiling and turning in a slow circle, checking every corner. He followed her gaze and saw nothing moving, nothing remotely bat-like.

"I guess maybe they left," she said, taking a final look around before meeting his gaze. "You must be Mason." She reached behind her head to retie her hair, and looking past him, said, "and these are your colleagues."

Mason turned to find Ned and Peggy in the doorway, and introduced them.

"Welcome, all of you," Astrid said, and took the

net from Mason, setting it on her desk. "Sorry for the confusion. I don't know how they get in here, and I don't know how they get out."

"Have you ever caught one?" Ned asked.

"Not yet." She grinned at him. "I have a room where we can sit. Come."

Astrid walked past them toward the door. Ned shot Mason an amused look, and Mason shrugged, turning to follow her.

"Is there someone in your yard?" Peggy asked. She was looking at the windows, and stepped closer to the glass.

As Mason turned to look, he saw it too—a flash of movement, barely visible in the darkness outside. Astrid turned back and approached the window.

"I told you to beat it," she shouted, pounding the heel of her fist on the glass.

Peggy recoiled, taking a step away from her, but Astrid was instantly calm again.

She smiled at Peggy. "Sorry to startle you."

"Who's out there?" Peggy demanded, her tone agitated.

"My little visitors. Nothing to worry about."

Peggy took a deep breath, and they followed Astrid into the next room. To Mason it felt like stepping into a design magazine.

"Your home is gorgeous," Ned said.

Astrid bobbed her head in acknowledgment and waved her arm. "Please—sit."

Mason knew the furniture was high-end, and avoided the Barcelona chair—why was there always one of those? He picked one that looked sturdier, facing the windows. They were in the same picture-window style as in the studio, and equally black to the darkness outside. Astrid took the Barcelona chair, her back to the windows, and Peggy and Ned sat at either end of the luxy sofa.

"So, Ned," Astrid said, meeting his eye, "Your name is English, but you look Latin."

"*Ned* is an Anglo derivative of *Edgar,*" he said, pronouncing it with the clipped Spanish vowels. "I'm not sure where it came from. I don't think it was my parents."

"*¿Hablas español?*" she asked him.

Ned responded with what must have been the equivalent of "Of course," and they had a short conversation.

Looking at Mason, Astrid said something that started with "*Y tú …*"

"I don't speak Spanish," Mason said, flipping his palms upward in the universal gesture for *no comprendo.*

"It's OK," she said, "but I'm not going to apologize for speaking Spanish to someone who lives in a city of five million Latin people and still doesn't speak Spanish."

"Fair enough," Mason said. From the corner of his eye, he noticed movement at the windows again.

"Did you see that?" Peggy asked, sitting up. "Seriously, someone is out there."

"I saw it too," Ned said. "They looked like little kids, just beyond the reach of the light from in here."

"They're not children," Astrid said, not bothering to look at the windows.

"Then who are they?" Peggy asked.

"Paranormal renderings."

"That sounds like my field," Mason said.

"I thought you worked in property management," Astrid said.

"I do, but I'm interested in paranormal stuff."

"Go after them if you want," she said, gesturing languidly. "You'll never catch them."

Mason stood up. "Is that open?" he asked, pointing to the glass door at the end of the windows.

"You just have to unlock the deadbolt," Astrid said.

"Is this really necessary?" Ned called after him as he moved toward it.

"I'm just going to check it out," Mason said.

"It seems like asking for trouble."

"I'm not afraid of paranormal renderings," he said, frowning at Ned, and pulled open the door.

"Do you want company?" Peggy asked.

"It's better if I go alone," Mason said. "The psychic channels are clearer." Stepping out, he didn't wait for a reply, knowing that Ned would have a snarky one, and pulled the door closed behind him.

Walking away from the house, into the inky night, he didn't look back, wanting his eyes to adjust to the dark. There were no outdoor lights here, and all was blackness at first, save the glow of the city above the distant treetops. As the trees themselves became visible, and the grass stretching toward them began to resolve in fuzzy gray, he knew that there was nothing moving out here. He decided to try his psychic senses, and sat down on the grass.

Working the Penstock Canyon case, he'd had success visualizing liminal entities that went unseen by the regular senses by using a technique called hidden mind.

It was a powerful state of altered perception, and he spent a minute with his eyes closed, getting into it by willing his mind to disperse outward, around his head, thinning as it expanded, like a cloud of smoke.

Even though he knew he was in hidden mind, and he opened his eyes slightly with dramatically improved night vision to perceive what he could, nothing moved on the lawn, liminal or otherwise. He sat that way for a few minutes, the only sound lazy crickets and the distant subsonic rumble of the traffic. Eventually he rose and turned back toward the house. Squinting at the bright light from the windows, he finally saw them—four dark shapes, no taller than preschoolers. They were inside the picture window, looking out at him, their hands cupped to the glass.

Still in hidden mind, he was able to suppress his fear reaction, like swallowing bile, and strode toward the house, peering at them. As he approached, they melted, faded, until there was only Astrid's living room. Peggy looked up at him, squinting, as he got close to the door.

"You've got intense paranormal activity all around you," Mason said, stepping inside.

Astrid raised her eyebrows. "Most people just think I'm crazy."

"I've seen a lot of this stuff," he said, putting his hands on his hips. "Are you a psychic, or a channel? Have you cultivated this?"

"Does it look cultivated?" she asked. "I have no control over it. It's like a piece of toilet paper permanently stuck to my heel."

"I'm glad you haven't let it intimidate you. You

seem completely functional. Lots of people would find it terrifying."

Astrid turned to Ned. "I like this one," she said, gesturing to Mason. "He's open-minded, for a corporate type."

Ned nodded. "I guess the risk in being too open-minded is that your brains fall out."

Astrid cackled and got to her feet. "I'm going to make coffee, and then we can talk about your building."

Ned rose and said something in Spanish, following her out of the room.

Mason rubbed his eyes, working to recover his regular consciousness. Hidden mind tended to persist more than other psychic states, lingering like fog.

"Too bad you can't tell her what you really do for a living," Peggy said in a low voice, stretching an arm over the back of the sofa. "You might be able to help her."

"I'm not sure what I could do. There's something different about her—she's not psychic, but she's caught up in this paranormal stuff."

Mason walked around the room, examining her wall art and a couple of sculptures, scanning the small collection of books in a bookcase, most of them in Spanish. Everything was carefully positioned, with no clutter, nothing overlooked, no randomness. It was like a room meant to be admired rather than used.

Astrid came back, carrying a tray of steaming cups, and set it on the table in front of the sofa.

"Your boyfriend said you take it black," she said, offering a cup to Mason.

"It's a little late for me."

"I made decaf," she said impatiently, and Mason took the cup.

"Tasty," he said, after taking a sip.

"It's Costa Rican," Astrid said, handing a cup to Peggy.

They sat down again, and Mason was itching to talk business, but Astrid wasn't paying any attention to him, focused instead on Peggy.

"You have great hair," Astrid said. "It must be a lot of work."

"Not that much. I've thought about butching it, like yours. It would be so much easier."

"Mine's not that short," Astrid said, absently touching the back of her head. "And it's not that easy. I prefer it this way—I don't want to be a fembot." She waved her arms like a mechanical toy.

"I have long hair, but I don't consider myself a fembot," Peggy said affably.

"You're not, it's true. I guess I'm thinking of the femme fatale type. I don't want to be that way, using men for my income."

"I thought you were gay," Peggy said.

"I am gay."

Mason looked at her, and then at Peggy, wondering how Peggy could have known that.

"Well, don't make assumptions about me based on my hair," Peggy said. "I'm not a femme fatale. I make my own money."

"But you are straight. Burn your bridges in the daytime, then build them again at night."

Peggy laughed. "Come on—it's not that simple. Besides, I did go to college."

"Aha," Astrid said. "A has-bian."

"Stop labeling me," Peggy said.

A sudden *crack* came from the windows, and they all looked. Two more sharp reports came, the sound of something small and hard hitting glass.

"What the hell?" Ned said.

"Just ignore them," Astrid said. "They're throwing pebbles or something."

Mason rose and cupped his hands on the glass. Just beyond the reach of the light from the windows, three shadowy figures dashed away.

"It has to be neighborhood kids," Ned said.

"It's not kids," Mason said grimly. He sat down again, leaning toward Astrid. "Can we talk about the renovation of the Primavera Building? The company I work for acquired it quite recently, and something unusual came up in the floor plans. I have a photo of your renovation drawings."

Mason reached into his pants pocket for his phone, but Astrid waved dismissively.

"I don't need to see that. I know why you're here." Her eyes narrowed. "The shaft."

"Is that what it is?" Peggy said. "Like an elevator shaft? The voids are connected?"

Astrid frowned. "You didn't know that?"

"In the plans it looks like there's a void on each floor," Mason said.

"It sounds like you've been operating on the wrong assumptions," Ned said, and sipped his coffee.

"So you haven't been inside." Astrid looked from him to Mason.

Mason shook his head. "We couldn't find a way in."

She smiled knowingly. "It exists."

"The safe," Mason said.

"At least you've done your research," she said.

"The combination seems to be lost."

"Lost to the bean counters, but not lost to an artist."

He frowned. "I don't understand."

"Take a closer look at the door."

"Do you know the combination?" Mason said. "Can you just give it to me?"

"It's written on the door."

"We looked at it pretty closely," Peggy said. "I didn't see any numbers."

Astrid met Peggy's eye, and gestured to Mason. "This one is open-minded. Go back and see if he can see them."

"What's inside?" Peggy asked. "Is it an elevator, or just an empty shaft? What was it supposed to be in the original design?"

"My dear, reality must be experienced firsthand. It's like art—I can't tell you what to see, and anyone who does is a fascist. Go see it for yourself."

"I'm so intrigued now," Mason said.

A loud *bang* came from the direction of the kitchen, the sound of metal on tile, like a pot had struck the floor. Mason started, and Ned and Peggy both looked alarmed.

"I don't know why," Astrid said, seemingly unperturbed, "but my little guests are acting worse since you've been here. I don't want to be rude, but I think you'll have to leave. We can talk again once you've been inside the shaft."

Mason sighed and got to his feet. He'd hoped to learn more.

Ned spoke to Astrid in Spanish as she walked them to the front door. The only words Mason could pull out were *gracias* and *café*.

"I won't say good-bye, because I'm sure we'll talk again soon," Astrid said, standing in the doorway.

"I don't have your number," Mason said.

She rattled it off impatiently, and he scrambled for his phone, thumb-typing it and reading it back to her.

At the car, Peggy said, "Mason, sit up front. I want to stretch out."

Ned twisted the key in the ignition and revved the engine, pulling around Astrid's SUV and back down the driveway.

"Man, she is intense," Ned said.

"I feel bad for her, with all that paranormal stuff going on," Mason said. "It's really disruptive."

"She said it was worse with us there," Peggy said. "That has to be about you."

"A psychic can ramp up the ambient metaphysical energy sometimes," he said. "Some people are like those card keys—they're inert until they're next to a terminal, then *bam*, they're energized, and you have psychic experiences."

"It wasn't psychic induction," Ned said. "It was neighborhood kids. They redoubled their efforts when they saw you looking for them outside."

Mason sighed. "That may be how it happens on Planet Denial, but not on this one, toots. When I was outside, I saw them inside with you, looking out at me."

"Seriously?" Peggy said, leaning between the front seats. "I was there the whole time, and I never saw anything."

"They weren't really there—it was a projection for my benefit."

Ned scoffed. "It's hilarious that in this equation, I'm the one from another planet."

Mason ignored him, turning to Peggy. "What was all that with Astrid, about butching your hair and burning bridges?"

She mimicked Astrid's accent. "It's called fliting, my dear."

"Seriously? How come I couldn't see that?"

"Well, she was flirting with me a lot, and in a rough way, and I was only doing it a little."

Mason turned to Ned. "Did you know that's what was going on?"

"I don't want to make you feel like you're the only one not getting it," he said.

"I'll take that as a yes," Mason said. "I guess I need to take a lesbian awareness class."

"We have that at my school," Peggy said.

"I may be clueless sometimes," Mason said, "but I'm not buying that."

Ned laughed, reaching for Mason's hand and giving it a squeeze as he turned onto the quiet boulevard.

"I cannot wait to look at that safe," Mason said. "I hope Owen comes home tomorrow."

"Tomorrow's Monday," Ned said. "Doesn't he have school? Where is he?"

"In Santa Barbara with Sweet Marie's family," Mason said.

"It's actually a long weekend for the students," Peggy said. "I have to be there, though. They're called professional development days."

"Will you actually be doing anything professional?" Ned asked.

"I'll find out tomorrow. It's all new to me."

Mason slid his phone from his pants and tuned out Peggy and Ned's conversation. He thumb-typed a text to Owen:

Let me know when you're home. I need to look at your safe.

His reply came soon after:

We'll be back sometime tomorrow.

That, Mason thought, was very good news.

In bed later, Mason drifted off quickly, and became aware of the darkness all around. The only thing visible was a pale blue dot, and he focused on it, watching as it swelled up into a sphere right in front of him. He tried to reach for it, but it morphed into something else, busy with noise and color, the constant eternal blue lost.

Forcing himself to wake up, he scrabbled for his pen and bedside notepad, wincing at the brightness when he clicked on the lamp on the nightstand, and wrote down what he remembered.

pale blue sphere
cold
inert

Four

In the morning he woke up latish and stuck his head into Ned's office to say hello on his way to the kitchen. He could hear Ned's keyboard clicking but otherwise the house was quiet; Peggy was long gone to work. He started the espresso machine and poured some berries into a bowl with his muesli, and ate it sitting on a stool at the counter. Once the coffee started to kick in, he checked his phone and found a message from Owen.

At home. Come any time.

Finishing his breakfast, he slammed the rest of his coffee, then got dressed and pulled on his backpack. After he said good-bye to Ned, he flew down the hill and locked up his bicycle at the station, then rode the train downtown. As he climbed up out of the ground, he took a good look at the Primavera Building across the street. *You're almost a centenarian,* he thought. *What are your secrets?*

"Hey, Marcus," he called to the familiar security guard as he walked into the lobby, happy that he could remember the guy's name.

As he approached his office, he stopped to admire the lettering on the door for a moment. It was so loud, the bright yellow on black, like the brilliant light of psychic power in the darkness, so absolutely perfect. He dropped his backpack on the sofa, then went out again, locking his door behind him. It was only two flights up to the penthouse, so he took the stairs, bounding up two at a time. At the door that Owen had led them through on Saturday he couldn't find a bell, so he rapped on it with his knuckles.

Owen pulled it open and flashed a smile, waving him inside. He was dressed for a day off, in jeans and a blue plaid shirt. Sweet Marie stepped over to greet Mason. He was a year or two older than Owen but still looked like a kid, despite his regal Roman nose. His mousy brown hair was carefully coiffed to look untouched, as if tousled only by the forces of nature. Over his T-shirt and gray sweatpants he was wearing a dark-green garment with big droopy sleeves, maybe a *haori* or a *yukata.*

"How are you?" Mason asked, leaning in for an air kiss. Today Sweet Marie wasn't wearing any makeup that he might muss, but avoiding direct physical contact must be a habit he'd developed when he did drag. Mason had seen him perform; he was pretty talented.

"Owen met my family this weekend," Sweet Marie said. "I think it went well."

"It must have gone extremely well, if you put it that way," Mason said.

Sweet Marie grinned. "Miss Cassie wants me to reconnect with my family now that I'm independent of them and supporting myself."

"Miss Cassie is your therapist too?" Mason said, trying not to sound surprised.

"I figured she's right in the building," he said, and shrugged. "I like her, and she pushes me outside my comfort zone. The consensus online is that's what you need from a shrink."

"Yeah, she's pretty good at it," Mason said, and to Owen, "What did you think of his family?"

"In two words," Owen said, "bougie zombies."

"If you want bougie, look in the mirror, mister teenage landlord," Sweet Marie said, waving his arms and flapping the fabric of his kimono jacket. "And my people are not as expressive as your people because they're Anglo. Cut them some slack."

"I'm glad I'm not the only one who has that experience," Mason said. "Ned's Latin family thinks I'm pretty uptight."

"You?" Owen said, raising his eyebrows in mock disbelief. He clapped Mason on the shoulder and steered him toward the closet doors. "So what was Astrid Luna like? I didn't get the selfie I requested."

"She's not really the selfie type," Mason said, eyeing the outside of the closet and mentally positioning the hidden space behind it. "She said that the voids are connected—she called it a shaft."

"Really?" Owen said. "That's so not what I was imagining."

"She also said that the way in is through the safe."

"We were told that the combination was lost," Sweet Marie said.

"Astrid said it's written on the door."

Owen frowned and pulled open the closet, striding back to the midnight-blue safe door with its brass handle. "You'd think we would have noticed that."

The three of them stood looking at the safe door, between the racks of shirts and jackets, and Mason leaned close, craning to examine the aging paint of the MONTCLAIR SECURITY logo, then spent some time studying the circular design below it. It was a mesh of stylized flowers entwined on a lattice, he decided, the constituent lines boxy in places and swirling in others.

"There aren't any numbers," Sweet Marie said, folding his arms. "Isn't that what a safe combination would be, a bunch of numbers?"

"Numbers plus directions," Mason said, "like clockwise and counterclockwise, or left and right."

Owen pressed his cheek to one side of the door, gazing across its surface. "I don't see any scratches in the paint."

"It has to be about this design," Mason said. "It's a bunch of flowers. Isn't that a little out of place on a safe?"

"Is it maybe the Montclair Security company's logo?" Sweet Marie asked.

"Too artistic, and too complex for that," Owen said.

"I think it's just a decoration," Mason said. "But why? Flowers don't really imply 'strong' or 'secure' or anything else you'd want from a locked box."

"It's nice, though," Owen said. "It was definitely done by an artist."

68

"I have an idea," Mason said. "Give me a minute or two to read it."

"Ooh, psychically?" Sweet Marie asked. "How do you do that, exactly?"

"When he says 'give me a minute,' he means shut up," Owen said, and moved a few steps away.

Sweet Marie just scoffed and stepped back with him.

Mason grinned at that and then planted his feet apart, fixing his gaze on the floral design. Working to shift his state of mind and be more open, more receptive to insights, he focused on the gold paint. Soon the lines seemed to move slightly, curling away and then snapping back into place—maybe it was just eyestrain, or the rough surface under the paint in the play of light from the bright fixtures above, or maybe his perception really was shifting. Reaching up to touch the paint, he traced a line with his finger, the golden stem of a gilded rose, feeling the smooth surface. As his finger moved, a number popped out behind it, part of the woven stems and latticework. He cocked his head and blinked, then looked again with his rational mind.

"That could be a five," he said, tracing the digit. "And the open space here could be a zero."

Owen came closer and leaned in to look. "I'll be damned. You're right—I can see it too."

"I don't," Sweet Marie said, unself-consciously putting a hand on Mason's shoulder and leaning in. "Show me."

Owen traced the five for him, and the zero, and added a seven. "This could be a six, or another five."

"I see it now," Sweet Marie said, leaning closer, his tone hushed. "Six—it's definitely a six. Once you know what to look for, you can't not see it." He looked to Mason. "So it's not really from a psychic reading, huh."

Mason sighed. "I'm not sure. I think it's partly psychic. Astrid said the way in would be clear to an artist."

"I'm kind of an artist," Owen said, "or at least a wannabe. I didn't see it until you did."

They spent a minute parsing the image, pulling out information, eventually agreeing that there were four two-digit numbers.

"I guess we can just try the numbers in both directions," Mason said. "It might take a while."

"Maybe not," Owen said, still gazing at the design. "Look at the slope of the number shapes. The five and the zero are kind of leaning forward, so maybe that means clockwise. This one is leaning back, so counterclockwise. See? They all have one slant or the other."

"You're right," Mason said, suddenly seeing it too. "Brilliant observation. You definitely have the soul of an artist."

Owen beamed, and Mason pulled out his phone, thumb-typing a list of the numbers and directions.

"So how do you enter the numbers on the dial?" Sweet Marie asked.

"You spin it completely around a few times to reset the tumblers, then start from zero at the alignment mark. That's here," Mason said, pointing out the white hairline above the dial.

"You should spin it, bae," Sweet Marie said, looking at Owen.

Owen crouched in front of the dial as Mason read back the numbers.

"That's all of them?" Owen asked, looking up.

"Try the handle," Mason said.

He wrapped his hand around the brass lever and pulled. It didn't budge, making the same dull mechanical *thunk* it had before.

"Don't worry," Mason said. "We're not beat. Sometimes you have to go back past zero when you move to the next number, or sometimes you pass zero twice."

"How do you know all this?" Sweet Marie asked. "Are you old enough that you've used one of these?"

Mason grinned. "Not quite, but I've done a lot of reading about how to get into a safe in the last two days."

Owen recited the first number, carefully twisting the dial, then asked Mason for the next one. "Back past zero," he said, half to himself, and dialed in the rest. He reached for the handle again, pulling it up, to no effect, but when he pushed it downward, this time it twisted freely, and they could hear the mechanism unlocking.

"Oh, what a lovely sound," Mason said.

Owen's eyes grew wide. "We did it."

"Right on," Sweet Marie said.

"This is it, boys," Owen said, meeting Mason's gaze, and then Sweet Marie's, his hand still on the lever. Mason gestured impatiently, and Owen stepped back, pulling on the handle. The door swung outward easily, noiselessly, like it was well oiled and brand-new.

It took Mason a moment to process what he was seeing as he stepped into the doorway. There was no safe, only the shaft. He stepped onto the square pad of concrete just inside, finding himself in the corner of a stairwell. There was a handrail, and steps leading up to another landing, and more steps going down, the flights at right angles. Stepping closer, he saw that there was a landing above and below, the stairs turning ninety degrees at each corner. The bizarre part, however, was the illumination. Surrounded by the winding stairs, in the few feet of empty space at the center of the shaft, was a column, maybe ten inches in diameter, that looked like a dim oversize fluorescent tube. It emanated a muted white glow, just enough to illuminate the stairwell. Mason stepped closer to the railing and looked down.

"Whoa," he exclaimed, and pulled back a little, reacting to the height, his heart starting to pound. The luminous column stretching downward, seemingly endlessly, interrupted only by the metal support rings that held it in place, braced beneath the stairs every other flight.

He felt Owen at his side, and in his peripheral vision saw his fingers tentatively grasp the railing.

"It looks like the stairs go all the way down," Mason said quietly, "and so does … this." His gaze followed the glowing column upward, where it ended abruptly at the concrete slab of the ceiling, just a little higher up.

"What the hell is it?" Sweet Marie demanded, standing in the doorway behind them. His sharp tone was jarring; clearly Sweet Marie wasn't as enthralled as Mason was.

Mason kept his eyes on the column. "I've no idea."

"It's lit up," Sweet Marie said. "There are no other lights in here, so it must be plugged in somewhere."

"Did Astrid build this?" Owen said, his tone soft, awed.

"She didn't build the stairwell," Mason said, finally pulling his gaze away from the diffuse light. "Look at the detail in the metalwork. This has to be from the 1920s."

"The railing and the treads are the same design as the other stairwells," Sweet Marie said, "and those ones are definitely restored originals."

"It's dusty in here, but the construction looks new," Owen said. "There's no wear on the steps." He squatted to run his hand along the edge of the landing. "See? The treads are still even."

"It's not new," Sweet Marie said. "Just unused."

Mason walked down to the next landing, then a few steps farther, and peered over the railing into the void. "It looks like there's a landing every quarter turn all the way down, but no doors."

Owen gestured helplessly. "So who builds a stairwell with only one door? And why is there a glowing tube down the center of it?"

Sweet Marie looked down at Mason. "Astrid Luna didn't tell you anything about it?"

"She said I needed to see it for myself first. I think figuring out the combination to the safe was like a test. If I could see the numbers, I'd be worthy of seeing this."

"Let's see if there are any other doors," Sweet Marie said.

"There can't be," Owen said. "We've looked at the outside of these walls on every floor."

"He's right, though," Mason said. "We should check it out."

Owen frowned, peering down along the column. "Do you think that's safe?"

"It's been sealed up at least since Astrid renovated the building," Sweet Marie said. "If there was anything dangerous in here, it would have starved to death long ago." He walked past Owen, and then Mason, trotting down the stairs.

Mason waited for Owen to pass and then followed him down, mostly examining the column as they descended. The surface was remarkably even, and he stopped for a moment to touch it. It felt cool, and definitely like glass. When he rapped his knuckles on it, there was no sound—it was solid, not hollow like a fluorescent tube.

The exterior walls of the stairwell were the same unfinished concrete all the way down, and with no visual cues, he soon lost track of which were the interior walls and which faced the street.

"See how the walls have board marks in the concrete?" Mason called down to them. "That's from the 1920s. It's like the ceiling in your penthouse. If Astrid had built this, she would have used some newer technology that doesn't leave marks."

Sweet Marie called back to him. "Every side looks the same. Have you been counting the landings? I'm assuming every fourth one lines up with a floor, but that's just a guess."

"I'm completely turned around," Mason said. "Up and down is the best I've got right now."

They trudged downward until somewhere below he heard Sweet Marie vocalize surprise, followed a moment later by Owen. The two of them had stopped walking.

"Guys?" Mason said, and quickened his pace, hopping downward two steps at a time.

He found them at the very bottom, standing on the concrete floor at the foot of the last step. The luminous column was anchored here on a squat concrete pad with a snug lip that concealed its base, but Owen and Sweet Marie had their backs to it, staring at a heavy metal door opposite the last flight of stairs. In the dim glow Mason could see that it had a latch on this side, and it was hinged to swing inward.

"It has to be in the coffee place," Owen said.

Sweet Marie shook his head. "No way. We'd have seen it."

"Maybe it got drywalled over on that side," Mason said.

"There's one way to find out," Owen said, and reached for the door handle, twisting up the latch.

As he pulled on it, the door started to move, but the hinges resisted audibly, so Mason moved to help him, the two of them heaving on it until it swung open.

A scuffed and blackened leather box—an ancient steamer trunk, Mason realized—blocked the lower part of the doorway, and beyond that was blackness, the dim glow of the column casting insufficient light to illuminate the space. Mason pulled out his phone and switched on its flashlight, aiming it through the doorway. Owen climbed onto the trunk and then down again, and Mason followed, wobbling to maintain his balance as he briefly stood on top of it while holding his phone aloft. They were in a storage room, it seemed, piled with boxes, some old and made of wood, others newer cardboard, along with haphazard stacks of lumber, lengths of pipe, and pieces of thin-walled metal ductwork. On the opposite side was a much larger rolling door, like in an old warehouse, with a single handle to slide it open.

"I know where this is," Owen said. "I parked on the other side of that door this morning. It's at the end of the underground garage."

"I didn't even think of looking in the garage on Saturday," Mason said. "How did I miss that?"

Sweet Marie clambered over the trunk and joined them, his sleeves billowing as he hopped down. "Here's why we never noticed the door into the stairwell," he said, holding up his phone to illuminate the surrounding wall. "It's covered with the same kind of boards."

He was right, Mason saw—the others were bare concrete, but the wall with the door to the stairwell was covered with rough-cut lumber, as was the back of the door. When it was closed, it would have been next to impossible to notice, the irregular wood blending together.

"I remember thinking it was weird that only one wall had a wood surface," Owen said. "And that the boards are mounted vertically. I wondered if it was some old-timey way to protect stored furniture or something."

Mason panned his phone light along the boarded wall. "The purpose was to hide the way into the stairwell, I'd say."

Sweet Marie stepped back onto the trunk and hopped down to examine the door. "There's no handle on this side," he said grimly. "Just the boards. It was definitely meant to be hidden."

"A twelve-story stairwell with only two doors," Owen said, "and both of them are hidden. Why?"

"Don't forget the glowing tube," Sweet Marie said. "That's actually the weirdest part."

"We need to look at the roof," Mason said. "Can we go out through the garage and take the elevator?"

Owen shook his head. "We thought this was just a storage room. It's padlocked from the outside."

Mason clambered over the steamer trunk, followed by Owen, who pushed the door closed but didn't latch it. Mason was not looking forward to climbing twelve flights; he was already sweaty from hiking down in the dead air. But the inscrutable glowing column was a distraction, and he watched it in wonder as they spiraled around it on the way up.

"I'm glad the stairwell isn't a total death trap," Sweet Marie said. "We could use it to escape."

"We'll need to stop padlocking the storage room door in the garage," Owen said, "and put access to the lock on the inside."

The three of them were winded by the time they got to the door into the penthouse, breathing heavily. Mason glanced into the closet, where the boys had stopped, the warm lighting and colorful clothes such a contrast to the rough gray stairwell. He climbed past them, up the four short quarter flights to the last landing, right below the ceiling. He didn't have to stoop to stand in the little space, but the ceiling was just inches above his head. Feeble daylight filtered through a ventilation grate at chest level.

"I know where this is," Owen said, coming up behind him. "On the roof there's a box—I remember the air grate. It's on a small protrusion, like two feet tall. We must be right inside it."

"There's no door here either," Mason said.

"You could climb through the air grate, if you

unscrewed it," Sweet Marie said.

"The column doesn't end here. See the black stuff?" Mason reached up and tentatively prodded the material that oozed around the glass where it met the concrete ceiling. "It's dry, but I think it's sealant to keep the rain out. The column goes through to the roof."

"We've been up there plenty of times. Wouldn't we have noticed that?" Sweet Marie said.

"I know where it is," Owen said, and grinned. "Let's go up on the roof. I'll show you."

He trotted back down to the safe door and led them through the closet, then out of the penthouse into the elevator lobby. In the main stairwell, which was much larger than the hidden one, Mason realized, there was a fire door marked with ALARMED—EMERGENCY USE ONLY in big red letters. It was the way up to the roof. Owen punched a four-digit code into the alarm's keypad, not trying to conceal the numbers, then pushed the crash bar and propped the door open by flipping down the little foot pedal at the bottom. As they walked up the stairs to the roof, Mason committed the alarm code to memory, in case he needed it one day.

The door at the top wasn't alarmed, and Owen pushed it open. The roof was mostly flat, except for the long windowless box at the top of the stairs; probably the elevator machinery, Mason thought. It was painted that industrial pinkish-tan color that so many structures had been assigned, including everything else on the roof. The crisp fresh air felt good, and he took a deep breath.

Over near a corner of the roof was a squat protrusion with a ventilation grate in the side, the same one they'd just seen from the hidden stairwell. Owen strode toward it, and Mason followed, feeling his heart start to pound with the proximity to the edge—there was a structural wall at the side of the roof, but it was only a few feet high, and the yawning void felt much too close.

On top of the innocuous squat cube was a smoky-gray dome, bolted down at the corners and oozing black sealant around the edges.

"That's why you never saw the top of the column," Mason said. "It's under a skylight."

"That's new, though," Sweet Marie said. "It's plastic—it can't be 1920s."

"I'd bet money that Astrid put it there," Mason said.

"Is that why the column is glowing, because it's exposed to the sky?" Owen said, leaning over the opaque bubble to peer inside. "Fiber-optic cables do that."

Mason thought about it. "That's actually a good insight. It feels like the column is conducting light, not generating it, doesn't it?"

"I wonder if Astrid Luna knows what it's for?" Owen said.

"Let's ask her," Mason said, and pulled out his phone. The call went to voice mail, and he left her a message, staring at the cloudy skylight dome as he spoke. "It's Mason. I've been inside the shaft, and I have questions."

"I wish Peggy could see all this too," Owen said, still staring at the skylight. "She was really into it on Saturday."

Mason checked the time on his phone. "She drives right by here on the way home from school. Can I tell her to drop by?"

"I'll be here," Owen said.

"I won't," Sweet Marie said. "I'm performing tonight. I have to get to rehearsal."

"I'm glad you're still doing that," Mason said.

Sweet Marie grinned. "Why's that?"

Mason swung his arm around, gesturing at the building. "All of this could start to consume all your time. It's important to have a community too." It was a gentler way of saying he was glad all the money hadn't gone to his head.

They trudged down the stairs, and Mason said good-bye in the elevator lobby. "I'll knock on your door if Peggy stops by," he said, and to Sweet Marie, "Are you competing tonight?"

"No—just having fun."

"Send me some pictures," he said, and walked down the stairs to his office. Stretching out on the sofa with his phone, he texted Peggy:

Stop by my office after work if you can. You're going to want to see this.

She soon responded: a single exclamation mark. Mason smiled to himself. He knew she'd come. He sent her a second text:

If the coffee place happens to be open on your way in, please bring me up a triple espresso.

It was cheeky, because of course the coffee place would be open, but he knew she wouldn't mind.

He wanted to go to his computer and research 1920s glass, and fiber-optics, but he couldn't muster the energy to get up off the sofa. Instead he closed his eyes for a minute, and thought about the shaft, the glowing column. The light it was diffusing was white, like daylight, certainly like the kind of light that came through a skylight. But what was the purpose, hidden away in the center of a stairwell?

Starting awake at a sharp knock on the door, he sprang up and called, "It's open."

"I love your door sign," Peggy said, breezing into the room. "It's very retro."

"It's great, right? No ambiguity about what I'm all about."

She handed him a paper cup. "You owe me five bucks."

"I know this didn't cost that much," he said, frowning and taking a sip.

"I tip well when I'm running errands for someone else."

Mason chuckled. "Let's go see Owen."

"So did you get into the safe?" she asked, as Mason paused to lock his door.

"We did."

"So what's inside?" she demanded.

"Like Astrid said, you have to see for yourself. If I tried to explain it to you, I'd be a fascist."

She laughed but didn't press it, and followed Mason up the stairs. By the time they'd reached the penthouse floor, he'd finished his espresso, and folded the little paper cup into a ball, slipping it into his pocket.

"I was hoping you'd come by," Owen said to Peggy when he answered Mason's knock.

"How's the picking and grinning going?" she asked.

"Great," he said, and beckoned them into the penthouse.

Mason had no idea what they were talking about, but he didn't bother to ask.

"Did Mason tell you what we found?" Owen asked.

"He declined."

"I didn't want to bias her first impression," Mason said.

Owen nodded. "Smart."

Following him into the closet, Mason saw that he had pushed the safe door mostly closed, but it was still slightly ajar.

"You got it open," Peggy said. "How?"

"Psychic power," Owen said. "His, not mine."

"You helped," Mason said, and to Peggy, "We'll explain all that after, but first, you should go inside."

"Behold," Owen said, taking the cue, and with a flourish pulled on the safe's handle, revealing the dim glow of the stairwell.

Peggy walked through the doorway, pausing to look around, then slowly stepped up to the railing.

"What the hell is that?" she said finally.

"No idea," Mason said. "I'm going to ask Astrid."

"It's not meant to be a light fixture, suspended in the middle of a stairwell. No way."

"Owen thought it might be conducting sunlight," Mason said. "It pokes through the roof, and the end of it is under a skylight."

Peggy looked up toward the ceiling, then down through the central gap. "How far down does it go?"

"All the way to the underground parking garage," Owen said. "The only other door is down there."

She wandered down to the next landing, and then farther, leaning over the railing and looking downward.

"Do you want to walk down?" Owen asked. "You'll have to walk back up. We're going to fix it, but for now there's no way out at the bottom."

"Twelve floors? I don't think so," she said.

"It's all the same the whole way anyway," Mason said. "Concrete and stairs."

"Whatever this is," she said, gazing upward along the column, her eyes glinting in the light, "it's magnificent." She reached out to touch the luminous surface, then knocked on it. "Glass?"

"That's what I thought," Mason said, and felt his phone buzz in his pocket. When he pulled it out to check, he said, "It's Astrid," and answered the call, "Braithwaite."

"You found it," Astrid said, her voice so energetic that Mason had to pull the phone away from his ear.

"I'm inside the stairwell right now," he said. "It's kind of beautiful. What am I looking at?"

"I have theories," Astrid said, "but I don't really know."

"So you didn't build any of it."

"Of course not. It was there when I got there."

"You put the skylight dome on the roof, though, correct? What was there before?"

"I would love to come and look at it again," she said. "I can tell you what I know. Will you be available tomorrow?"

"Let me check." He muted the call. "She wants to come by and look at it tomorrow," he said to Owen, "but you have school."

Owen shrugged. "Sweet Marie will be here. He'll be interested to meet her, and he can fill me in."

"Cool," Mason said, and unmuted his phone. "What time tomorrow?" he asked Astrid.

"After lunch. The light is better in the afternoon."

He made a mental note to find out why that was important, and said, "Call me when you're half an hour away, and I'll meet you here."

"Are you sure you're OK to miss Astrid?" Peggy asked Owen, walking up the stairs to join them in the doorway. "I could probably write you an absence note."

"I have stuff I need to do at school. That has to be the priority."

"Aw." Peggy beamed and put her arm around him to squeeze his shoulder, making him take a step to regain his balance.

Grinning, Owen turned to Mason. "Just make sure you take a selfie this time."

"Deal," Mason said.

"So, are you ready to go home?" Peggy asked, but she seemed reluctant to leave, again staring at the column.

"You'll have to drop me at my bike," Mason said.

Stepping out of the stairwell through the safe door, Peggy turned back and said wistfully, "Good-bye, giant glow stick." Owen walked them to the door. "Thanks for showing me," she said.

"I'm thinking there will be more opportunities. It seems there's much more to learn," Owen said.

"That is a great attitude," Peggy said.

Mason followed her down the stairs to his office, where he grabbed his backpack and locked up again. On the elevator ride down to the street, Peggy seemed lost in thought.

"Are you OK?" he asked.

"I'm just thinking about that thing. I'm not sure how to fit it into my mind. Bizarre things are routine for you, but not for me."

"I can't tell you how to interpret it. Astrid was right—you don't need someone else's words to describe it. What you said to her last night was meaningful too: 'Don't label me.' Maybe we shouldn't try to name it and define it yet. Maybe its meaning will turn up in some other way."

"That sounds really wise." Peggy met his eye. "I'm not saying that just because you're quoting me, either."

Her car was just up the block, parked at a meter, and once they'd climbed in, Peggy pulled into the sluggish end-of-day traffic. Mason knew he could have been home in half the time on the metro, but he didn't mind making the trip with her.

By the time he'd put away his bicycle in the garage, Peggy had already changed clothes, and Ned had food waiting for them, tomato soup and focaccia bread that he'd baked, flavored with rosemary. After dinner Mason spent some time at the dining table writing up his notes about the day, eventually tearing the sheets off the pad and stuffing them in his backpack, to be filed later at his office.

He wanted to just go to bed, but his mind was still roiling with the excitement of the day. He pulled open his laptop and sat on the sofa to read about glass. It was a jazz night for Ned, which meant he put on an album and listened to the entire thing, beginning to end, as his sole evening's activity, sometimes followed by another. Visual distractions were not allowed on jazz night, and Ned reclined in an easy chair, the audio cranked up, a tumbler of soda water at hand, eyes closed, no screens to mar the experience. Mason would never verbalize his suspicion that no music could be so valuable as to dedicate a whole evening, never mind even a whole hour, just to listening to it, but it was pleasant to work here with the music as background, and Ned didn't seem to mind having company, as long as Mason didn't interrupt.

Fiber-optic glass, it turned out, didn't exist in the 1920s, so that's not what was mounted in the hidden stairwell. The strands of optical fiber in use today for communication carried light from one end to the other, but the column in the Primavera Building felt more like it was leaking light, not passing it anywhere. Still, it seemed like the right model: the column was transmitting rather than generating light.

After the last strains of Dave Brubeck had faded, they climbed into bed. Ned was relaxed and content from the music, and Mason drifted into the hypnagogic state, where he found himself painting a wall with a floppy brush, working to make it look right. No matter how many times he went over it with the brush, it looked off, his strokes uneven in the new paint, that bland industrial pinkish-tan. Why was he even doing this, when the color below was the same as what he was slapping on top of it? He struggled to become lucid enough to control the dream, but he lost hold of it just as he turned away from the wall, just as he felt he was ready to manipulate things.

Five

A strid was smart, he decided, wanting to meet in the afternoon, because it gave Mason the chance to sleep in and have a leisurely breakfast. He got dressed and put his computer into his backpack, and was just draining his second mugful of espresso when Astrid texted:

I'm leaving my house now.

After he ducked into Ned's office to kiss him goodbye, he cycled to the metro, and once he'd settled into a seat on the train, pulled out his phone and texted Sweet Marie:

We'll be there in twenty.

Sweet Marie's reply came soon after:

I eagerly anticipate your strong manly fingers … knocking on my door.

Mason smiled at the silly innuendo, which was de rigueur for drag queens. It was a good sign, he thought, that the kid was being mentored by pros.

Coming up out of the ground at his station downtown, he admired the Primavera Building, as he always did, and as he stepped into the crosswalk he caught sight of Astrid, at the curb in front of the building, stepping out of a car with a ride-sharing sticker in the windshield. She was wearing a dark suit today, but the way she moved as she climbed out of the vehicle was unmistakable. He trotted across the street to catch up to her, but didn't get too close, knowing his physical size could be intimidating, especially if he caught someone by surprise. Instead he called to her as he approached.

"Right on time."

Astrid smiled when she recognized him. "I was so happy you were able to get through the safe door. I knew you could do it. You're open-minded."

"I'm not sure if that's why I got it, but it's certainly a clever way to encode the numbers. Do you know who did that—who created the design?"

But she was looking past him, and her face contorted with alarm. "Oh, no, no, no … don't look; don't look."

Despite her admonition, Mason spun around, but he couldn't see anything worthy of such a reaction. A man was crossing the street, in the same crosswalk Mason had just used, and he stepped up onto the curb, leisurely making his way up the sidewalk. He was a bit odd looking, in a black trench coat, a floppy black hat, and black sunglasses, but it was a big city, and he certainly wasn't the oddest person around.

"Do you know him?" Mason asked, turning back to her.

"No, no, no," Astrid cried, squeezing her eyes shut.

Mason turned to watch as the black-clad man walked behind the corner of the building, confused as to what Astrid was seeing. The moment he disappeared from view, in the middle of the intersection a car plowed into the back end of another with a sickening crunch.

"Ay, ay, ay," Astride cried, vocalizing her emotional distress.

Mason had seen the crash in the periphery of his view, but now watched closely as both drivers climbed out of their vehicles. They hadn't been moving fast enough for anyone to get injured, it seemed, but the guy from the car in front was already shouting.

"How did you not see me stopped there?" he demanded.

They talked at high volume, but neither one of them was too angry, just understandably freaked out. Another driver honked as he pulled around them, shouting at them about blocking the intersection. Several people on the sidewalk stopped to rubberneck, and one of them had a cell phone out, filming the scene. Watching seemed pointless, and Mason turned away.

"How did you know that was going to happen?" he asked Astrid.

"Did you see the guy?" she demanded.

"The one with the big black hat?"

She nodded, looking relieved. "I wasn't sure if it's only me who sees him or if other people do too."

"What does he have to do with the fender bender?"

"I don't know." She gestured to the crash scene. "When he shows up, something like this always happens. I'm glad you can see him too."

Mason had a sudden thought, and ran to the corner to look for the man in the floppy hat.

"Don't bother," Astrid called after him. "He won't be there."

She was right, he saw—there was no sign of the guy, but he could have stepped into a shop farther up the block, or a car parked at the curb, even the coffee place on the ground floor of Mason's building.

"He did look out of place," Mason said, returning to where Astrid stood on the sidewalk. "Not so much that most people would notice, but something was off. Maybe the hat."

"He dresses like that in summer or winter, whenever I see him, in Buenos Aires or Los Angeles. He's always the same."

"So he's a paranormal entity?"

"I don't know who or what he is." She gestured helplessly, then met Mason's gaze. "But you can see him. It makes me wonder if you're psychic."

"I'm totally psychic. I do psychic research for a living."

Her eyebrows rose. "That explains a lot. You don't really work for the building's new owners?"

"I do, but I'm kind of a subcontractor."

Astrid nodded. "Let's go inside. We don't need to watch this ugliness." She gestured to the crash. "Standing out here makes me feel like a siren on the rocks."

Mason took a last look at the crash, where both men were bent over the hood of the second car, examining paperwork, and followed Astrid into the building. She really did have an intense cloud of paranormal energy surrounding her.

Astrid clearly knew the place, leading the way inside, ignoring the security guard and striding into the elevator lobby.

"So why did a real estate company hire a psychic?" she asked, standing in front of the middle elevator but not pressing the button to summon it.

"To figure out what was in that stairwell."

Astrid cackled in response, and stepped away from him, looking up at the murals that ringed the walls above the doorways. "It's not the best example of the genre," she said, "but at least he had heart."

Mason looked up at the familiar artwork, a pair of oxen pulling a plow with a laborer clad in nineteenth-century garb walking behind them. He hardly ever bothered to give them even a passing glance.

"I never really liked these," he said. "They're too dark, and kind of oily looking."

Astrid scoffed, and pressed the elevator call button. "Art isn't about what you like," she said, using her fingers to put air quotes around the word *like*. "What you *like* is called entertainment. Art is something that gives you a glimpse of a tiny shard of the true nature of reality."

There was a soft *ding,* and the sign above one of the elevator doors lit up in red, signaling THIS CAR UP. Mason followed Astrid into the car.

"That sounds important," he said, and hesitated, looking at her. Finally he said, "I'm going to write it down," and pulled off his backpack, fishing in it for a pen and pad.

Astrid grinned. "You won't just remember it?"

"It sounds like something I'm going to have to think about. I don't understand it yet, so it's better to commit it to paper."

Still writing as the doors opened, Mason followed her off and put his pad away, then knocked firmly on the penthouse door. When Sweet Marie pulled it open, he was wearing chinos and a conservative blue dress shirt.

"Hey, man," Sweet Marie said, his tone lower than usual, puffing out his chest a little.

Mason had to grin. Was he doing that because of Astrid? Mason introduced them, and Sweet Marie waved them in.

"Are you an intern for the holding company?" Astrid asked him.

"I actually own the holding company, with my boyfriend," Sweet Marie said.

"Wow." She looked him over. "You certainly married well."

Fleeting annoyance flashed in Sweet Marie's eyes, but his words were gentle. "I love the renovation—you did a really beautiful job."

"Thank you," Astrid said, and did a little neck bow. "I tried to stay true to the original architect's intentions."

"Well, your restraint and minimalism allow it to shine. That's why we bought it."

Astrid preened, smiling broadly. "It makes me happy that you appreciate it. The last owners saw it just as an investment, no different from a warehouse or a factory or a parking lot."

"So what's with the glowing column thing?" Sweet Marie asked.

"Can I look at it?"

"Of course," he said, and before he could move, Astrid was headed toward the closet, clicking on the room lights like she lived there herself. Mason followed them inside, and watched as Astrid pulled open the safe door and stepped into the stairwell. He joined Sweet Marie inside as Astrid walked down to the next landing.

"Such a beautiful thing," she said, her tone reverent. She reached out and touched the column, and the light pooled around her fingers, intensifying in the glass where she touched it. That definitely had not happened when he'd touched it, Mason thought, watching her closely, but she let her hand drop away. He reached out, pressing his fingers on the column, just to make sure. There was no reaction in the glass, just the smooth, cool texture of the surface. Watching Astrid again, she seemed enchanted, her eyes bright.

"What's it for?" Sweet Marie asked.

"I don't know," she said, gazing at the glass. "But I have a theory. I think it's an avant-garde skylight."

"In a sealed stairwell?" Mason asked. "Why not just put up lightbulbs? And why are there only two doors to this stairwell?"

"The light is not just for the stairs. I think it was meant to illuminate the whole building. The original design had doors and windows into this shaft: a door on each floor, and a big window on the perpendicular wall. That would distribute the light beyond the shaft. Every floor has two knockouts. I wanted to use them."

"What's a knockout?" Mason asked.

Astrid walked down the next flight of stairs, beckoning them to follow. Mason and Sweet Marie joined her farther down, directly below the safe door. If it lined up with the eleventh floor, it meant they were standing inches from Miss Cassie's restroom.

"This looks like just a concrete wall, yes?" She slapped her palm on the gray surface. "On the other side we found the frame of a door." She drew a rectangular shape with her finger. "This is concrete fill, but the door frame is there, designed so you can easily knock out the filler. Ten minutes with a sledgehammer and you could expose a nice neat door frame. On the adjacent wall, a little higher because of the stairs, there's a window knockout. They're on every floor, all the way down to the ground."

"So the original architect planned to add doors and windows later?" Mason asked.

"Yeah," Sweet Marie said, frowning. "Why wouldn't he just do it when they put up the building?"

"Excellent questions." She shrugged. "I also can't explain why the shaft is hidden behind the safe door."

"Wait a minute," Mason said, thinking it through. "If it's supposed to be a skylight, this stairwell is on an outside wall. If you wanted light, why wouldn't you just put in windows?"

"That is more logical, yes," Astrid said. "That's why I can't say for certain that it's a skylight. Maybe there's something I'm not seeing." She nodded to the column. "The glass, for example, has unusual properties. Just a little bit of it is exposed to the sky, but it's transmitting a remarkable amount of light. At first I assumed it was a light fixture, but it's not plugged into any power source."

Mason looked at the column again. It didn't really seem very bright, but considering it was twelve stories tall, maybe it was.

"Isn't it odd that you'd build a glass column," he said, "whatever the purpose was, and then hide it?"

Astrid smiled. "And there is the mystery." She looked at the column again, stepping close to the railing, following it upward with her eyes. "Maybe it was here before the building was, and they did the construction around it, rather than tearing it down."

"Are you serious?" Sweet Marie demanded. "I think I would have heard about that."

"Or maybe the original architect planted a moon rock in the garage, and it grew into this, reaching skyward for its mother. There's no reason we can't create mythology for it," she said, her gaze fixed on the light. "It's definitely something out of the ordinary."

"A glimpse of the true nature of reality?" Mason asked.

"A very good observation," she said. "I think that's exactly what it is."

They stood there in silence, gazing at the column. Even Sweet Marie seemed content just to look at it for a while.

Without really thinking about doing it, Mason started to perceive the column with his nonphysical senses. When he realized what was happening, he considered interrupting it; after all, drifting out of consensus reality seemed like something that should be carefully managed. But he let it happen, closing his eyes and feeling the column. It felt dense, and energized— not just passively, with light streaming through it, but with power of its own. An image came to mind of a slice of banana bread, studded with pieces of walnut. Envisioning that, he could taste it, moist and delicious, the way Ned made it, with the crunchy nutty bits.

Opening his eyes, he shook off the imagery. "You didn't change anything during the renovation?"

"I wanted to," Astrid said. "I was going to remove the knockouts and put a nice door and a window where they were meant to be. White frosted glass, and locking doors, of course. Every office would always have natural light."

"So the window knockouts are where the restrooms are?" Sweet Marie asked.

"Right—and the door knockouts open into the main room. If you decide to implement them, you'll have lovely windows in the back wall of the restrooms, and another exit in those suites."

"Why didn't you do that?" Mason asked.

Her face clouded. "Because the Texas real estate men thought it would look too strange."

"It would," Mason said. "The whole idea is strange. It makes me think it wasn't meant to be functional."

Astrid scoffed. "Spare me your postmodern bull-shit."

"What are you talking about?" Mason said, looking at her.

"You can agree that the man who designed this building was a genius, yes?" she demanded. To Sweet Marie, she said, "You said you bought it because you loved it. The architect's reasons are unimportant. All that matters are his intentions. What was it supposed to look like? I wanted to honor that, and the knockouts gave me a clue. As for his reasons, we can't read each other's minds, and speculating is selfish."

"Why is that selfish?" Mason asked. "It seems like a reasonable question."

"Because it makes it about you, not the work," she said, her voice rising. "Our work and our actions have to stand on their own, and be judged for themselves."

"Trust the art, not the artist," Sweet Marie said.

"Exactly." Astrid nodded emphatically.

Mason looked at Sweet Marie. "I didn't know your opinions on art were so evolved."

"They're not. I'm just reiterating what she's saying, because I've heard it before. When I took English lit, the prof said, 'Trust the tale, not the teller.' I'm with you, though—I want to know what it's for."

"Bah," Astrid said, waving her hand. "In ancient Greece, you two would have been ascetics. They would stare at their belly button for seven days to achieve enlightenment."

"People actually did that?" Sweet Marie asked.

"A beam of light was supposed to shine out of your belly button, giving you all the wisdom of the world. Your generation is doing it now, but you use your telephones instead of your belly button. Standing alone in a crowd of people, staring at a screen, questing for enlightenment." She sighed, and rolled her shoulders. "Anyway, it's pointless to talk about his reasons, unless you can communicate with the dead."

"I can't, although lots of psychics do," Mason said, eyeing her. "So, do you know anything about the original architect?"

"What was his name?" Sweet Marie asked.

"Augustus Hawley," Mason said.

Astrid smiled. "I'm glad you know him. But I can't tell you much—everything I know you can read yourself at the library."

Latin blood, Mason thought. She was like Ned: quick to get upset and then quick to calm down.

Moving up the stairs, Astrid said, "Thank you for letting me come in. I had many arguments about this shaft. It's like seeing an old friend."

Mason followed her and Sweet Marie out into the closet and then the penthouse, where Astrid spent a moment assessing the space.

"Good furniture," she said. "I'm glad you didn't build any walls. This space is too dramatic for that."

"That's what I thought too," Sweet Marie said. "I'll call you if it comes up again and I need backup."

Astrid grinned at him. "I'd be happy to help if you need to win that argument."

"Can I take a photo of you two?" Mason said, suddenly remembering. "Owen asked."

"He wanted a selfie, so you have to be in it," Sweet Marie said.

Astrid threw up her hands. "Go ahead, but what you see is what you get."

Mason stood beside her, and urged Sweet Marie to crowd in on her other side, then flashed his best smile and snapped the photo. He gave it a cursory assessment. The two of them looked fine, but Mason's smile looked pained and forced, his skin an unearthly pasty pink. There was no point trying again, he knew, as that was as good as it was going to get.

They said good-bye to Sweet Marie and stepped

across to the elevators. Mason pushed the call button, and it stayed lit for a second, but then winked
out. The up and down arrows lit simultaneously, then
flickered off.

"OK," Astrid said, staring at the arrows, her eyes
narrowing.

Mason pushed the button again, and instead of the
usual cheerful *ding* announcing an arriving car, they
heard a muted metallic *thunk*.

"That's it," Astrid said. "I'm taking the stairs."

"Do you think it's something paranormal?"

"These elevators and all the wiring were all redone
under my supervision. I know it's not a mechanical
problem." She turned to the stairwell and started down.

Mason followed her as far as his floor. "This is where
my office is."

Astrid turned to him. "Then I shall say *Hasta luego*."

"Listen—I know a lot of psychics. Maybe one of
them could help you with this paranormal stuff."

"I appreciate the offer, but this is a chronic condition. It's not really fixable."

"How long has it been happening?"

"Many years." She smiled. "But that's a story for
another day. As for your architectural mystery, now you
know as much as I do. I'd love to hear if you find out
anything more." She waved good-bye and turned to
continue her descent.

Returning to his office, Mason admired his bright-
yellow name on the door, thinking again how right-on
it was, then sat at his desk, first sending Owen the selfie, then making notes about Astrid and everything
she'd told them. He pulled out his computer and

searched again for Augustus Hawley, looking specifically for other structures that he'd designed. There were a couple in Chicago from the early 1920s, including a high-rise, the Asia Commerce Building, that had deco styling similar to this one. Mason made notes about specific details of Hawley's life, how he'd worked on this building and then settled in LA—much the way Astrid had, he thought—and died here in 1956. There was a reference to a short biography of the man in a book titled *Stalwarts of California Design*. Mason knew exactly where he could find a copy.

Packing up his computer and pulling on his backpack, he walked the few blocks to the central library, and in a few minutes had found the book and settled into a desk. There were dozens of architects and designers profiled, and Hawley occupied only a few pages, but it was interesting reading. The author explained that Hawley was "known as an occultist," and there was much symbolism and hidden meaning in his work.

As a psychic, Mason heard that word, *occult,* a lot, and knew it basically meant hidden information. But it meant different kinds of information for different people: information hidden from scientific instruments, which meant basically everything Mason did for work and everything that Ned discounted as bunkum; or information hidden from the mainstream, meaning religious groups and other organizations with secrets, like his friend Yoshida, a hard-core freemason. The biographer, sloppily, didn't explain what kind of occultist Hawley was, perhaps forgivable in light of the fact that it was just a few pages outlining the man's work more than an in-depth biography.

There were some hints in the examples provided, though: Hawley used alchemical symbols in his designs, including the symbol for water in the Asia Commerce Building, his deco tower in Chicago. The author speculated that this was done because the structure bordered a river.

There were no images of it in the book, but Mason pulled out his computer and quickly found the water symbol: a simple equilateral triangle with one corner pointing straight down. That would be easy to integrate into lots of designs, he thought, especially in art deco, with its zigzags and chevrons. He spent some time looking at alchemical symbols and reading about their meanings. Hawley was clearly a privileged-info occultist rather than a paranormal occultist, he decided.

Reading to the end of the piece, he found a small footnote that made his pulse quicken: Hawley had left his papers to Live Oak College. Mason had heard of it, and knew it was a design school somewhere in Southern California. He found it online, and saw that it wasn't even that far away, out in the Valley. It took some time digging through the school's website to find the right person, but eventually he did—Claire, the "manager of special collections and archives" at Live Oak's library. He composed an email:

> I work for the owners of the Primavera Building, one of Augustus Hawley's architecture projects, and I'm researching some of his design choices. I understand his papers are in your care. How can I gain access to the collection?

Reading through it again, he hit SEND and then packed up his computer, walking out to the street and back to his office. At street level the building was just unadorned stone, but higher up, out of reach, it was richly decorated in shiny terra-cotta. He stood at the curb, across the sidewalk from the lobby, and stared up at the stonework and the copper trim, now dark green with age.

The copper had chevrons in it, which weren't really alchemical symbols, from what he'd just read, but higher up was a decoration that looked like a series of ascending bubbles, perfect circles with a dot inside each. They were integrated into the design, so it was hard to say whether it was independently symbolic, but thinking about it, he'd just seen a symbol like that in the library. He'd have to check again.

A woman approached him, homeless, he knew, based on her aimless meandering, and he saw her stop beside him at the curb. He kept his eyes on the building, hoping she wouldn't try to engage. Once he caught a whiff of her familiar Skid Row tang, like old shoes and vinegar and window cleaner, he started to breathe through his mouth to avoid smelling it, but he stood his ground.

She followed his eyes upward and stared for a moment, then asked, "What are you looking for, Stretch?"

"A glimpse into the true nature of reality."

"Sounds fancy. Can you spare ten dollars?"

"No," Mason said firmly, and stepped across the sidewalk into the lobby.

Greeting the guard, he took a minute to look around at the stonework and the fixtures, all of them presumably Hawley's originals. He ignored the mural of the oxen and the plowman, as that hadn't been Hawley's work. Suddenly he saw it: above the elevator doors and all around the lobby were light fixtures, six of them, in the same form—the circle with a central dot. He felt the hair stand up on his neck. It was an odd experience, seeing something so familiar with fresh eyes and new information, like suddenly being able to understand a foreign language. Whatever it meant, it had been important to Hawley.

A quick check of his box in the mail room revealed it was still empty, so he said good night to the guard as he left and headed to the metro. Once he was waiting on the platform, he pulled out his phone and found the page describing alchemical symbols. The circle with the dot was one of the fundamental ones: it meant the sun.

Sitting on the train, he mulled the meaning of that in relation to the Primavera Building. It had been commissioned by an insurance company. Insurance was an esoteric construct not fundamental to anything, not like the sun and water and the planets, the stuff of transformative alchemy. Maybe Hawley had just used it as a pleasing design element. But would a man who went to the trouble of building a hidden stairwell with a glowing column running through it really use a symbol that didn't have a connection to the overall project?

Darkness was falling as he rode up the hill to home, and he found Ned still in his office.

"You're working late," he said, going in to kiss him hello.

"I'm on a deadline," Ned said, glancing up. "But let's have something simple for dinner when I'm done."

"Perfect," Mason said, and went out to check his

phone, which had just vibrated with an email.

It was from Claire at Live Oak College, and he sat on the sofa to read it. She explained that Mason should outline his research goals and his affiliation on letterhead and email it back to her.

Easy, he thought, and wrote to Sweet Marie.

> Does your company have letterhead? I need to write a proposal on it to get access to some research material.

Relaxing on the sofa, he read through more emails, then got distracted reading news until Sweet Marie's reply came.

> Letterhead attached. It has the building's street address already on it, but you can just add your phone number or email or whatever. Have fun.

Mason had to grin. Those two really did trust him unconditionally.

He grabbed his laptop and spent a few minutes crafting the letter to Claire at Live Oak College, explaining that he was researching Augustus Hawley's unusual stylistic choices. He didn't say anything about the hidden stairwell, but tried to use learned-sounding language, and threw in some flattery at the end:

> Your institution is so very fortunate to be in possession of the personal papers of this titan of California design.

Under that he typed his name, leaving space for his signature, and even though it was spelled out at the top of the page, added "Primavera Building." After he sent it to Ned's printer, he went into the office to find the sheet and scribble his signature on it, then asked Ned to scan it for him. Ned managed to run it through his document scanner without leaving his chair, barely glancing at the page, and to his credit not getting annoyed at the interruption. He handed the sheet back and said, "I'll email it to you now."

"Thanks," Mason said, and grinned as he went back to the living room.

After he emailed the letter to Claire, he started reading more about alchemy, the symbols and their layered meanings. Ned wandered into the kitchen, but Mason was only vaguely aware of the sound of him working, as he was engrossed in alchemy, which led him to articles about hermeticism. The thinking was so similar to freemasonry, he realized, and wondered if Hawley might have been a freemason. He knew who might know, and pulled up his email, banging out a quick note to Mr. Yoshida.

> Was the architect Augustus Hawley (died 1956) a freemason? He lived in LA, and I thought you might have run across the name.

It wasn't likely that he'd get a quick response, as Yoshida was in his sixties and wasn't tech-obsessed. He probably checked his email about as often as he checked his regular mail.

"Ready to eat?" Ned called to him from the kitchen counter, pulling Mason's attention away from the computer screen.

"Always," he said, and rose, helping Ned transfer their plates to the dining table.

"Seitan steaks au poivre," Ned said as they sat down.

"You call this simple?" Mason asked.

Ned grinned. "It didn't take that long."

"So what's in au poivre sauce?" Mason asked, and Ned explained it, and Mason enjoyed hearing about it. He set aside his research and hung out with Ned for the evening, helping him clean up the kitchen and watching some cringe-inducing television.

Whatever happened in the dream world wasn't clear in his mind, but when he awoke briefly, he had fleeting memories of circles and triangles, basic shapes rearranging themselves and building on one another. But the imagery brought no clear ideas or insight.

Once he'd had some fruit for breakfast and enough coffee to think clearly, sitting at the kitchen counter, Mason looked at his phone to check his messages. Yoshida had written back early in the day, when Mason, sensibly, had still been asleep. "It might be easier if you simply joined our order and did the research in the records yourself," Yoshida began, which made Mason smile. It was true that he'd asked Yoshida for help several times, but Mason had helped him out too. Yoshida continued:

> Membership is privileged information, but because he's so long deceased, I can tell you that he was a brother at our lodge for several years when it was new. He didn't rise very far in the organization, and there's nothing else about him in our records. And because I know you'll ask, no, I don't have any personal knowledge of him.

Mason thumb-typed a quick thank-you to Yoshida,

ending with "You're a rock star," then scrolled through the rest of his email, happy to see that Claire from Live Oak College had also written back:

> I understand your request, and the department head has approved your research. Because the Augustus Hawley collection is kept in the main library, you don't need an appointment. Visit us anytime during regular hours.

That was very good news, he thought, and spent a minute with his phone figuring out how to get to the Live Oak campus. The best option seemed to start with a metro ride, but it would still take him more than an hour. After he drained his mug, he got dressed and made sure all his notes about Hawley were in his backpack, kissed Ned good-bye, then rolled his bike out of the garage.

Standing with his wheels on the train for the long trip out to the Valley, he checked the map on his phone to plan the cycling part at the other end. Annoyingly the campus was at the edge of the hills, which meant it would be an uphill ride.

Carrying his bike up out of the ground again, he set off, cycling on side streets and boulevards when he had to. The Live Oak campus was leafy and pleasant, and not very big, so he quickly found the library. It was definitely a car-oriented place, with one little bike rack to lock his wheels to, put to use by only one other cyclist, who'd chained up a well-worn racing bike.

The library seemed quiet, with just a couple of people working at tables. At the circulation desk he asked for Claire, who soon appeared.

"You must be Mr. Braithwaite," she said, smiling affably, her accent subtly foreign, maybe Caribbean.

"You can just call me Mason."

"Of course. Come with me."

He followed her behind the desk, and realized she was almost as tall as he was; the swirl of her myriad little microlocs gathered behind her head was right at eye level. She showed him to a spacious desk between two narrow windows. It was at the side of the main room, with the stacks lined up just behind it, but it was the only desk along this wall—he'd be able to work in peace.

"I'll have someone bring the boxes," she said, and was gone.

Mason pulled out his computer and set it up, hanging his backpack on the back of the chair. Claire soon returned with a dark-green box under each arm, and a man behind her, young enough that he was likely a student, carried two more.

"These are Hawley's letters and journals," she explained. "There are several more boxes. Kyle here will bring them out. There are also drawings and artworks stored separately because of their size."

"Let's start with this stuff," Mason said, as Kyle left again. "Do I need to wear gloves or anything?"

Claire smiled. "This collection is not that old. Ask Kyle or one of the people on the desk if you need help. They can track me down too if necessary."

"Thanks," he said, and sat down to examine the boxes.

They were made of heavy cardboard but smaller than a banker's box, and numbered sequentially, so he started with the lowest number, sliding off the cover and pulling out the contents. Kyle appeared and deposited two more boxes. The papers inside looked old, wrinkled by the touch of many hands and scented with age. In this stack were letters Hawley had received, filed in sequence with carbon copies of his typed letters of response. Even though they were about his work, not personal matters, Mason decided they were too old to provide any useful insight, dating from the early twenties.

Kyle deposited two more boxes on the side of the desk. "That's all of them," he said. "You're researching art deco?"

Mason leaned back to look at him. He was wearing a natty vest and tie, and wore his faux-blond hair swept back. Definitely a student, Mason thought, if he was interested in the content of these files.

"I'm looking into Hawley himself."

Kyle nodded. "Augustus Hawley was totally deco. There's a great piece of his downtown. The Primavera Building."

Mason grinned. "My office is in that building."

Kyle's eyebrows shot up. "Sweet—so you already know how glam it is."

"I'm trying to figure out some of his design choices."

"One of my profs talked about him. Apparently he had a falling-out with the owners of the building while they were building it. It's always the way, right, the creatives and the money people don't see eye to eye."

"Interesting," Mason said. "I guess we're lucky it got built."

Kyle waved a hand. "Art triumphs once in a while. Let me know if you need anything."

As Kyle left, Mason realized he should have asked for an introduction to his professor, if that person knew about Hawley's experience with the Primavera Building. But maybe the same information would be in these boxes. He surveyed the now crowded desktop and shuffled the paper back into the first box, then checked the numbered labels and opened the next one in the sequence. These were journals, softbound day books filled with neat blocky handwriting. Architects must be trained to write this way, he thought, as the notes on Astrid's blueprints were in a remarkably similar hand.

These were also from the early twenties, and Hawley's journal entries were terse, mostly about meetings and progress on projects. Flipping through the pages, he noticed that some entries were marked with a C in the margin, always near the last note for that day. He pondered the meaning of it. What started with C and only happened intermittently? It wasn't written the same way as his blocky handwritten C's, he realized, but more open, almost a crescent rather than the letterform.

Definitely not a C, he thought, flipping through the next volume, also littered with the mark. Maybe it was a crescent, the alchemical symbol for the moon? Lots of the alchemical symbols had layers of meaning. The circle-dot for the sun also stood for the element gold, he remembered, and the crescent moon meant silver.

The words next to one of the crescents caught his eye:

Found a turtle hiding high up the wall. Came down when I demanded it do so. Was actually a bird with beautiful feathers, no eyes.

He flipped to the next page to find the next crescent, and read the line next to it:

> Grandmother Rose sitting atop a zebra-striped carriage.
> Happy to see me.

Mason knew what these were—he did it himself. Hawley had kept a record of the content of his dreams.

He read through dozens of them before he decided that they weren't really insightful, at least not the kind of insight that he wanted. A lot of them seemed to involve animals, and they were entertaining, and he loved that they shared that habit, but he needed to focus.

Opening three more of the boxes, he found Hawley's journals from the time the Primavera Building was under construction. They were easy reading, as Hawley's language was concise, just the facts. But there were no references to the hidden stairwell or the luminous column, just notes on meetings with the construction company, queries about materials and their supply, and who he met with from the insurance company. It seemed odd that he was involved in the project through its construction and completion; Mason had assumed that an architect's work would be done when the plans had been drawn, but in these journals, Hawley was consulting with the contractors almost daily.

In late 1928 Hawley had left several weeks blank, which was unusual compared to his other journals. After the empty pages, his notes resumed with a cryptic entry:

> Morgan is the only one supportive of original design.
> Will talk to McLeay about using knockouts.

Astrid had explained what knockouts were—this had to be about the stairwell. He shifted his chair closer, eagerly flipping back through the pages. He'd seen the name McLeay written earlier that year, and soon found it. McLeay was the main contractor, the one who was putting up the building.

Mason glanced around to make sure he wasn't being observed, then pulled out his phone to photograph the page with the reference to knockouts, and the one inferring who McLeay was. No one had said he couldn't make copies, but it would be easier if the issue didn't even come up.

On his laptop he found the site with the rundown of the Cudahy Mutual Insurance Company's history that he'd seen when he'd first started researching the building. As he'd suspected from the context, Morgan worked for the company, listed as "head payroll accountant." Did Hawley's note mean that Morgan was the only one at the company who wanted to expose the column in the stairwell? Maybe Hawley had run into the same kind of pushback from the owners that Astrid had when she did the renovation.

Back in Hawley's journal, he kept reading, but it didn't reveal anything about the hidden stairwell beyond that one tantalizing reference, and Mason folded it closed after reading the entry describing the building's dedication and opening for business in 1929. Turning to the letters from that period, most of his correspondence was about other projects that he had pitched or had been contracted to work on, but nothing mentioned the Primavera Building.

Slumping back in his chair, Mason rubbed his eyes, then went out to the circulation desk. Kyle was parked there, gazing at a computer screen.

"Where can I get a coffee?" Mason asked him.

Kyle directed him to the cafeteria, which Mason located after a short walk across a lush grassy lawn. There was an espresso machine, thankfully, and he even found a sandwich with a little green label on its plastic wrap that promised VEGAN. He ate it on the leisurely stroll back to the library, and the caffeine gave him renewed energy to keep digging into Hawley's life.

The 1930s were an employment drought for Hawley, understandable given the worldwide economic collapse, and based on his journals, even in the 1940s and 1950s he seemed to be working less than during the age of art deco, building houses, libraries, and swimming clubs rather than grand towers. He still made note of his dreams, but he never mentioned anything personal. Didn't he have a family, a wife?

Opening the box labeled as the last in the sequence, he found Hawley's correspondence from the 1950s, feeling a twinge of sadness as he started into it, knowing that at this point Hawley was near the end of his life. The addressee on one of Hawley's carbon-copy letters jumped out as he flipped to it: "To the Society for Subconscious Research, NYC." This sounded a lot like Mason's world.

> Sirs, with respect to the proposal put forward by Mrs. Wilson at last month's symposium, I encourage you to seek funding for her project. Her work has demonstrated the veracity of premonitory dreaming. The time to act is now. We must establish the protocols to interpret our dream lives for the benefit of all men.

There was no response filed with the letter, but it implied that Hawley might also be a paranormal occultist, not just the esoteric type. Mason photographed it, then read and scanned through the rest of the contents of the last box, but there was nothing as juicy as the letter about dreaming, and nothing else relating to Hawley's occult ideas.

He closed the box and stacked it neatly with the others at the back of the desk, then went to the front to find Kyle.

"Can I look at the large-format stuff for Augustus Hawley?" Mason asked him.

"Let me find out where it is," Kyle said, and spent a minute absorbed in the computer screen, then rose and led Mason back into the stacks and a row of deep, low cabinets with extremely thin drawers.

"His stuff is this entire unit," Kyle said, pointing it out. "You can spread out the drawings on top."

"Sweet," Mason said, and pulled out the top drawer as Kyle left. It contained blueprints that were actually blue, unlike Astrid's, and fading with age, the lines still visible but faint. Each sheet was dated, but they weren't filed sequentially. It took a while to thumb through all of the drawers, and there was nothing from the Primavera Building until he reached the bottom one, and a sheaf of pages that weren't blueprints, but rather ordinary drawings on yellowing paper. They were done in pencil, he saw when he looked closely, and bore the title PRIMAVERA. He dropped to his knees, fingers trembling—this was it. These were Hawley's plans.

Pulling the sheets out, he rose and spread them on top of the cabinet. First was the one marked 10TH, where his own office was today. He tried to parse the drawing's lines. The style was different than Astrid's plans, and of course the office space was laid out differently, so it took a minute to make sense of it. That had to be the bank of elevators, and that was the main stairwell beside them. Following the outside wall, he found the corner where his office was today.

The missing space was marked, but in this drawing it included the stairs, in a neat square with a landing at each corner. In the back wall of what was now the restroom were thin hairlines—a window. The adjacent side of the shaft had the markings for a door. This confirmed that Astrid was right: Hawley's original plan was to have doors and windows into the stairwell. In the square space at the center of the stairs, representing the column, was a simple circle with a dot in the middle.

Glancing around to make sure he was alone, he photographed the sheet, then compared it to the rest in the sheaf, seeing that on all the floors the shaft was marked identically, even the one labeled 12TH, the penthouse in Astrid's version but in this plan just another warren of offices.

After he shuffled them back in their drawer, he went to get his laptop and pulled on his backpack, then headed out to the circulation desk to talk to Kyle.

"I'm headed out," Mason said. "Thanks for your help."

"Will you be back?" Kyle asked, looking up from his work.

"Possibly—should I let you know in advance?"

Kyle waved dismissively. "Not necessary. Just ask for me or Claire. We're closed quite a lot during the December holidays, so check the schedule before you schlep all the way out here."

Cycling always gave Mason time to think, and it was

an easy downhill ride to the boulevard and the metro. It was a rush to have everything he'd learned so far confirmed by the original source, or at least by his drawings and journals. Hawley was more interesting than he'd expected, with his paranormal pursuits, recording his dreams and lobbying the Society for Subconscious Research. He wanted to talk to the guy now. The big question was still unanswered: what was the column for? Hawley was the only person who could explain it, and despite Astrid's dismissal of trying to ascertain the designer's motives, he really wanted to know.

His train of thought was interrupted when he had to dodge a driver who didn't think taking turns at a four-way stop applied to bicycles, but once he was rolling again, a plan started to coalesce.

There was a way, he knew, to get access to Hawley. Almost from the start of this career Mason had learned the temporal bleed-through technique. It wasn't too difficult to shift perception by a few days, and get a glimpse of the past. A bleed-through was akin to a psychic insight, a shift in perception, albeit vivid and very real rather than vague and symbolic. Actually taking his body with him and being in the past was a lot more work, but he knew it was possible—he'd done it. The problem was that Hawley had lived so long ago. He'd need help getting there, and help getting back. There was only one person to ask.

Once he was underground, waiting on the platform for the train, his bicycle leaning against his thigh, he pulled out his phone and found Pretty Nail Blowout, Ned's nail salon on Sunset Boulevard, in his contacts.

"Is Hanh working today?" he asked the receptionist.

"She's with a client, but she'll be here until nine."

"Can she take a drop-in?" He glanced at the tunnel at the end of the platform as the lights of the approaching train appeared. "I can be there in about twenty minutes."

"It's Mr. Mason, it sounds like?" the receptionist asked.

"That's me," he said, grinning, happy that she knew his name.

"That's fine," she said. "Please visit us."

Hanh had shown up the very first time he'd bled through to the past, which had happened completely unintentionally, and since then she'd never been far away when he was contemplating a bleed-through. She'd asked for his help a couple of times in her own psychic work, usually in tandem with Peggy's boyfriend, Matt, and even though she was tight-lipped about it, Mason had surmised that she had some kind of supervisory role in the supernatural world. There had been signs that she might even be a supernatural being.

Ned knew her only as his manicurist, coincidentally, and had a vague notion that she participated in séances with Mason from time to time. Climbing up out of the ground in Hollywood, Mason pedaled to the familiar strip mall, just a few minutes from the station.

He locked up his bike and went inside, where he found Hanh at the reception desk. She looked up and smiled in greeting. It was only recently that she'd started to treat him with personal warmth, rather than her previous perfunctory businesslike demeanor, and he still found it a bit disconcerting.

"Your digits need some work?" she asked.

"Probably," he said, glancing briefly at his nails. "I also wanted to ask you something."

"I thought so," she said, and beckoned for him to follow her to a nail station farther back.

Despite her commanding presence, she was only as tall as Mason's clavicle, and wore her hair in a severe wedge. One of the other manicurists, working on a woman's nails, looked up at him as they went by, unsuccessfully suppressing a giggle. Hanh said something to her in what Mason assumed was Vietnamese, and the woman laughed out loud.

Mason could feel his face heating up. He knew he wasn't the source of so much entertainment because he was a big mooky guy in a woman's world; lots of guys came in to get their nails done. It was all about the red hair, and it was irritating that Hanh was participating in it.

"You should come in more often," she said, dropping into her seat and taking Mason's hands in hers. "There's only so much I can do when they get like this. We call it salvage work."

Mason flexed his fingers and peered at them. "They don't seem that bad."

"So what did you want to talk about?" she asked, setting to work with a nail clipper.

"You know that time I went to the 1950s?" he asked.

"Of course. I was there."

"Good," he said, relieved that she remembered. She didn't seem to experience time in a linear way, so it was equally possible that it hadn't happened for her yet.

"I want to go back," he continued, "and interview a guy about a case I'm working on. I'll need your help because it's too far for me to do it alone."

Hanh's eyes flicked up at him, and she gestured for his other hand. "What information does this man have that you need?"

Mason explained about the hidden stairwell, and the luminous column, and Augustus Hawley.

"It seems like a lot of work for a vanity project," she said.

"Why would you call it that?"

"It's not about someone's physical or mental well-being. You're just curious about it because your office is there."

"That's true, but it doesn't mean it's not important." He watched her working on his cuticles. "Maybe this column has some significance that no one knows about except Augustus, and it's languishing, hidden away, when it could be put to good use. Besides, it's just a small favor. I'm the one who'll be doing most of the work."

"What if I said I can't help you with this?" She focused on his fingers, not looking up.

"Well, I guess I'd be very sad."

"But you'd do it anyway?"

"Of course not," Mason said. "I could probably get there with help from a couple of other psychics, Matt and Anna, maybe, but I don't think I could get back without you. It's way too risky—I wouldn't even attempt it."

A smile played on her lips. "I'm glad to hear you have a realistic understanding of the world." She met his eye. "Almost anyone else would have said, 'I'm going to do it anyway.' If it was anyone else, Mason, I'd probably say no. But I will help you, if it's something you really want."

"I do," Mason said, holding her gaze.

"You'll need to ask Matt for help," she said, returning to his nails, her tone businesslike. "We'll send you and retrieve you at the same time on this end. Pick your arrival time carefully—you don't want to waste the trip if he's overseas or something and you can't meet with him."

"I will," he said, and broke into a smile. He was so glad she was willing to help. Matt was easy to work with too—they'd become friends in the psychic world before he was Peggy's boyfriend; Mason had introduced them.

"Did you notice anything unusual about Astrid Luna?" she asked, her brow furrowing.

"Totally," Mason said, not bothering to ask how she knew about Astrid. Not bounded by the flow of time like most people—and Hanh wasn't, moving back and forth like other people strolled around an art museum—questions about time lines fell apart. "That woman is surrounded by paranormal weirdness."

"She's been on my radar for a while."

"What's going on with her?"

"You know how some windows are just a pane of glass in the wall, and don't open," she said, "and some windows open wide, and some open just a crack?"

"Sure," he said, suppressing a sigh. He could rarely make sense of her convoluted analogies. "Like the windows in my office. They're big, but they only open a few inches. It's annoying. I think it's some kind of safety code thing because they're on a high floor."

"Most people are fixed panes that never open," she

continued. "They never experience the wider universe beyond their physical senses. Some people experience paranormal events but ignore them, or discount them, like a window that opens a crack and then quickly gets sealed up again. Very few are like you and Matt—windows that open wide to the other layers of reality."

"So Astrid is like us?"

Hanh shook her head, rubbing something cold and viscous onto Mason's fingers. "The frame around Astrid's window is loose. The pane is there, but rain comes in, and wind whistles through, like a window without a decent wall."

"I can see that," he said. "It sort of feels like weirdness is leaking in around her."

"It's no coincidence that you've run across her. I think you can help her."

"You know, I had that instinct too. How would I go about that?"

"Psychic window repair," she said flatly.

Mason laughed. "Can you be more specific?"

"One thing at a time, as people always say. Let's send you to meet your architect first."

"Great," Mason said. "When can we do that?"

"Whenever you're ready. Late at night works best, so any evening after eleven." She finished wiping the goop off Mason's hands, and wiped her own on a towel. "Do your prep work and let me know."

"These look really good," he said, inspecting his nails. "Thanks for salvaging them."

He paid the receptionist on the way out, and decided to cycle all the way home along Sunset. It wasn't far. Peggy and Ned were both in the kitchen when he got in, happily collaborating, both in food-stained kitchen aprons.

"Dinner in half an hour," Ned told him, after he'd leaned across the counter to kiss Mason hello.

"Yay," Mason said, and went to their bedroom. His plan was to relax for a minute and reflect on the day, but as soon as he'd stretched out, Ned was waking him for dinner.

Joining them at the table, Mason saw that they'd prepared a spaghetti squash with a creamy dill sauce, sharp and cheesy, and roasted cauliflower on the side.

After he'd told them both how delicious it was, he asked Peggy, "So how's school?"

"You might be surprised to hear this," she said, twirling squash around her fork, "but not every child is capable of learning music."

Ned laughed. "They're lucky to have you to extract from them what little there is."

"For most of them, it's zero. For a few it might even be in the negative range—when they play it actually sucks goodness and light out of the world."

Mason eyed her. "But it's still worth it for the ones with some talent."

"More than worth it. One kid like Owen balances a hundred who don't want to be there," she said. "So what's the progress on the giant glow-stick?"

Mason speared a cauliflower floret with his fork and told them about Astrid visiting the building, and his trip to Live Oak College to dig through Augustus Hawley's papers. "I'm actually planning to talk to Augustus."

"He's dead, isn't he?" Ned asked, meeting his eye.

"I thought you didn't believe in communicating with the dead."

"It's not really like that. It's called a bleed-through. A psychic experience where I send my mind to when he was alive." He wasn't about to explain that he planned to take his body with him, to actually go there. Ned would never believe it.

"Ah," Ned said, shifting his focus to gathering a forkful of squash. He added vaguely, "I think you've talked about that."

He wasn't trying to be dismissive, Mason reminded himself, pushing aside his annoyance. He knew Ned was actually trying to stay civil.

"I hope you do talk to him," Peggy said. "I'd love to know what the column is for."

Mason nodded. "Finding out might not change anything, though. Hanh actually called it a vanity project."

She frowned. "That sounds judgmental."

"You're consulting Hanh on this?" Ned asked.

"She's going to help me with the bleed-through."

"OK," Ned said, eyeing him thoughtfully.

After they'd eaten, Peggy left to spend the night at Matt's, and Mason helped Ned clean up.

"Want to unwind with an old movie?" Ned asked. "One of the services just added a film noir section."

"I've got some work to do, but I might watch the end with you later," Mason said.

The evening was pleasant enough that Mason decided he could sit on the balcony. He put on a sweater and took his computer out, getting comfortable on a lounge chair and looking out at the lights of the hilly neighborhood.

It was like walking a tightrope, navigating what he told Ned about his work and what he glossed over. Miss Cassie was of the opinion that he should tell him everything, but Mason wasn't completely on board with that yet. Explaining reality as Mason saw it would devolve into an argument or a stand-off. Ned knew there were things Mason didn't explain—he had to know—but he seemed content not having all the information, as he usually didn't press for details.

He sighed and pulled open his laptop, wincing at the brightness of the screen. Looking through the photos of documents that he'd taken at Live Oak College, he found the letter Hawley had written to the Society for Subconscious Research. It had been written in 1949, and the key phrase was "premonitory dreaming." Searching for that phrase turned up a lot of results. The scientific establishment seemed to consider any mention of it to be pseudoscience. Less dogmatic writers called it "fringe" rather than unscientific, but overall, Mason decided, it definitely fit the definition of occult.

Hawley's letter mentioned "Mrs. Wilson." It took him a few minutes to find a connection between that name and the field of premonitory dream research, but eventually he found her by searching with the word *subconscious* instead of *dream*. The reference was to a book on the history of U.S. psychology, and with a little more digging Mason found a relevant extract. It had to be the person Hawley had written about:

> Jane Wilson's postwar research into the possibility that dreams could predict widely reported events, such as

hurricanes and earthquakes, was cut short when the threat of funding cuts in the increasingly conformist McCarthy era forced her to focus on more palatable pursuits in psychology. Her subsequent work was far less innovative, and her published research papers are a footnote in the long ascendancy of behaviorism.

It implied that Hawley never got his wish, that her research never achieved anything. But this was an invaluable bit of information, a puzzle piece dropping into place. It was going to help Mason gain Hawley's confidence.

He had to approach Hawley in the 1950s, he knew that now, not in the hectic 1920s when the Primavera Building was going up. Besides, he'd been there before, just for a few hours, when he'd been working for some futuristic scientists. They'd even outfitted him with a vintage suit that he still wore sometimes.

LA in the 1950s was well documented, he found, doing a cursory search, and even though he'd been there, and had a feel for the place, he spent some time now reading about it, scanning photographs from the era. Funny that Ned was watching film noir on television right now, probably made in the period Mason was researching.

Next he searched for writing about McCarthyism and conformity in that era, becoming increasingly disheartened as he read. It hadn't just been fringe scientific research; hundreds of authors and filmmakers, even people in roles behind the camera, had been branded disloyal and were unable to work. Some emigrated, never to return.

Eventually he couldn't read any more, and folded

his computer closed. Ned was already in bed, hands folded behind his head, watching Mason as he peeled off his clothes and climbed in.

"You know what the surgeon general says you should do before doing a bleed-in?" Ned asked.

"It's a bleed-through."

"Right—that's what I said."

"Um … obey the speed limit?" he said, draping his arm across Ned's belly.

"Nope. They recommend raunchy sex."

Mason laughed. "I'm in, but I really hope the surgeon general isn't interested in my sex life." He ran his hand over Ned's toned chest, quickly getting turned on. "I wouldn't be surprised, though—I've been reading about the McCarthy era. It's scary how much damage one backwoods totalitarian can do."

"You obviously haven't been reading about the Senate lately," Ned said, leaning in and kissing him hard.

They both forgot about politics, getting into the familiar satisfying rhythm.

Later on, Mason was walking down a flight of stairs—Augustus's hidden stairwell, he realized. Sure enough, the column was right there when he checked, but it was brighter than before, to the point that he had to squint to look at it. Now he was seeing it from above, outside the stairwell, through the roof, still glowing blindingly white. Pushing himself up into consciousness, he scrabbled in the nightstand drawer for his bedside pad, and wrote down what he could remember.

bird's-eye view of the column
extremely bright

Seven

His alarm sounded early, and he slapped it off, sitting up so that he wouldn't drift back to sleep. Last night he'd checked the opening time of the library at Live Oak College, and he wanted to get there early. After he slammed an espresso and munched on an apple and a persimmon, waiting for his body to catch up to the pace of the rest of the world, he gathered his computer and his notes and started the long commute.

Kyle was on the circulation desk, Mason was happy to see when he walked in.

"You're back," he said, looking up at Mason, and then frowned. "Are you OK? You're kind of red."

"Just a little winded. It's uphill all the way, and I'm on a bicycle."

Kyle's eyes grew wide. "I'm sorry to hear that."

"It's not a tragedy," Mason said. "I cycle because I want to."

He didn't look convinced, but said, "You know, I don't think we even refiled the Hawley papers. I'll take you back there." He rose from his chair. "Can I get you some water or something?"

"I'm fine," Mason said firmly, following him inside to the desk he'd occupied yesterday.

As Kyle had promised, the boxes were just as Mason had left them. Once he got settled he found Hawley's journals for the 1950s. He had spent much more time previously on 1928 and 1929, but today he did a closer reading of the later years. Hawley's letter about Jane Wilson had given him the seed of an idea, and maybe he could find more.

Flipping through and reading the mundane details of a life lived long ago, Mason's focus started to flag, until he flipped to a page in 1952 with a word written at the top in Hawley's neat draftsman's hand, and twice underlined: "Exonerated."

It was the only thing written on that day, with no explanation following. It seemed like something important—the word implied it was a legal matter. There had been something else in that vein, he remembered, the year before, and after he snapped a surreptitious photo of the entry with his phone, capturing the lone word and the date beside it, he started flipping backward through the pages. It had been two years earlier, he found, after hunting through many days. A single line: "Deposed for four hours," with no further explanation. That was clearly for a legal matter too, but about what?

He sighed and kept flipping backward, scanning Hawley's notes. At least his handwriting was easy to read. A few weeks before the "deposed" entry he found "Subpoenaed for Miller house." Again he photographed the entries, making sure the date was visible. This was juicy: Augustus had been involved in a lawsuit, and now he had a name.

Walking back to the circulation desk, Kyle was nowhere to be seen, but Claire sat in his place.

"Is it possible to get connected to the county court filings database, and the newspaper archive?" he asked.

"You have your own computer, if I remember correctly?"

"I do."

"Give me a minute," she said, "and I'll bring you the login details."

Once he was in the court database, he found a case with *Miller* and *Hawley* in the 1950s. There was only one—this had to be it.

It was hard to parse the legalese, but it was a civil case, and it read like Hawley was getting sued because a house he had designed had collapsed. *Ouch,* Mason thought, and searched again for additional records, wanting to read about the resolution of the case, the outcome of the trial. Hawley had proclaimed his exoneration several years later; how had that come about? But he couldn't find anything more from the court.

Giving up on it, he shifted to the newspaper index, searching for the same names and limiting the results to the 1950s. The first article that came up was from the *Los Angeles Daily Bugle* in 1950: "Palos Verdes Mansion Collapses into Sea." He definitely wanted to read that, but it was too old to have had the text transcribed. The other entry was titled simply "Interview with Augustus Hawley" in a journal called *Western Architect and Designer*, but again no digital version of the text was available.

Back at the circulation desk, he spoke to Claire. "Do you have microfilm for the *Bugle* in the 1950s?"

"Unfortunately, we don't," she said. "We could order it from one of our partner libraries."

"Thanks anyway," he said, and flashed her a smile as he went back to his desk.

It took a few hours to read through the rest of Hawley's journals. Mason got the sense that the guy hadn't been doing much of anything in the 1950s, apart from the occasional "lodge meeting," probably meaning his time with the Rugley Hall freemasons that Yoshida had told him about. Not once did he mention a wife, or any other family matter. That was worrying. Mason needed to know, needed a fuller picture of the man's life. Toward the middle of 1955 a new entry appeared, repeated more frequently until there was almost nothing else: "Doctor." The last months of that year were blank. It was the final journal in the series, and Mason knew he'd died in 1956. It was sad, he thought, staring at the last entries he'd made. It was as if Hawley had just faded away.

Once he'd put the journals back in their boxes, he packed up his computer and made his way to the circulation desk.

"I'm on my way out," he told Claire. "I won't need to come back."

She smiled. "I hope you learned everything you needed."

"Enough, I think," he said. "Thank Kyle for me."

On the ride back to the metro, he thought through the plan for his excursion. It was coming together, but he wanted to read more about that court case. To gain Hawley's confidence, that proclamation, "Exonerated," might be the key.

Locking up his bike outside the central library, he went in to the atrium and descended the escalators to the history department. That's where the spools of microfilm containing old newspapers were kept, and soon he had the right one in hand, and got set up at a reader. Zooming through the white-on-black pages and stopping to check the date printed along the top, eventually he found the article: "Palos Verdes Mansion Collapses into Sea." The subhead elaborated: "No Injuries; Construction Debris Litters Beach."

Hawley had designed the house, as the legal filing had said, and while it had been under construction, it was swept in a landslide ninety feet down to the water. A grainy photo showed jumbled and broken wood and other detritus on a narrow stretch of sand. There had been no victims because it had happened at night when no one was working. Mason knew that neighborhood—plenty of old houses lined the cliffs above the sea, and there had been landslides in recent years, even an entire neighborhood red-tagged and fenced off when it started to collapse.

The house had been commissioned by a man named Ernest Miller, and now that Mason had that name, he could probably find out more. He sent the article to the printer and pulled out his computer, connecting to the library's newspaper index, which led him to a subsequent article in the *Bugle*. It was dated just a few weeks later, and when Mason checked the microfilm box, as luck would have it, that issue was also on this spool.

He zoomed through the pages until he found it. This article covered the lawsuit, and Mason soon read that Ernest Miller had sued everyone involved—Hawley, the contractor, even the city office that had granted the permits. He pressed PRINT and went back to the counter, where he filled out a request slip for a different spool of the *Bugle,* two years later, for an article that explained how the lawsuit ended, the day Hawley had marked his exoneration in his journal.

Back at the microfilm reader he installed the spool and located the article. There hadn't even been a trial, just a summary judgment, whatever that was, assigning all the blame to a geologist who had misunderstood the nature of the ground the house was built on. It made sense that Hawley wasn't at fault if the problem was the land itself.

The other thing he wanted to read was the interview in *Western Architect and Designer.* He filled out a slip and left it with one of the librarians, who soon came over to the machine where he was sitting.

"This one is in hard copy," she said, handing the slip back to him. "I wrote down the shelf number for you. It's right over there."

Walking in the direction she'd pointed and perusing the stacks, he pulled down the hardbound volume of the journal labeled 1954 and carried it to a desk. It was easy to understand why it hadn't been relegated to microfilm—there were a lot of photos in splashy old-timey color as well as stylish page layouts. The price printed on the cover, $2, seemed like a lot for the time, but then color printing would have cost a premium. Flipping through the magazine, he found the interview with Hawley. It was just a few pages, mostly with photos of his recently designed houses, along with a post office somewhere, and one of the Primavera Building. There was a black-and-white photo of Hawley, reclining on a sleek midcentury sofa, one arm draped casually over the back, eyeing the camera, his expression confident and relaxed. He was in his sixties by this time, Mason knew, and he looked it. His hair was dark and slicked back, and he wore a thin little pencil mustache. Under a dark sweater-vest he wore a necktie, as they all did back then, but no jacket.

The reference he'd found to this article meant it discussed the Miller house at some point, but the first line on the page instantly eclipsed that:

> In tony Los Feliz, at the end of leafy Mount Clemens Drive, I sat down with architect Augustus Hawley in his gracious 1932 Tudor Revival.

Mason couldn't help but smile. It was a stalker's dream—now he knew where the guy lived, even how to identify the house. He opened his computer and searched for "Tudor Revival." Perusing the images that came up, it seemed to be distinguished by dark vertical wood beams over white walls, and the roofs had a sharp pitch.

Got it, he thought, and went to a mapping site, zooming in on the Los Feliz neighborhood, soon locating Mount Clemens Drive. It had two ends, of course, but one was at the boulevard, so Hawley's house must be at the other, farther up in the hills. The street view revealed only one Tudor near the end of the road, and it looked like it could easily date to 1932. He copied down the address.

The interview in *Western Architect and Designer* started directly with the Miller lawsuit, and consisted mostly of the journalist asking softball questions about the righteousness of Hawley being found not legally culpable for the incident, more generally implying how architects shouldn't be held responsible for structural issues; those pesky problems were for the engineers. In his responses, though, Hawley had clearly been worried about being blamed:

> When you hear something shocking, the environment you're in seems to become cemented in memory. I'll never forget the moment the call came from my lawyer. I was listening to the radio, the 10 o'clock news, and he called me from the courthouse. At first I was annoyed at the interruption, but it was wonderful to be exonerated, and wholly unexpected. I felt liberated for the first time in years.

Mason sat back in his chair, amazed at his luck, elated that his plan was coming together. He knew exactly what day that had been. Hawley had recorded it in his journal: "Exonerated." That was the day he had to approach him.

Standing over the heavy volume splayed open on the desk, he positioned his phone to photograph the portrait of Hawley, and then the textual parts of the story.

After he replaced the volume on the shelf, he packed up and headed out to the atrium. Despite how early he'd woken up, and all the work he'd done, he bounded up the escalator, energized by what he'd learned—he had almost everything he needed, and it made his heart soar.

Once he was out of the building, he unlocked his bike and then paused beside the library's little lawn to phone Matt.

"Are you still at school?" he asked when Matt picked up.

"Hell, no—I don't have classes until Monday," he said. "I'm at home."

"The sweet life of the academic," Mason said. "Do you have time for a coffee? I'm downtown."

"I'll meet you at the place with the courtyard."

Pedaling over to the Arts District, Mason thought about the other time he'd been in the 1950s. It took a minute to remember the dates, but he was right— this excursion was happening only a couple of months later. It meant he had contacts there. He could look up Mamie, a canny drag queen who'd planted a kiss on him, uninvited but not unappreciated. It seemed like an oddly convenient coincidence that the two trips aligned so closely, but as he was wont to tell people, there are no coincidences. This was meaningful, a syn- chronicity. Maybe it was happening so that he could connect with Mamie. No way was he going to kiss her again—that was just asking for trouble.

The Arts District had morphed from a neighborhood of outmoded warehouses and industrial spaces, where art had been produced in makeshift conversions, into a sparkling zone where art was sold in upscale galleries, meaning the artists had moved on to more affordable places. But at least there were lots of dining options.

Matt was already there when Mason walked into the bistro, nursing a coffee at a table for two, and Mason hung his backpack on the other chair before sitting down.

Despite the fact that the academic year was in full swing, and Matt had presumably been teaching today, he wore several days' worth of stubble, and his brown hair was wild and unkempt, his red plaid shirt open a few buttons.

"I get the feeling you have some work on," Matt said, lacing his fingers around his coffee cup.

Mason grinned. "You had a psychic insight?"

"No, but it's one of the two reasons you call me."

The server stopped by, and Mason ordered a double espresso. Turning back to Matt, he asked, "What's the other reason?"

"You've got no work on, and you're bored."

He chuckled. "This is a work one."

"For Hanh?" Matt asked, concern clouding his expression.

"It's for me, but she's going to help. I'm going to do a bleed-through to the 1950s."

"Wow—that's far."

"Hanh says I'll need the combined efforts of the three of us to send me there."

"And to bring you back, presumably," Matt said. "I hope you have a good reason. The farther you go, the more fucked-up it is to get back."

"I remember," Mason said, eyeing him. He'd helped Hanh pull Matt back from the eighteenth century, where he'd become stranded. He'd returned looking like a homeless person, grubby and emaciated, and

138

it had taken him days to recover from the trauma of the journey.

"I'm happy to help," Matt said, and paused as the server set down Mason's coffee. "When will these events be taking place?"

"Hanh said you'll send me and pull me back at the same time, so it's only one event."

"That's new," he said, raising his eyebrows. "But I guess I didn't have a return plan when I did it." He scoffed at the memory. "What a fucking moron I was."

Mason sipped at his espresso. "More of an oversight, don't you think? You didn't know what you were getting into."

Matt shrugged.

"Hanh said we'd do it late at night," Mason continued, "so tomorrow, I'm thinking, or maybe even tonight. We'll do it at my office."

"I'm around. Just give me a few hours' notice. My only plan for the weekend is to see Peggy."

"How's it going with her?"

"Fucking great," he said emphatically. "The *L* word has been mentioned."

Mason frowned. "Lesbian?"

"No, you dipshit, *love.*"

"Oh, right—that sounds serious."

"In the best possible way." He hesitated, but then spoke. "Dude, she makes me feel happy."

"That," Mason said, "is huge."

Cycling back toward his office, he texted Peggy while he was stopped at a light.

Are you available to work on a graphics project? I can actually pay you.

A few blocks later, he felt his phone buzz softly in his pocket, and glanced at her reply:

Sure. Home in an hour.

It would take Mason longer to get there, as he had stops to make. There was an office supply store on the way to his office, and he locked up his bike out front, then went in to pick up what he'd need. It took a minute to assess the cardstock and the photo paper, with so many kinds for sale, but eventually he picked the best options, tucking them into his backpack at the register.

At his office, he wheeled his bicycle into the lobby and took it up in the elevator, dropping its kickstand and parking it in the broad open space beyond his bookshelves. Sitting at his desk, he pulled out the middle drawer and reached for the stack of cash he kept at the back. It was probably foolish to leave it lying around, and there was a lot of it, he thought, thumbing through the pile, more than he'd realized. But people tended to pay him in cash, presumably to avoid creating a visible record of their dealings with a psychic, and it had started accumulating in that drawer.

Counting out the amount he thought he'd need and stuffing it in his pants pocket, he hid the stack under a packet of envelopes again and closed the drawer, then wheeled his bike back to the elevator and down to the street. His next stop took more thought than the office supply store, as he needed a less ubiquitous item. He knew of a couple of antique coin dealers who might be able to help him, in the Jewelry District, just a few blocks from his office. Outside the storefront of the first one he came to, he locked his bicycle to a street sign and went in.

At the sound of the front door's electronic chime, a gray-haired guy, in a dress shirt that was struggling to stay in his pants over his bulging belly, emerged from the back and put his hands on the counter.

"Buying or selling?" he asked affably. He had the authoritative air of a proprietor.

"Buying."

"My favorite," he said. "What are you looking for?"

"Antique paper money. Do you sell that, or only coins?"

"I've got paper. U.S. currency?"

"Specifically late 1940s or early 1950s. Nothing dated after 1952. I don't need pristine bills—anything with the right dates will do."

"Let me see what I've got," he said, and stepped into the back.

Mason was relieved the guy hadn't asked why his request was so specific. It meant he didn't need to spew some half-baked story about being a collector, inevitably to get caught out in the lie. While he waited he admired the coins on display inside the glass counter, strategically lit to make them shine. It seemed like such an inane hobby, collecting old money, but obviously enough people did it to keep this place afloat.

The owner returned with an accordion box, labeled in felt pen USA 1928–1953, and flipped it open on the counter.

"The design changed in 1953, so your ask is easy," he said. "All of these have been in circulation. Are you looking for specific denominations?"

"Smaller is better," Mason said. "Anything up to twenties."

"How old is too old?"

"I'm thinking the end of the war."

The man nodded and started leafing through the compartments in the folder, pulling out singles, fives, tens, and twenties, checking the dates and stacking them in neat piles.

"I have lots, it seems," he said, and paused, eyeing Mason. "Which of these do you want?"

"Maybe a couple hundred dollars' worth? Face value, I mean."

His eyebrows shot up, but he said simply, "OK," and continued riffling through the pockets.

Once he'd searched to the end of the box, he assessed what he'd set on the counter, tapping the piles and counting.

"That's three hundred and twelve."

"What's it going to cost me?" Mason asked.

"Each bill is different, depending on the quality."

"For example?"

"Well, these extra-fine twenties are going to cost you fifty." He tapped them. "But some of these singles are not in great shape, so they're a buck and a quarter."

"That sounds reasonable," Mason said. "Can I get a discount for volume?"

He smiled. "I'll see what I can do. Which ones do you want?"

"Total up everything here, and pull out anything that's more than double the face value. I'll decide if I really need those."

Beside the register was an old-school adding machine, and the owner pulled it over, deftly punching in numbers with three fingers as he went through the piles of bills. When he was finished, he pointed to a thin sheaf of tens and twenties.

"These are the extra-fine and uncirculated bills. Including them, the total is five-eighty. I can deduct them if you want."

"No—I'll take them all."

The man nodded and rang up the sale, and Mason produced his own cash, which the owner inspected closely, smoothing out the bills that had become rumpled in Mason's pants and holding the hundreds under a UV light beside the till. Eventually he looked satisfied, and made change, and put the old bills in a clear plastic folder.

"So are you a collector?" he asked as he handed them over.

"Not me—they're for a friend," Mason said, moving toward the door. He thanked him as he stepped out to the street. The guy probably wondered why Mason hadn't inspected any of the bills, checked how worn they were, but no matter. It was a good deal—even at almost double the face value, the cash would stretch much farther where he was going.

Tucking his purchase into his backpack and unlocking his bicycle, he cycled to the metro, the long shadows and feeble sunlight of the late afternoon darkening the streets. There was one more stop to make, and he got off the train near the massive thrift store in Lincoln Heights. He knew they'd have what he needed—he'd seen it here before.

As he explored the vast space, he resisted the urge to look at shoes, and shirts, and office furniture, and eventually found them: a selection of antique embossers. In the pre-digital age, companies used them to officialize paper documents, affixing a neat round seal with the name of the business. They always looked the same, these devices, heavy and black with a swooping handle to create sufficient pressure. It was no surprise that there were always some in the thrift store. Made of cast iron, they would last for centuries.

Slinging off his backpack, he pulled a sheet from his notepad and set to work testing the embossers. Most of them still created a crisp impression of the company seal, with the words and graphic details clearly legible. Mason settled on one that didn't print cleanly, its dies worn down from much use. It was priced at just a few dollars—so reasonable he didn't even bother to haggle at the register.

When he got home, Peggy was in the kitchen, wearing her apron. Thursday—Ned had an AA meeting, he remembered, and he usually ate out with the group afterward as part of the fellowship. Mason put his backpack beside the door, setting it down gently so that the extra weight of the cast-iron embosser wouldn't smash his computer.

"So are you making a meal, or just puttering?" he called to Peggy, approaching the counter.

She looked up from what she was working on, a tray of pastry and spinach. "Are you worried about going hungry?"

"Not at all. Ned's mom sends me food. I can microwave a frozen tamale."

She grinned. "I've seen those packages in the freezer. They're hard to miss: you labeled them FOR MASON'S USE ONLY in Sharpie."

"That's just so there won't be any misunderstandings."

"I know they're good tamales. Anyway, I'd planned to feed us both."

"Right on," Mason said.

"I've perfected the cashew feta, so I want to see how it works in spanakopita."

"Do you need some help?"

"No—it's almost ready. Then we'll work on your graphic thing."

Mason washed up and collapsed on the sofa, grateful for being excused from food prep. He usually got a pass, because kitchen work was like doing the laundry—turn a white shirt blotchy pink or blue, throw a good sweater in a hot dryer, or burn something on the stove, and you wouldn't be asked to do it again for a while.

He closed his eyes but resisted the urge to sleep, thinking through what he'd learned today, looking at the photos on his phone occasionally to memorize details he'd need—Hawley's address, the names and dates of the court case, what Hawley had told the journalist about talking to his lawyer. If Peggy could get the ID cards right, he might even try to go tonight. His heart pounded at the thought, and he sank into a sensory memory of that era, the smoke in the air, the street noise.

When Peggy woke him, food was on the table, spanakopita with a tomato salad on the side. It was delicious, of course, and he answered her detailed debriefing questions about the flavors and textures and combinations as thoughtfully as he could.

After he'd helped her clean up, Peggy dried her hands on a kitchen towel and eyed him. "So—we've got some work to do."

"I need to make two 1950s documents. The first one is a Washington, D.C., driver's license."

"What does that look like?"

"I emailed you a photo of one I found online before dinner. We just need to print out a photo of me on shiny paper to attach to the card. I have both kinds of paper." He picked up his backpack and followed Peggy to her bedroom, where her computer was set up.

She sat down and pulled up her email, examining the image Mason had sent.

"I get it—a portrait photo glued to a gray card. It's not laminated?"

"When I went before, the anachronism team gave me one, and it was just paper."

Peggy turned to look at him. "I forgot you've been there already. You're becoming a regular tourist."

Mason grinned. "Shout when you're ready, and I'll give you the names and numbers to plug in."

"What about your photo?"

"I figured we'd use the one in my passport." He went to the bedroom to get it, and when he returned, Peggy was already at work on reproducing the design of the document.

"Take a close-up of your passport photo with your phone, and send it to me," she said, not looking away from the screen. "I should be able to match these fonts quite closely. It's just a basic thick sans, and then an old typewriter."

146

"Good news," Mason said, not completely sure what she was talking about, then went to Ned's office and turned on the desk lamp, setting his passport under it and photographing his portrait. Making sure it wasn't blurry, he cropped the image and sent it to Peggy.

Eventually Peggy printed her reconstruction of the license on the gray cardstock, cut it to the right size, and glued on Mason's photo, which she'd converted to black-and-white. She held it up beside her screen to compare it to the image of the original. Mason leaned over her shoulder.

"It looks perfect," he said.

"What about the seal? That's hard to fake."

"It's actually easy," he said, and pulled the embosser from his backpack. "I got it at the thrift store."

Peggy set the device on the corner of her desk and slid a blank sheet of paper between the dies, pulling down firmly on the handle and then peering at the resulting circular impression in the paper.

"Eleanor's Frozen Foods, founded 1939," she read.

"I figured we could do it so that it's not really legible. You want to be able to see that it's been embossed, but not what it says."

"It doesn't make a very clean impression," she said. "I'm sure we'll be able to make it indistinct."

She spent a few minutes experimenting with a sheet of the cardstock, pressing gently, shifting the sheet slightly and embossing it again over the first impression. Finally she was satisfied with her technique, and did it on the fake license. She inspected it closely, holding it up to the light at an angle.

"It looks good to me," she said, and handed it

to Mason. "You can kind of make out 'Eleanor' on your photo because it's thicker there, but it's not that noticeable."

"I'm thinking no one is going to look that closely," Mason said, peering at the document. "Peggy, you're a genius."

Next they set to work on the other ID, and Mason found his old metro pass holder, a black folding wallet from the time before everything went to electronic cards. He slid the ID into it and admired Peggy's handiwork. It really did look official, he decided.

Stretched out on his bed, he spent a minute running through his plan again in his mind, making sure there was no reason he should wait a day or two, soberly taking time to gather additional information rather than heedlessly leaping forward. This had to be done right. But nothing seemed to be missing.

Checking the time on his phone, he saw that Pretty Nail Blowout would still be open, and he dialed. To his surprise, Hanh answered. She never did that—but maybe she already knew why he was calling.

"Would you be available tonight to help with my excursion?" he asked.

"Of course—where?"

"I'm thinking at my office building. It was definitely there in 1952. The lobby has been the same since the day it opened."

"That sounds wise," she said. "I'll come to your office after midnight."

After he ended the call, he tried to remember whether he'd ever talked to her about which building, specifically, his office was in, or which suite was his. It didn't really matter, he decided; either way, she knew.

He texted Matt:

Are you available tonight? Departing from my office at 12 midnight.

Matt soon texted back:

I'll be there.

That was still several hours away, but the plan was in motion now—no turning back. He took a deep breath to calm his nerves, then went to the bathroom to shave, getting it as close as he could. His electric-orange stubble didn't stand out too much on his ruddy face, so he could usually go for a few days before he looked unkempt, but the standards were different where he was going.

Pulling his vintage suit out of the closet, he hung it on the bedroom door, then dug through his underwear drawer for the heavy baggy boxers that had come with it. He found the fedora that went with the suit, and dusted off the black oxfords that completed the outfit. They'd never needed polishing, and had the same slightly worn sheen as the day he'd been given them. The suit had never needed pressing either, which made him think it was made out of some futuristic material that held its shape and repelled grime. Any other garment Mason had ever put on was quickly wrinkled and askew, but the suit always looked sharp.

He set his alarm and stretched out on the bed, but he was too nervous to sleep. Eventually he got up and went to the bathroom, running a glob of Ned's luxe pomade through his hair, and styling it to look like guys did back then. He changed into the suit, which still fit him perfectly, he thought with some satisfaction, then texted Ned that he'd be home very late, and said good-bye to Peggy.

"Be careful there," she admonished him, standing in the living room with her arms folded as he made for the front door. "When will you be back?"

"Late tonight."

"Does Ned know what's going on?"

"The broad strokes," he said. "I told him I was doing a psychic thing."

She looked dubious.

"I will come back," he said, grinning confidently. "It'll be fine." He waved good-bye and went out to the garage, hoping that was true.

If things went to plan, Mason would be heading home well after the trains had stopped, so he'd need his bike. He tied his pant leg with a strap to keep it from getting caught in his bicycle chain, then climbed on and headed for the metro. Standing with his wheels on the train, he got a few curious looks at his suit, but it wasn't all that unusual, he decided, even with the fedora, and with his backpack rumpling the jacket around his armpits.

Wheeling his bike into the lobby of his building, he greeted the security guard. "Janet, right? I'm Mason."

"Correct," she said. "You're in 1020."

"Wow—great memory."

She shot him a gap-toothed smile, flattered. "Just part of the job."

"I've got two guests coming up a bit later," he said, and recited their names.

Janet typed them into her computer, and as he walked toward the elevators, she called after him, "Nice hat, 1020."

Upstairs he wheeled his bike into his office, thankful that the front door was painted black when he bumped it with his front tire as he maneuvered to get the key into the lock. He parked the bike and dropped his backpack on the sofa.

His case files had outgrown his bottom desk drawer, so one of his thrift-store investments had been a low file cabinet. Digging through it now, he pulled out the folder labeled QUALTROUGH, from the Invisible Arrow case, and found the little paper membership card for the Blue Moon, a gay bar he'd hung out at the last time he'd gone. It was where he'd met Mamie. He grinned at the memory as he scanned the card—her confident feminine stride in spike heels, her excitement at getting caught up in Mason's case.

Tucking it into his jacket, he went to his backpack and pulled out the folder of antique cash, separating it into different pockets—the front and back of his pants, and inside his jacket. He couldn't take his keys or his phone or his wallet, so he put them in a desk drawer. He'd have to leave his office unlocked, but it wasn't much of a risk at this time of night. There was a knock at the door.

"Come in," he shouted, and Matt entered, wearing a khaki cargo jacket.

"I love the way you put your name on the door," he said. "Very retro. It suits the building." Catching sight of Mason, he added, "Whoa—it suits your suit too."

"I can give you the guy's contact info," Mason said.

"He could put that kind of lettering on your office too."

"Nah—the university is fussy about that kind of thing." He slid his hands into the pockets of his jeans and looked around the room. "You're getting settled. It looks better than when it was empty. I wonder, though, if your expansive bicycle parking area might be repurposed as something more functional."

Mason chuckled. "Peggy is adamant that I find some furniture for that space."

"So what's the plan? Are we waiting on the boss?"

"When she gets here, we'll do the transfer in the lobby. I know the layout is the same as it was then."

"Smart," Matt said. "Who knows what these offices looked like then? We wouldn't want to send you into the middle of a desk or a wall."

Mason frowned, not happy to be confronted with the possibility.

Hanh knocked on the door, and pushed it open before Mason could answer.

"Gentlemen," she called in greeting.

"Where?" Mason said, and turned to look at the empty space behind him.

"Funny," Hanh said, but she wasn't smiling, all trace of lightheartedness absent. "Are you prepared for your excursion?"

"I'm ready," Mason said firmly. "I'm not too nervous, because I've been there before."

"You're very trusting if you're not worried about letting me help you," Matt said.

"I'll be doing the steering." Hanh shot him a sharp look. "You just need to focus your power." She looked to Mason. "You said you want to use the lobby."

"Right—there's the security guard, but her desk is out of view of the mail room. We can work there, in the doorway into the lobby."

"Let's do the prep here, so we can keep silent when we do this," Hanh said. "Remember when we pushed that knucklehead at the racetrack?"

"You pushed," Matt said. "We were just backup."

Hanh nodded. "Same deal tonight. I'll push, and you both focus your energy on me. I suspect you have a precise date in mind?"

"I do," Mason said, and recited it.

"We'll send you to late the night before, so no one is around to see you drop in," Hanh said.

"That makes sense," Mason said. It would also give him time to get oriented before he approached Hawley.

"So you'll stand facing me." Hanh stepped into the empty part of the room near Mason's bicycle, waving for him to join her. "Matt, you'll be behind my left shoulder." She waited for him to move into position. "When I give the high sign, you have to focus." She held up both palms and eyed Mason. "This is not a free ride—you'll have to use your energy too."

"Right," Mason said, remembering how that had felt when he'd done it before.

"Stand closer," Hanh instructed, "and on your toes. Be ready to land on your buttocks."

Mason stood facing her, and Hanh gestured for him to crouch a little. He bent his knees, bringing himself to her eye level, and nodded.

"Let's do a run through, without the energy transfer," she said. "Matt, watch my hands."

She gazed at Mason for a moment, then brought

up her palms, pausing for a beat before lunging toward him and shoving him firmly backward. As he'd been on tiptoe, he easily tumbled backward, landing on his butt.

Matt laughed. "Nice."

"Perfect," Hanh said. "So we know that's the right stance for you."

"It felt like I was flying," Mason said ruefully, rising to one knee and rubbing his thigh.

"Shall we?" Hanh said, her businesslike demeanor unwavering, and walked toward the door.

Once they were in the elevator and headed down, she turned to Mason. "I know I don't need to say this, but don't change anything. Don't advise people about what stocks to buy, or what neighborhood to move to, or who to vote for."

"I know the rules," he said quietly.

When the doors opened, Hanh stepped into the lobby and headed for the mail room, wordlessly, seemingly knowing exactly where it was without being prompted.

Matt followed and quietly stood behind her, inside the fluorescent-lit utilitarian space with its rows of little numbered boxes, while Mason positioned himself facing her, in the doorway, on the threshold of the warm light of the restored lobby. He glanced toward the front entrance and the security guard's desk. She might have heard them step off the elevator, but they were out of her view here.

Hanh closed her eyes, then opened them a moment later. They looked larger, and much darker. Mason felt a flash of fear—maybe she really was a supernatural being. She dipped her head, determination palpable in her expression. Mason crouched, balancing on his toes, his oxfords creaking with the effort. Breathing hard, he scrambled to muster the power he'd need. Hanh raised her palms.

This is it, he thought, and closed his eyes, focusing on projecting all the energy he could into her. He imagined a ball of white light in his core arcing toward her. Then he felt her hands connect with his chest, felt himself losing balance, flying backward, painfully connecting with the stone floor.

Dazed, Mason opened his eyes, looking into the mail room, now dark and empty. Scanning the lobby, the familiar light fixtures and the elevator doors, the painting of the plowman and oxen far above, it seemed darker. Maybe the lighting was different here. *Here*— he was here, he thought, shaking off the fog shrouding his thoughts. Hanh and Matt were gone. He'd made it.

Rising slowly and brushing off the seat of his pants, he saw the lobby really was deserted, the lighting minimal. Where the security guard's desk had been was just open floor. He went to the front door and pushed gently, but it was locked. Of course it would be; it was dark out, late at night.

A hulking, curvy auto with huge bumpers drove by on the street, its engine rumbling audibly. It was dark red—that had surprised him last time. Period photos were usually in black and white. The style was right for the era, even though he didn't know what make it was—this was real. He took a breath and watched the street for a minute, gazing at the other old-time cars parked on the opposite side, trying to get grounded. No reason to be afraid of this place—he already knew it.

Eventually he felt calmer, ready to move. Besides the main entrance, there was one other way out, and he went to the stairwell, trotting down to the parking garage. Again he was struck by the old cars, and as he made his way past he ogled them like he was in a museum. As he walked up the sloping floor, he saw that the street entrance was ungated, with only a length chain stretched across to prevent vehicles from turning in. He smiled to himself. That had been easy.

"Where did you come from?" a voice demanded from the darkness.

Mason spun toward the sound. "Hello?" he said.

A gray-haired man stepped out of the shadows, dressed in a blue uniform, a metal badge on his breast. Security, not a cop, Mason realized with relief.

"Howdy," Mason said. "I was upstairs, working late. Insurance never sleeps." He continued walking, pulling the brim of his hat low on his brow.

"Hold on a minute," the watchman called after him.

"Sorry—no time," Mason said, and stepped over the chain. He walked quickly toward the corner, and waited until he'd hustled across the street before he looked back. The watchman was staring at him, hands on his hips, still in the entryway rather than following him.

Once he was farther up the block and out of the watchman's view, he slowed down and took a breath. The guy had just stood there, looking puzzled, which probably meant he wasn't about to raise an alarm. He pushed that concern away and focused on his surroundings.

Nothing looked familiar. The shops on the deserted street felt dangerously vulnerable, plate glass windows lit from within and unprotected by bars or steel shutters. Office supplies, lamps, vintage clothing that was new here, even a smoke shop with cigars arrayed in plain view, all ripe for the taking by anyone with a sledgehammer and a getaway car. But that was his world, not this one. He needed to focus.

Hanging over the sidewalk at the next corner was a clock, part of a drugstore's facade. If it was accurate, the time was 5:30. He wanted to be at Augustus's house in Los Feliz later in the morning, but that was hours from now. Turning the corner and strolling up the next block, he shoved his hands in his pockets and thought about what to do. The sun would be up soon, he reasoned, looking over his shoulder again, relieved to see no one in pursuit. He'd walk to Los Feliz and soak in the atmosphere of the city as it woke up. It was a long walk, but he had the time.

In the next block, as he strolled along the sidewalk, a prowl car pulled up beside him and slowed, its engine chugging. The cop on the passenger side leaned out the window, wearing the familiar navy-black peaked cap with the insignia on the front, and eyed him with that look they got when the hammer was about to drop. Mason felt his heart start to pound.

"Where are you off to at this late hour?" the cop said.

Mason stopped and turned to face him. "I'm just taking a walk. That's not illegal yet, is it?"

"Vagrancy is, wise guy. Where do you live?"

"I've got a room on Bunker Hill," Mason said,

gesturing vaguely in that direction. "On Clay Street."

The cop sighed and looked him up and down. "Have you got any money?"

"Why?"

"If you don't, you qualify as a vagrant. Show me your cash."

Mason pulled a wad of folded bills out of his front pocket and fanned them out, then held them up.

"All right," the cop said. "I've got my eye on you. Keep your nose clean."

The car pulled away, and Mason pocketed his cash, watching as the taillights turned the corner. The street was silent again, and he took a few deep breaths to calm down, then resumed his gait. Getting popped so soon after arriving would make this a completely wasted trip.

Looking in the shop windows, he didn't know any of these places, their low security and retro contents instead evoking old photographs and Ned's film noir. But the street names were the same, and he soon got oriented again, heading toward Bunker Hill. It was a lot steeper to climb than in his day, and once he was at the top, panting with the exertion, he quickly got lost again.

It was a residential neighborhood with dilapidated grand Victorians, all of them razed sometime after this to make way for the office towers and concert halls of Mason's LA. Even the street names were unfamiliar, having been consolidated and reorganized on a neighborhood scale.

When he found the far side of the hill, there were no bridges over the freeway, like in his day—the freeway was still a massive construction site, a long pile of dirt littered with heavy machinery. There had to be a street that crossed it eventually, he reasoned, and walked north.

Once he was across the future highway, he started recognizing the street names again, and even some buildings had an air of familiarity. Others were completely alien, like something from an Old West town, low-slung and sprawling and sided with narrow strips of wood.

The city itself was the focus when no one was around, allowing him to take it all in, but as the sky lightened with dawn, people gradually started to appear on the streets. Every single man wore a hat, either in business dress, like Mason was, or a workman's cap, and all the women wore dresses that ran well below their knees. It was a Friday, he knew, and people were going to work, hustling despite their heavy clothes, but there was also time for civility—when he strolled up a leafy residential street, several people greeted him.

Sunset Boulevard felt more walkable than it did in his day, the shops closer together, the traffic less frantic. A streetcar rolled by, olive green and school-bus yellow, laden with people. Mason smiled at its silly-looking current collector, arching up to the overhead wires like a tail.

Ahead he saw the marquee for a diner, and found it open, and not too crowded. He ducked inside, remembering to hang his hat on a peg by the door, and took a stool at one end of the counter.

"Coffee?" the waitress asked him, setting down a mug and filling it before he could reply.

He thanked her and watched her stride away, marveling at her elaborate uniform, green and white with a little apron and cap sleeves, with a matching hat pinned in her curly mass of hair.

Mason yawned and sipped at the suspiciously pale liquid, and as he suspected, it was cowboy coffee—thin, more like coffee-flavored tea than actual java. This wasn't going to wake him up much, and he had jet lag, having skipped most of the night to get here.

"Want some grub, hon?" the waitress asked, pausing in front of him. It felt like she was moving in fast-forward.

"A bowl of oatmeal," Mason said. "And do you have any fruit?"

"Fruit cup?"

"That works," he said, and she was gone.

Mason twisted on his stool and scanned the other diners. Most of them seemed to be blue-collar men, with a lone woman sitting with one of them at a table by the window. One guy was in coveralls, and there were a couple of cops. Everyone was white and Anglo, he realized, even the waitress. It was eerie, once he noticed it. California hadn't seen the worst of Jim Crow, but he knew it had always been segregated.

The oatmeal was salty and little improved by dumping sugar on it, but the fruit was especially tasty. Maybe it was because of his long walk, but whatever the reason, he savored it, then ordered another. After he'd finished he caught the waitress's eye and asked her for the check. It came as a handwritten slip torn off a pad, and he had to grin at the cost: $1.24. He left two singles on the counter and headed for the door, nodding to one of the cops, who was openly eyeing him as he put on his hat.

Like the cop in the prowl car downtown, it was just his job to keep an eye on people. Mason took a deep breath and stepped out to the street. Even with his red hair, and probably looking flushed, he wasn't inherently suspicious, and he wasn't acting oddly, no matter how out of place he felt.

Reaching absently for his phone, he remembered why it wasn't there. He should have checked the time in the diner. Looking in store windows, eventually he saw a clock on the back wall of a barbershop. By the time he got up into Los Feliz, it wouldn't be too early to knock on Hawley's door. The food had perked him up, and he felt upbeat now as he walked. The novelty and awe of this place were wearing off, and now he could revel in the high that came with the success of actually getting here.

The route to Hawley's house was relatively simple, and he remembered the layout of the neighborhood from the map he'd studied on his computer. That kind of tech was so removed from this era, he thought, watching the lumbering smoky vehicles roll by.

Hawley's street twisted up into the hills, and he was winded by the time the familiar Tudor came into view. Mason paused for a minute on the sidewalk, catching his breath and steeling himself for the encounter. He'd come a long way for this.

A car was parked in the brick portico over the driveway that led uphill behind the house. Farther up was a garage, finished in the same Tudor style. Black and low-slung, the car looked expensive, with fat whitewalls. As he approached he read the chrome label on the trunk: ROADMASTER. Ned would love this.

Even without the car, Mason knew Hawley was home, based on his journals, and took a deep breath, heart pounding, and rang the bell. There was no sound of movement inside. Maybe Hawley wasn't going to answer. Mason certainly wasn't expected; maybe the guy would just ignore the doorbell. He waited a minute and then rang again, and this time heard someone approach the door. A woman in a blue and white maid's uniform pulled it open. Unlike the waitress at the diner, she wore no hat in her carefully coiffed African hair. There was suspicion in her eyes.

"Can I help you?"

"I'm here to see Mr. Hawley," Mason said.

"Your name?" she asked, one eyebrow rising, almost imperceptibly.

"Mason Braithwaite," he said, enunciating carefully.

"Just a moment," she said, and closed the door.

Mason glanced around at the quiet street. He could feel his cheeks burning, such an annoying giveaway to his emotional state. It was several minutes before the door opened again, revealing Hawley himself, with the same pencil mustache as in the photo Mason had seen, wearing an open-collared shirt and tweed pants, clearly not prepared to engage with the world.

"Mr. Hawley," Mason said, trying to sound formal despite his great relief that the man had appeared.

"Can I help you?" Hawley said, his tone barely masking annoyance.

"Mason Braithwaite. I'm from the Premonitions Bureau," he said, and pulled out his transit-pass folder with the fake ID, flipping it open for Hawley to read.

"I've never heard of that."

"That's not surprising," Mason said. "We don't advertise. But I know you were an early supporter of Jane Wilson's work."

Hawley's eyes grew wide. "The dream researcher? I haven't heard anything about her in years."

"That's because she's been working for us."

"Who are you?" Hawley demanded, his brow furrowing.

"I just told you that," Mason said firmly. "Is there somewhere we could talk? I'd like to ask you a few questions."

"Am I in some kind of trouble?"

"Quite the opposite, Mr. Hawley. We'd like to interview you about a project you worked on."

Hawley hesitated, but Mason could see the curiosity burning in his eyes. He'd bought it.

"Come in," Hawley said, pulling the door open and stepping aside.

Mason remembered to take his hat off when he saw the hat rack in the little foyer, and hung it on one of the pegs. Hawley led him to the living room. The housekeeper was nowhere to be seen. It was a glammy space, befitting a great architect, and Mason admired it for a minute, the high ceilings and modernist furniture. He may have been a titan of art deco, but he'd clearly embraced the newer design trends. Half the shelves on a bookcase were filled with an array of crystals, large and small, in a riot of colors, some raw, some polished. Mason wondered if it was just a mundane mineral collection or something New Age.

"This is a lovely home," Mason said, noticing that Hawley was quietly assessing him, watching him as he scoped out the room.

"Thank you," he said, and gestured to a chair. Once they were sitting, Hawley called loudly, "Dorothy," and waited for the housekeeper to appear in the doorway.

"Yes, Mr. Hawley," she said, her tone perfunctory.

"Could you bring us some coffee?" he asked.

"Yes, sir," she said, and was gone.

This was the dark side of the era, Mason thought. A woman of color keeping house for an old white guy; a diner in a big city where every single person was the same race.

"Do you know Mrs. Wilson?" Hawley asked, leaning toward him.

"Not personally," Mason said, "but I know her work. I know that three years ago you wrote a letter supporting her research."

"You said she was working for your agency," Hawley said, frowning.

"The Premonitions Bureau." Mason just smiled, knowing Hawley would ask.

"What is that, exactly?"

"We're using Wilson's theoretical work to conduct a mass study," Mason said, gesturing broadly. "The goal is to track down individuals who are adept at premonitory dreaming. The results have been so compelling that we've expanded to twenty-two offices around the country. We have dozens of these skilled dreamers working on contract."

"What kind of results? People are dreaming accurately about the future?"

"Some of them are," Mason said, meeting his eye. "I can't get into specific cases, but premonitory dreaming works, and the bureau has started collecting massive amounts of data."

"Why have I never heard of it?"

Mason sat forward and lowered his voice. "In this political climate, anything that strays very far from the mainstream becomes a target. Dr. Wilson herself was pressured to end her research."

"I remember," Hawley said, nodding vigorously.

"Besides all that, we don't really want our friend Ivan to have access to the same tools that we do."

Hawley sighed. "Enemies in Congress, enemies abroad. A lot of good people are lying low these days."

Dorothy reappeared, carrying a tray with coffee cups, and set one on the table in front of Mason.

"Cream or sugar?" she asked.

"Just black, thanks," he said, and smiled appreciatively, trying to catch her eye, but she remained impassive.

"If your project is a secret," Hawley said, once they were alone again, "why would you share it with me?"

"A couple of reasons," Mason said, picking up his cup and trying to look thoughtful. "We know you're sympathetic to the cause, so you can be trusted not to endanger the project by gossiping about it. Also, we think you may have information that can help us, and we suspected you wouldn't be forthcoming with it unless you understood our reasons for asking."

"I guess I should be flattered," Hawley said, "but what information could I possibly have that you'd want? The whole thing sounds so far-fetched."

Mason sipped at his cup before answering. It was real coffee—Dorothy, at least, made decent joe, so it wasn't unknown here. "I may be able to dispel your doubts. Our dream models predicted that this is an auspicious day for you. That's why I waited until today to visit."

"Dream models?" he said, raising his eyebrows.

"Information is collated from the dreamers on staff, and then cross-referenced."

"They dreamed about me?"

Mason shrugged. "I don't see the data directly, only the end reports. The long-term goal, as you can imagine, is to be able to predict things like natural disasters, and political events overseas. How will the next typhoon season affect the food supply in Red China? I can't comment on those results, but lots of incidental information comes up."

Hawley sighed. "When you say that today is auspicious, that sounds about as specific as my horoscope in the newspaper. Or a fortune cookie."

"I can be much more detailed," Mason said. "Around ten o'clock you're going to get a call from your representative at the courthouse. I don't know his name, but he's going to tell you that you've been fully exonerated in the Miller house affair."

Hawley looked startled. "That's pretty specific. There's a preliminary hearing today, and Lloyd is there, but he's not expecting a resolution for several weeks." He watched Mason for a moment. "You know an awful lot about my affairs. I like the way you think, though. If there's any justice in this world, I will be released from that lawsuit."

As casually as he could, Mason said, "I may be wrong. Our accuracy isn't a hundred percent, although the analysts said this one looked firm."

"I guess we'll see." Hawley glanced at his wrist-watch. "Ten o'clock isn't far off." Reaching for his coffee, he said, "What is it that you think I can help with?"

Mason shifted in his chair. "I've seen a lot of your work: the Asia Commerce Building in Chicago, where you used the water motif, integrated with the overall design."

Hawley grinned over his cup. "Most people don't notice things like that."

"I didn't notice it myself. I had it pointed out to me."

"When I was working on that project, I found the plot of land had once been on a riverbed." His eyes were bright, talking about something he loved. "In Chicago they moved the rivers around and buried some of them. I used a lot of cobalt blue in the finishings, and incorporated symbols of that hidden riparian history."

"Fascinating," Mason said. "The Primavera Building here in town has the symbol for the sun. It's everywhere, once you know where to look."

"I'm glad you looked. I used the ocher tile on the facade for the same reason. It represents the tone of the light at sunset."

"In both cases you used alchemical symbols. They're also Hermetic symbols."

"It sounds like you're fishing for my inspirations," Hawley said.

"I am, if you're willing to share them." Mason glanced at Hawley's wristwatch. It was just a hair past the hour. "Of more immediate concern is the matter of the hidden stairwell and the glass column."

He sat up. "How do you know about that?"

"I see the future, Mr. Hawley," Mason said carefully. "People are going to want to know what's really going on. After climbing those stairs, I have the feeling there isn't a simple explanation."

The phone rang, an old-fashioned vibrating bell, loud and jarring even though it was muffled, in another room. Hawley didn't move, but sat staring at Mason.

"You should answer that," Mason said. "I'm pretty sure it's your lawyer."

"Dorothy will answer."

The phone stopped, and Hawley watched Mason, wordless, until Dorothy appeared.

"I'm sorry to interrupt," she said. "Mr. Hawley, telephone. It's Mr. Lloyd at the courthouse. He says it's important."

Hawley scowled and leaped out of his chair, pushing past her into the next room. Dorothy closed the door again, and Mason couldn't make out Hawley's voice, except a lone exclamation of "Oh." He slurped at his coffee while he waited.

When Hawley returned, he spoke breathlessly. "I don't know how you knew that would happen, but you knew."

"I'm glad our data was valid."

"Lloyd said it just came down, so it happened well after you were already here. There's no way you could have heard about it before you arrived."

Mason shrugged. "Like I said, it's my job." *What a relief,* he thought—it had worked. Hawley fully believed him now.

"This calls for a celebration. Do you drink scotch?"

"Not usually at this time of day," Mason said, setting down his coffee cup.

"Doesn't this seem like a good reason to break the rules?" Hawley gestured wildly. "I've been exonerated, my good man, and you've successfully predicted the future."

"Good point," Mason said. "Scotch it is."

Hawley cackled and led him into a smaller space beyond the living room, an office with a drafting table and big windows onto the garden. It looked a lot like Astrid's studio. He pulled a bottle from a bookcase, where Mason saw there were even more crystals—white and blue and purple, clumped together and separate, some inside split-open rocks, their dull exterior belying the dramatic color inside. Hawley poured from the bottle into two little glasses and handed one to Mason. He needn't have worried about his judgment becoming impaired—the volume in each glass was a dribble, barely more than a spoonful.

"To the power of the subconscious."

"Hear, hear," Mason said, and lifted the glass, then slammed its contents. "That's good stuff."

Hawley sat on the stool at his drafting table, his back to the windows. "This has been hanging over my head for years, and I'm finally free of it. I never should have taken that commission. Even then it seemed like folly to build a house crowded up to the edge of the world."

"It must feel great to be vindicated."

Hawley met his eye, frowning slightly. "And then you show up to tell me that it was going to happen."

"When our dreamers turned up data on you," Mason said quickly, "we started looking into your work, in case you're more important to the future than it appears."

"Am I?"

"We're not sure yet. That's why we studied the metaphysical aspects. The Primavera Building is truly beautiful. I spent quite a bit of time there. I'm no art critic, but I'm certain it'll be a lasting classic for future generations."

Hawley tipped his glass toward Mason. "That's the best any designer can hope for."

"As I said before, I found the stairwell," Mason said, setting his glass on the shelf beside the scotch bottle. "I really want to know what it is."

"Did Morgan show you? Is he still there?"

Mason had to think quickly to remember who that was. He shook his head. "I never met Morgan, although I know he was the payroll guy."

"It's such a long time ago," he said, looking away. "The war changed everything."

"Was it his office where you put the safe door?"

"That's right," he said, focusing on Mason again.

"Was encoding the combination in the artwork your idea too?"

"You found the combination." Hawley sipped from his glass, affecting a casual tone, but his eyes burned with curiosity. "Or did someone show you?"

"I found it myself. Not right away—I had to think about it for a while."

"Then you have the soul of an artist." He grinned. "Encoding the numbers was my way of making sure they wouldn't get lost."

"Well, it worked—I never met Morgan, but I found

the combination. Why are there only two doors to the stairwell?"

Hawley drained his glass. "What are you going to do with this information if I explain it?"

"My job is using metaphysics to make the world a better place. If there's something of value in that stairwell, I want to maximize it."

He cocked his head. "You're not going to suppress it?"

Mason subtly emulated his body language, folding his arms and tilting his head. "It's already suppressed, wouldn't you say? Hidden away for decades in a windowless stairwell that no one knows about? I'm not in Congress, Mr. Hawley. We try to avoid the notice of those knuckleheads."

Hawley broke into a smile. "I never thought I'd see this day."

Mason grinned, happy that he seemed to have convinced him. "What do you mean?"

"The day when someone took an interest in that aspect of my work. Do you know anything about crystals?"

"The kind you have here? Not really."

"Nature creates a wide variety of them," he said, rising from his stool and crossing to the bookshelves, then handing a hexagonal stone to Mason. "That's quartz. Feel it."

It was almost clear, like cloudy glass, and felt cool to the touch.

Hawley took it back and handed him another, much more bizarre object, iridescent metallic stacks of spiraling right angles. Mason had a flashback to peering over the railing in the Primavera Building, the spiraling square stairwell descending below him.

"That's bismuth."

"Such an odd pattern," Mason said.

"Their shapes spring naturally from the shapes of the constituent molecules. Each type of crystal has inherent resonance. That means a kind of vibration."

Mason knew that much was scientific, as crystal resonance was used in building very accurate clocks, but he suspected there was more. "What do you use them for?"

"They can change the vibrations in people—change their energy."

"To what end?"

Hawley gestured vaguely. "Well, I personally don't believe they can cure illnesses. They act more like sunshine, or coffee. They can perk you up, help you operate at your best. Some are like moonlight, to calm you down and induce patience."

He sounded like a proto–New Ager, Mason thought, and handed back the hunk of bismuth. "Is that what the column in the stairwell is made of? Crystal?"

"It's called the melioreum," Hawley said. "There's no crystal that takes on that tubular form. It's made of a kind of glass with a lot of crystals in it. It had to be made of glass to be cast in that shape."

"Melioreum—can you spell that?" Mason asked, wishing he could write it down.

Hawley did, and added, "It's from the same root as *ameliorate,* to make things better."

"What were you trying to make better?"

"My intention was to bring the light of the crystals

to every floor, and beneficial vibrations to everyone inside."

"That's why you built the knockouts," Mason said, half to himself.

"You really did a thorough inspection," Hawley said thoughtfully. "Any evidence of those would have been covered up by the finishing work."

"Why not just put in exterior windows?"

Hawley smiled. "That's the metaphysical part. The melioreum and the corona transform mere sunlight into positive energy. With the originally planned windows and glass doors onto the stairwell, it would have kept everyone in the building thoroughly invigorated."

"So why the knockouts for future use? Why wasn't it built with the actual doors and windows into the stairwell when you were involved?"

"The building owners saw the melioreum being put together, and they thought it was too strange to have windows onto a stairwell." His face clouded at the memory. "It was too late to rework the design. Originally they'd thought it was just a set of fire stairs. Rather than use the light from the melioreum, they insisted it be sealed up."

"Such small minds," Mason said.

"Morgan was the only one intrigued by the idea. He agreed to install the false safe door as a way to preserve access for later. And of course the basement egress is for safety."

"The column wasn't shedding much light when I was in there, even on a beautiful sunny day. It would have been a fairly muted effect."

Hawley gestured impatiently, setting the bismuth

on the shelf. "That's because the corona was never installed. All the melioreum is doing now is shedding ambient light."

"What's the corona?"

"It was supposed to be attached to the top of the melioreum, on the roof, to concentrate light. I worked with a physicist on the design to maximize its energy-gathering capability. It cost a fortune to plan, to do all the math. For two decades that building has sat there without the corona, like a burned-out lightbulb, not living up to its potential."

"Is that why you used the alchemical symbol for the sun in the design?" Mason asked.

Hawley went back to his drafting table and perched on the stool, hands on his knees, facing Mason. "In alchemy and Hermetic practice, the sun means the divine spark in man. It also means incorruptibility. The whole building was designed to be a solar temple, to enrich and purify everyone who worked in it—not just with sunlight but with metaphysical solar energy."

"The building definitely has a vibe," Mason said. "It attracts me, and just being there invigorates me."

"I'm glad you can feel that, but it's incomplete," he said, with a sad smile. "I was more successful with the Asia Commerce Building. It was designed to be calming. I ran pipes from the water table through the entire structure. The owners thought it was a cooling system, which actually is an ancillary effect, but it was meant to be a calming system. You said you haven't been in that building?"

"My colleague in the Chicago office did a walk-through."

"Well, if you're sensitive enough to feel that the Primavera Building is stimulating, you'd feel the opposite in the Asia Commerce Building. The site of each building suggested those elements—the old riverbed, and sunny California. When I came out here to work, I was thinking of the Chinese idea of yin and yang. Those two buildings balance each other like yin and yang, even though they're thousands of miles apart."

"Primavera is definitely a yang space, with the big windows. So why didn't you install the corona?"

"It's pretty outlandish-looking for an insurance company, even out of view up on the roof. They outright refused." He scowled, remembering. "They sealed the top of the melioreum in a box and walked away."

"Did you actually build the corona, or is it just an idea?"

Hawley met his eye. "It's sitting in my garage."

Nine

"**S**eriously? Can I see it?" Mason asked.

"It's packed away in an oil drum. I can show you sketches of it." He rose and went to a map cabinet, like the ones at Live Oak College, set against the wall behind his desk, and slid out one of the shallow drawers. Mason stepped over as he pulled out a broad sheet and spread it on top. It was pencil on white paper, depicting myriad curving lines, a mesh of red guidelines positioned all around, and numbers scrawled everywhere, seemingly at random.

Like with Astrid's drawings, it wasn't instantly clear what he was looking at, but taking in the overall image, Mason could get a sense of the object's shape. What it most resembled, he thought, was an asymmetrical artichoke with elongated spikes.

"Is this space between the sharp bits open?" Mason asked, pointing at the drawing.

"Only on the top two layers. Below that, it's solid."

Mason followed Hawley's finger as he traced the lines and explained, trying to envision it.

"Even though the sun crosses the sky every day," Hawley said, "its elevation varies with the seasons. But still, the sun only appears in a limited band. This device and its projections"—he tapped on the drawing—"maximize transmission of solar energy. The longest spike is oriented due south."

"How big is it?"

"The vertical aspect is thirty-one inches." He pointed out the number, written at one side of the drawing. "And just over twenty at the widest."

"It's made out of the same material as the meli …"

"The melioreum. It's similar, yes—crystal-glass."

Mason studied the drawing. "How would installing this change the melioreum?"

"It would all work," he said emphatically. "It would channel metaphysical energy, and it would be visibly much brighter."

"I wish I could see it."

He threw up his hands. "If you're willing to help me open the drum, I can show you."

"Let's do it," Mason said.

Hawley eyed him dubiously but walked back into the living room, leading him through a swinging door into the kitchen, where Dorothy was folding linen.

Hawley stopped abruptly. "Will you join me for luncheon, Mr. Braithwaite?"

"Sure," Mason said, "but I have some unusual food issues."

"I might be able to accommodate," Dorothy said.

"What would you like?"

"Fruit and nuts?" Mason said tentatively.

"Nothing more substantial? I was going to make Mr. Hawley a chicken sandwich."

"No, just some fruit would be great. And maybe some more of that coffee?"

Dorothy nodded confidently, and Hawley continued out the kitchen door. It opened onto the driveway that Mason had seen earlier as he approached the house. Hawley headed up the incline toward the garage, and Mason looked back at the car in the portico. From this side he could see its grill, huge and dramatic, with lots of chrome.

Hawley folded open the garage doors and clicked on the lights. The garage was neatly arranged, Mason saw, but like lots of people he was using the space for storage rather than to shelter a car.

"Help me move these boxes," Hawley said, and he set to work.

Mason pulled off his suit jacket and hung it on a nail, then spent a few minutes heaving the heavy cardboard boxes across the space. Each one had a three-digit number written on it in the neat hand of a draftsman. As they stacked them at the other side of the garage, Mason worked up a sweat. Gradually, in the feeble light of the naked bulbs hanging from the ceiling, an oil drum emerged behind the cardboard. Sitting upright on a wooden pallet, it was painted black and bore the grime of age.

"It only weighs about two hundred pounds," Hawley said, shifting the last box out of the way, "so we can move it if we both pull on the pallet."

Mason stooped and reached under it, and the two of them awkwardly slid it out, a few inches at a time, into the middle of the floor. Hawley was strong, considering his age and sedentary career, shifting it farther with each tug than Mason could. Through the layer of dust Mason could see the drum was stenciled FRAGILE. The top was secured with a metal hoop, tightened in place with a simple nut and bolt.

Hawley stepped to the side wall and chose two adjustable wrenches from the rack of tools, tacitly handing one to Mason.

While Hawley waited, Mason fiddled with the adjustment wheel, then attached the wrench to the head of the bolt. Hawley put his on the nut, giving it a hard push. Mason's wrench instantly twisted out of his grasp, and with no resistance, Hawley's hand struck the drum, his wrench clattering to the concrete floor.

Hawley shouted in pain and examined the back of his hand, where a red mark was starting to ooze blood. "Son of a hoo-er."

Mason had to think about what he meant, but eventually he understood: *whore.* "Sorry about that," he said sheepishly. "Do you need a bandage?"

"It's just a little blood," Hawley said, annoyed. "Hold it steady, man."

It took all Mason's strength to keep the wrench from turning away and slipping off again, and he could feel the handle cutting into his palm. Soon, though, the nut was loose enough that Hawley could twist it the rest of the way with his fingers. He pulled off the hoop and set it aside, then used the wrench to bang loudly on the edge of the lid to loosen the top.

He pulled off the heavy lid and set it on the floor, propped against a stack of boxes. The drum was stuffed to the top with tan-colored material that looked like straw, but it wasn't, Mason could tell, as it was loopy and fibrous, and soft when he touched it. Hawley unceremoniously started pulling out armfuls of the stuff, and Mason stepped back. Bright red spots dotted the light-colored strands as he dumped it on the floor—Mason winced when he realized it was blood from the cut on Hawley's hand.

"What is that stuff?" he asked.

Hawley paused. "It's called excelsior. You've never seen it before?"

"I don't think so."

"I get the sense you've never done a lot of manual labor. You have no idea how to use a wrench."

"True," Mason said, and picked up a handful of the excelsior. "What's it made of?"

"Wood," Hawley said emphatically. "So no smoking in here." He went back to work, and eventually beckoned Mason to look inside.

The top of the corona was visible, poking up through more excelsior. A long projection of dark shiny glass curved upward, with other shorter spikes arrayed below it. The shapes looked like the drawing, and seeing it now, he got a sense of what it would look like fully exposed. It was a bizarre object, with spikes curling upward, like a stylized interpretation of flames, or even the sun itself. It was no surprise that the building's owners had declined to mount it atop the structure. They both stared it for a while, until Hawley's words interrupted Mason's thoughts.

"We'd need a block and tackle to pull it out of there, but you get the idea."

Mason pushed aside some of the excelsior and felt the cool surface of the glass. "This has just been sitting here in the drum for twenty years?"

"Sadly, yes."

"This needs to be put on the Primavera Building."

Hawley's eyes narrowed. "Do you have any sway with Cudahy Mutual? You seem to have unfettered access to the building."

"It's not something I can do now, but given enough time …"

Hawley looked away. "Well, I guess if the opportunity arises, you can let me know."

Mason stared at the Corona, the glint of the dark glass in the feeble light. "Would you entrust me with this? I can't promise it will go up soon, but I know I can make it happen eventually."

Hawley straightened his back and met Mason's eye, speaking intently. "This represents a huge part of my work. I'm not going to give it away to someone I just met—someone who works for a shadowy government agency I've never heard of."

"I understand that," Mason said. "You don't know me. But the corona isn't doing the world any good hidden away in your garage. You can leave it here another twenty years, or let me try to get it installed where it belongs."

"Why can't you arrange to put it on the building, and then come and pick it up?"

"I wish I could do that. But the way it has to work is that I take charge of it first."

Hawley eyed him, then started lifting excelsior back into the drum. Mason helped him, the two of them working in silence, stuffing the material in and punching it down. Hawley lifted the lid back on the drum, then the ring to seal it, and Mason held one of the wrenches on the bolt while Hawley tightened it. He could hardly keep the wrench in position as Hawley worked, even with both hands. What was he doing wrong?

Finally it was closed tight, and Hawley took his wrench, hanging them both on the wall.

"Let's have lunch," he said, and walked out of the garage, leaving the doors propped open.

Mason grabbed his jacket and followed him back to the house. When they stepped into the kitchen, Dorothy turned from the counter.

"Whenever you're ready, Mr. Hawley," she said.

"I'll just wash up first, and tend to this wound," he said. The blood had dried in a dark streak on the back of his hand. "Do you need to wash, Mr. Braithwaite?"

"I didn't do any work, remember?" Mason said.

Hawley scoffed and pushed through the swinging door into the living room.

Dorothy was pouring two glasses of milk from a bottle. She nodded to the doorway. "The dining room is just on the left."

"Thanks," Mason said, but he hesitated. "Have you worked for Mr. Hawley for long?"

"Many years," she said, eyeing him suspiciously, and then turned to the fridge, putting the milk bottle away.

"He must be a good employer."

"I wouldn't say any different."

Mason smiled. "Do you live here?"

"I live south of downtown. I come on the streetcar."

"Near Central Avenue?"

"That's right," she said.

"There's a great hotel there with a jazz club. I forget the name."

Dorothy raised her eyebrows. "The Dunbar?"

"That's the one. I haven't been to the club, but I love the architecture of the building. It's in the same style as some of Mr. Hawley's work."

"I guess I'm not surprised you know about the jazz club. It was integrated long ago, although the neighborhood isn't."

"Right," Mason said, and had to think about what she meant by "integrated"—racially mixed rather than segregated.

"We won't be living there for long, though. My husband and I are looking to buy a home."

"Your first one?"

"Yes, sir."

"Congratulations," Mason said. "Where are you looking?"

"Farther south," she said, leaning on the counter, her mistrust and formality evaporating. "Florence or Watts, or maybe west, Leimert Park."

"West," Mason said firmly. "That's the better choice."

"That's what my Albert says. I'm not so sure. It's a very white neighborhood."

"It won't be for long. You'll feel like pioneers, but it'll be worth it."

Dorothy grinned. "A man who knows the future."

That was insightful, Mason thought. He wondered

if she'd been eavesdropping on his conversation with Hawley.

He heard the muffled sound of feet on stairs, and Dorothy nodded toward the door to the living room, reassuming her formal tone.

"That's Mr. Hawley come for lunch. You'd best join him."

Mason pushed through the door and went into the dining room. Two places were set at one end of the long table. A sandwich on thick snow-white bread sat on a plate, and on the other placemat were two little bowls, one filled with cut strawberries and chunks of apple, and the other with peanuts. A little pitcher stood next to them; cream for the fruit, Mason realized. He hung his jacket on the back of the chair.

Hawley stepped in, wearing a different shirt, his collar buttoned, with a maroon sweater-vest over it. As they sat, Mason flicked his napkin into his lap. Dorothy brought in the two big glasses of milk and set them down.

"Thank you, Dorothy," Hawley said dismissively, and bit into his sandwich, holding it daintily with his pinkies extended, sitting bolt upright.

Mason surreptitiously watched him take a drink of his milk. He looked like a wizened nine-year-old playing tea-party, so stiff and formal in his own house.

"Where did you get the idea to build the melioreum?" Mason asked, forking up his fruit.

"The hermetic symbolism and imagery that I used in the building are things I learned through freemasonry. I know you're not a freemason, Mr. Braithwaite—"

"How could you know that?"

Hawley smiled. "We have our ways."

"I've worked with freemasons," Mason said, scooping up a handful of peanuts. "I love the image of Mercury that they use."

"You should go see Rugley Hall. It's not far from here. There's a lovely statue of Mercury on the roof."

"Interesting," Mason said. He'd seen that statue, when Yoshida had shown it to him, although it wasn't on the roof anymore.

"Sealing off the stairwell wasn't a new idea to me either. One of the reasons I got interested in architecture was an experience from my childhood."

Mason munched on the peanuts as he waited for Hawley to work through a bite of his sandwich.

"I grew up in Chicago, in the suburbs," Hawley said. "Specifically Elgin."

"I don't know Chicago."

"Well, it's a suburb now, but it was the countryside then. Anyway, we lived in a rambling old Victorian, and my younger brother and I shared a bedroom. It was the last room in the upstairs hall, on the left. Sometimes there was another room across the hall."

"Sometimes?" Mason asked, meeting his eye.

"Correct. It existed, and we'd go in, and play there. Then we'd forget all about it, but one day we'd remember it, and talk about going back inside, but it wasn't there. Where the door had been was just a wall. Then the room would reappear again, months later, as if it had always been there."

"How old were you?"

"The room was there intermittently from as early as I can remember until I was about eleven, when they shipped me off to boarding school."

"Does your brother remember it the same way?"

"We haven't spoken of it in many years, but yes, he had the same memory."

"What was in the room?" Mason asked, tipping the last of the peanuts into his hand.

"It was just a bedroom—a bed with ordinary bedding on it, curtains, a washstand. I remember it had a window seat, and we'd climb up to look out at the yard, and watch the gardener. I never asked Mother or the servants about it. We knew without being told that it was something secret."

"That's such an odd paranormal experience."

Hawley paused to finish his sandwich. "Thank you for not laughing in my face. I've never told that story to a living soul."

"I'm well aware that there are all sorts of unseen things beyond the edges of our perception. It would be arrogant to think that what we can see is all there is."

Hawley nodded in agreement.

"Have you been back to the house as an adult?"

"I examined it carefully after I'd had a bit of architectural training. Where that room should have been was part of mother's room. It doesn't really exist."

"Not in the regular sense, anyway. If you went into it, it exists somewhere." Mason toyed with his fork, watching Hawley nibble his spongy bread. "It almost sounds like a wrinkle in reality that the two of you created, conjuring a new room into existence."

Hawley set down his sandwich and studied Mason's face for a moment. "Do you know what the goal of the alchemists was?"

"Wasn't it about turning cheap metals into valuable ones? Lead into gold?"

"Exactly, but it wasn't just about the metals. Alchemy was also symbolic of turning man into something better—transmuting human nature into a higher form. My buildings are meant to enact that transmutation beyond the personal level. We can better society by bettering the people in it, wouldn't you agree? Freemasons use the alchemical symbols because their goal is also personal transmutation."

"That makes so much sense," Mason said. "I see it in the freemasons that I know. It also explains why you built the melioreum."

"And the water building in Chicago. I had plans for a third building that incorporated the symbolism and power of the air, but then the Depression struck, and the war."

"What you've achieved is remarkable," Mason said, but felt a twinge of sadness, knowing Hawley would never build another structure.

Hawley looked at his plate, studying the crumbs. "You can take it," he said quietly.

"The corona?" Mason said, surprised. "That's great."

"Just let me know when you get it installed."

"I'll do that," he said, feeling a little guilty at the lie—Hawley wasn't going to live to see that happen either.

"It really will complete the project," Hawley said, his tone brighter now. "I'd love to come and see it."

"Even after I get it mounted, I might not be able to convince anyone to install doors and windows where the knockouts are."

"That's less important than just installing the corona. Even in a sealed stairwell, the melioreum will energize the building and everyone in it."

Dorothy entered, with two cups on saucers, and set them down wordlessly before leaving again.

"Like pouring everyone in the building a strong cup of coffee," Hawley said, grinning.

"I can get behind that," Mason said, and picked up his cup, taking a sip.

Hawley nodded at Mason's untouched glass of milk. "Not a fan?"

"I can't drink it."

"I've never met anyone who doesn't drink milk. You're an unusual fellow."

"Thank you," Mason said emphatically, and raised his coffee cup in acknowledgment. "About the drum—I won't be able to take it with me today."

"I should think not. You'll need some laborers and a truck."

"Can it be set on its side?"

"Gently, and for a brief period, but it can't be stored that way. It must be transported upright."

"Can I come back for it tomorrow?"

"I'll be here," Hawley said, spreading his hands, as if to say he was rarely anywhere else.

"I should make the arrangements, then." Mason slurped at his coffee and set the cup down. It was too hot to guzzle. "Thanks for lunch, and thanks for explaining everything."

Hawley rose with him, grinning as Mason pulled on his jacket. "Until tomorrow, then."

Dorothy came out of the kitchen as he was leaving,

and saw him to the door. Hawley had disappeared.

"You said you take the streetcar to get here," Mason said. "I've never done that. How does it work?"

Dorothy frowned. "When it stops, you climb aboard, and pay the conductor."

"They take cash?"

"Yes, sir. Fifteen cents. The conductor can make change."

"Where is it?"

"Walk down to Glendale Boulevard. It's about twenty minutes."

"Got it. Thanks," he said, and pulled on his hat, waving good-bye.

He was jubilant at the success, and it put a spring in his step. The walk gave him time to think through it all. Hawley had told him everything he wanted to know, answered every question he had. Astrid had been right about a lot of it. Finding the corona had been pure gravy, and there was a way to get it on the Primavera Building—Mason had cooked it up on the fly, as he stood there with Hawley gawking at the contents of the oil drum. It was going to take some work, and there were unknowns that might slow him down, but if things went well, he was sure he'd be able to get it placed where it belonged.

Once he was on the boulevard, it wasn't hard to find the streetcar—the overhead electric wires led him right to it. The platform was just a low curb between the tracks in the middle of the street. He stood with a man in a dark suit who was also waiting, and considered asking him which line he should board, if there were different ones, but when the car approached, he knew exactly where it was going: it was labeled SUBWAY TERMINAL. Mason knew it well, had dined at a friend's apartment in that very building, now residential space, with the long abandoned train tunnels running underneath, downtown and not far from the Primavera Building.

Paying the conductor was straightforward, as the uniformed man made a beeline for him once he'd climbed on, and he got a handful of change for the dollar he proffered. The ride was surprisingly fast, he thought, sitting on a hard wooden bench and watching the city roll by, but also a lot rougher than the trains in his version of the city, which mostly ran on dedicated tracks and didn't often compete with cars for real estate.

The line ran through his own neighborhood, or close to it, and Mason craned to look out at the hillsides, not yet completely built out. The template was the same, the shape of the hills and the lay of the land, but this wasn't his town, not yet.

Walking up out of the station with the crowd of passengers was disorienting, but after half a block's walk he figured out where he was, and made his way toward Pershing Square, and into the Baltimore Hotel that fronted it, its Edwardian brick facade timeless and familiar. Things inside were different, though—he couldn't even count the uniformed staffers, so many of them were milling around.

He approached the reception counter and spoke to the clerk, who wore his hair oily and slicked back, with a pencil mustache like Hawley's.

"I need a single for two nights," Mason said.

"Certainly, sir. If I could get your name and address for the register?"

Mason dug his DC driver's license out of his pocket and handed it over.

"You're a long way from home," the clerk said. "Are you visiting our city for work?"

"Exactly," Mason said. "What's the room rate?"

"Fifteen dollars, plus tax."

He pulled out a wad of cash and peeled off the right bills, setting them on the counter.

"I'll have you sign here, and a bellman will help you with your bags."

"They're in my car. I'll take care of them later," Mason said, scrawling his signature into the ledger the man presented.

"Of course." He waved to a young man—he couldn't have been older than twenty—wearing a uniform with big gold buttons on the jacket, and handed him the room key. "Edward will show you upstairs."

"Thanks," Mason said, picking up his change and stuffing it in his pocket. He could find the room himself, of course, but he went along with the procedure.

"This way," the bellman said, leading him to the elevators, and as they rode up, asked, "Traveling on business?"

"That's right."

"What kind of business are you in?"

Mason looked at him. "Transmutation."

The bellman gave him the once over. "You're not wearing any masonic jewelry."

"I'm not a freemason," he said, surprised the kid knew what he was talking about. "I guess I'm traveling a path that's parallel to theirs right now."

"Sounds complicated," he said dubiously, looking away.

The elevator doors opened, and the bellman led him to his room, pushing open the door and handing over the key. Mason knew what was expected; he scrabbled in his pocket and found a couple of quarters, handing them over.

"Hey, thanks," the bellman said. He seemed genuinely grateful. "If you need anything special, just ask for Edward."

"I will," Mason said, and closed the door as he left. The kid probably meant "special" like bourbon and burlesque, but it didn't hurt to have a contact in the hotel.

It was a cute little room, he thought, looking around, sticking his head into the bathroom. He had to smile when he pulled back the curtains; the view of the city included the Primavera Building, beyond the square below. He couldn't see the box covering the top of the glass column—the melioreum—but the facade looked the same as it always had, the same as the day it had opened, the same as the day he'd first gone inside to consult Miss Cassie, the same as the day he'd moved into his office. He stood and stared at it for a minute. He really hoped he could pull this off.

Even though he was exhausted, he had an errand to run before he could sleep. Pocketing his room key, he retraced the route to the lobby and walked up the street to the Grand Central Market. Not much had changed here; there was sawdust on the floor, and the familiar neon signs of the vendors. He bought apples, oranges, and grapes, then found some beautiful tomatoes, loading everything into a paper sack, and carried it back to the hotel. There was a little shop in the lobby, he noticed, and remembered that he was traveling light, so he stopped and bought a toothbrush.

Upstairs he got undressed, and had a shower, and climbed into the bed, grateful to be horizontal. There was no alarm clock, he realized, just an old-timey telephone beside the bed, but it didn't have buttons or a dial. He picked it up and listened. A woman's voice answered, "Switchboard."

"Can someone wake me up at six?" he asked her.

"Six this evening?"

"That's right."

"Certainly, sir. A wakeup call at six P.M."

The line went dead, and he replaced the handset. Again he wasn't sure exactly what time it was, without his cell phone, but he knew he had at least several luxurious hours to catch up on sleep, and soon drifted off.

A strident alarm bell pulled Mason into consciousness, and he blinked awake, looking up at the ceiling. He couldn't remember seeing that crown molding before. The bell rang again—why all the racket? Then it all came to him in a flood of memory, and he sat up to grab the phone.

"I'm awake," he mumbled, rubbing his eyes.

"This is your wakeup call," a woman's voice said. "It's six o'clock."

"Thank you," he said, and hung up.

After he splashed cold water on his face in an effort to drag himself completely into consciousness, he ate a couple of apples and got dressed. His shirt had dried out and passed the sniff test, he found, to his great relief, surprising after his inept sweat-inducing box-moving in Hawley's garage, and of course the suit was perfect and unwrinkled, as it always was. Looking at his hair in the mirror, it was messed up, and he wished he had a comb, but Ned's pomade was resculptable, and after a minute's effort it looked presentable again. He double-checked his necktie in the mirror—he wanted to look sharp for Mamie—and then headed out.

On the short walk, he pulled out his membership card and examined it again, running through his memories of the Blue Moon bar. The card had a big blue dot on it, presumably representing the moon, and along with his name said "Member in good standing."

Walking into the alley behind the storefronts, he looked for the unmarked fire door with a faded ½ painted above it. That was part of the address, 482½, and because the whole-numbered doors were around on the main street, initially it had taken him ages to find it. But it was still here, unmistakable once he knew what to look for. Being hidden made it felt seedy, furtive—but he knew that the subterfuge was necessary for a gay club in an unenlightened time.

The door was unlocked, happily, and the noxious tang of cigarette smoke billowed into his face when he pulled it open. He took a deep breath and trotted down the stairs, hanging his hat on a peg at the bottom. The place wasn't busy, not this early in the evening, and he scanned the faces for Mamie, but she wasn't here. The bartender, completely bald and wearing a black vest over his white shirt, his meaty biceps bulging in his sleeves, looked up as Mason approached. There was a flash of recognition in his eyes, and he broke into a smile.

"Hey, Gus," Mason said.

"Mr. Braithwaite."

"You remembered my name." Mason grinned and took a stool at the bar.

Gus leaned toward him, hands splayed on the bar top. "It hasn't been that long. Also, you caused quite a commotion the last time you were in here."

"Sorry about that."

He shrugged. "It was entertaining, and no barware got broken, which in my mind means no harm done. Kronenbourg?"

"Set me up," Mason said, slapping the bar top, and looked around the room. He nodded to a man who met his gaze, but the guy quickly looked away. Mason turned back to the bar and put down a five-dollar bill.

Gus came back with his beer, and pulled the five, returning a moment later with his change.

"So is Mamie coming in these days?" Mason asked him.

Gus raised his eyebrows. "She is something of a barfly. It's Friday night, so I'll wager she'll be here, one way or another."

Mason nursed his beer and scanned faces as more guys came down the stairs, alone and in twos and threes, some of them in drag. They looked like ordinary women, with subtle makeup and sensible hairdos, not the exaggerated drag glamazons he was used to.

Gus's young bar-back came in, ducked under the gate in the bar, and tied on an apron. The noise level was rising, getting more boisterous as more bodies filled the tables and barstools. Once or twice he got a flirty glance from one of the patrons, but he just smiled and looked away—as bolstering as it was to his ego to get that kind of attention, it wasn't why he was here.

A guy in an open-collared shirt with broad verti-cal stripes came down the stairs and grinned at him. Mason nodded but turned back to his beer. The guy sat beside him, a big smile on his face.

"Hey, detective," he said.

Mason looked at him more closely. He knew those eyes, even though little else was familiar—his short-cropped jet-black hair, the baggy dungarees. "Mamie?"

"I go by Billy when I'm not wearing a dress," he said, his eyes bright.

"You look so different. Why aren't you in drag?"

"Do you have any idea how much work that is?" he said, and gestured dismissively. "I haven't seen you in months."

"I went home," Mason said.

"To Vermont—I remember. But you're here now." He reached around and gave Mason a side-hug. "It's good to see you."

Mason couldn't help but smile. "Can I buy you a drink? Mamie is a G-and-T kind of gal. What about Billy?"

"She and I have similar taste," he said.

Mason waved Gus over. "A gin and tonic for my friend here," he said.

Gus grinned, and before he left, said, "Good to see you, Billy."

"What brings you back to LA?" Billy asked, twist-ing back and forth on his barstool with the energy of a distracted kid.

"I'm on a job. I wanted to talk to you about that. I know you're resourceful, and I thought maybe you could give me some ideas."

"Aren't you the flatterer," Billy said, and dipped his chin, showing a hint of Mamie the coquette.

"Is it still flattery if it's true?" Mason said.

"Oh, I'm not complaining. Flatter me any old time. What kind of case are you working on?"

"I need to hire someone who has a truck."

"What kind of truck?"

"To move a small load. Maybe two hundred pounds."

Gus delivered Billy's drink in a highball glass, and deftly slipped a single from Mason's pile of change.

"I have a truck that'll work for that. What are you moving?"

"It's an oil drum."

"How far does it have to go?"

"Just a couple of miles. Right here in town."

"Easy," Billy said. "I'll do it. You don't even have to pay me."

"It's a little more complicated than just the move. I need someone to help me bury it."

Billy sipped at his drink. "I can scare up some shovels. Where are you going to do that?"

"In a backyard. The problem is, it's not my backyard. I don't know who lives there, and I don't want them to know I'm doing it."

Billy studied him as he sipped his Kronenbourg, then said quietly, "Mason, are you trying to get rid of a body?"

Mason laughed. "Nothing so lurid, I promise. None of this involves any felonies."

"Except maybe digging up someone's yard on the sly."

"The key to that is not getting caught. If no one notices, then no crime has been committed."

"I'm no lawyer," Billy said flatly, "but I don't think that's how it works. What's in the oil drum?"

"It's hard to describe. It's nothing illegal."

"Try."

Mason sighed. It wasn't unreasonable of him to ask, he knew, even though the truth was too out-there to explain coherently, and making up a lie was a lot of work.

"It's an artwork," Mason said. "Like a sculpture. I need to hide it in a safe place until it's time for it to be installed."

"How long will that be?"

"A few years."

"Why does it have to go in someone else's yard?"

"I can't tell you that. It's privileged information between me and my client."

A guy who'd just walked in put a hand on Billy's shoulder and said, "Hi, Billy." He glanced at Mason and said a shy "Hello" before he moved on. Mason remembered him, the blond with the flat brush cut; he'd been here last time too.

"Hey, Flattop," Billy said.

Mason watched as Flattop sat at the other end of the bar and gestured to Gus. He wore a short-sleeved plaid shirt, and he was blushing, perhaps from his encounter with Billy and Mason, or perhaps just from coming into such a secretive place. His face was almost as red as Mason's got on a daily basis.

"Is that his nickname because of the hair?" Mason asked Billy.

"It stands out, doesn't it? Maybe because he's so damn blond. You know what they say: blonds have more fun."

Mason scoffed, and took a sip of beer.

"So nobody gets hurt?" Billy asked.

"You mean burying the drum? No way. I know it sounds strange, but it's just a sculpture that needs to be stored in the ground for a while."

Billy nodded, and picked up his highball glass. "Burying something that big, you can't do it in the middle of the night—it's too much work to go unnoticed. If you can't hide the digging, logically you have to come up with an excuse to be doing it. You have to get rid of the occupants for a few hours, and tell them you're doing something else. Maybe you could install some of those lawn sprinkler pipes while you're at it, to cover what you've done farther down."

Mason grinned at him, amazed. "I knew you were the guy to ask."

Billy shrugged. "Like you said, I'm resourceful."

"So you're willing to help me, even without a clear explanation?"

"Why not? I don't know you very well, Stretch, but I know you're no murderer, no bank robber."

"An accurate assessment on both counts."

"So it'll be an adventure."

"That's such a good attitude, Billy." Mason studied him for a moment. "I remember you were in military intelligence during the war, but what do you do for a living these days?"

He grinned. "I paint houses. Isn't that a hoot?"

"Not really," Mason said. "I imagine it's hard work."

"It means I'm no stranger to manual labor. I know how to dig a hole in the ground."

"Plus you can walk in spike heels like you were born in them. You're a true polymath."

Billy threw his head back in a loud guffaw.

"Do you think two of us could do this without heavy machinery?"

"How deep does it have to be?"

"Deep enough not to be found accidentally by an enthusiastic gardener. It has to be buried upright."

"So an oil drum is about three feet tall, and you want maybe three feet of soil on top. That's a six-foot hole. It'll take a while, but it's doable. Gravediggers do it every day."

"You'll have to teach me how."

Billy frowned. "To dig a hole? It's not complicated. You just have to use your muscles. And since this job is getting more complicated, I will let you pay me."

"Good," Mason said emphatically. "It's my client's money anyway."

"When were you planning to undertake this skullduggery?"

"Are you free tomorrow?"

"It's Saturday, so I'm not working."

"I like your sprinkler idea," Mason said, "but that would mean convincing the homeowner to put them in. I'm thinking we need a ruse that doesn't give them any choice. Maybe we could tell them a waterline broke under their lawn."

"Then you'd have to show up dressed like the DWP. And how would you convince them not to watch us work?"

Before Mason could answer, Billy grabbed his forearm, his fingers gripping tightly. Mason looked at him, but Billy was looking down the bar, at Flattop.

"He's the guy," Billy said intently.

"What guy?"

"Flattop works for City Gas. He's a pipefitter, or something like that."

Mason glanced at Flattop, then back to Billy. "A gas leak."

"It's perfect. You can send the homeowner away and dig up as much lawn as you want. Nobody knows where their local gas lines are buried."

"How well do you know him?"

"We've had a couple of conversations, but we never had an affair."

"I wonder how scrupulous he is."

Billy scoffed. "He's in here, isn't he?"

Mason frowned. "Huh?"

"I don't know how things are in Vermont, but here it's illegal even to be in a place like this, Mason. The cops could bust it up any time they want—and they do. Anyone who walks down those stairs is already a premeditated sex criminal."

It was a depressing thought, but he knew it was true. "He's alone right now. Should I go talk to him?"

"We'll both go," Billy said, "but let me start the conversation." He slid off his stool, taking his drink.

Mason scooped his change off the bar top and pocketed it, leaving a single for Gus and following Billy with his beer bottle in hand.

"What are you drinking, Flattop?" Billy said, standing beside his barstool.

Flattop looked a little surprised, but grinned at them both. "I'm waiting on another beer."

"Mason's going to buy it for you, if you let us bend your ear for a minute," Billy said.

Flattop's eyebrows shot up. "For free beer, I've got all evening."

"Let's sit at a table," Billy said, and headed to an empty one in a back corner, only dimly visible through the smoke wafting in the air.

Mason introduced himself to Flattop as they waited at the bar.

"I've seen you in here before," he said. "I'm Eugene, although everyone here calls me Flattop."

Gus came with a beer bottle, and Mason set a dollar on the bar. Flattop took the bottle, and to Mason, said, "Thanks."

They went to sit with Billy, who clinked his glass against their bottles and said, "Cheers."

Mason watched Flattop as they drank, and he saw it right away—the way he looked at Billy, the undeniable attraction.

"So what's going on, fellas?" Flattop asked.

Billy furrowed his brow. "A friend of Mason's is going to have a gas leak tomorrow under his backyard. We were hoping you could help us convince them to vacate the premises for a few hours so we could dig it up."

Flattop frowned, glancing from him to Mason. "What would that involve, exactly?"

"A couple of pairs of coveralls with the company logo should do it," Billy said. "I can get shovels and a pickax myself."

Flattop looked to Mason. "What's buried in the yard?"

"I actually need to bury something," Mason said.

Flattop frowned. "I don't think I can be a part of that."

"It's not a body," Mason said quickly.

"Yeah, nobody gets hurt," Billy added.

"So what are you burying?"

"Nothing illegal," Mason said.

Flattop looked doubtful and sipped at his beer. "So who are these people you need to scare away?"

"I don't really know them, but I want to use their yard to store an oil drum for a few years. They won't even know it's down there. It'll be like the fossils in the tar pits, just waiting until someone digs them up."

"What kind of lettuce are we talking about?" Flattop asked.

"Lettuce?" Mason asked, confused.

"He means the money." Billy met his eye. "As in, what are you going to pay him?" To Flattop, he said, "Mason's from back east."

"What do you think it's worth?" Mason asked him.

"Well, for the uniforms, twenty bucks. And you'll have to give them back."

"My god, man," Billy exclaimed. "Are they gold-plated?"

"I don't know what you're going to do with them. I could get in big trouble."

"You know," Mason said, "maybe you could come with us. You already know what the gas company would tell people to convince them to vacate for the afternoon. It would work much better."

"I don't know if that's a good idea," Billy said, frowning.

"My time would cost you a little more," Flattop said, "but I'd feel better about loaning you the gear. I could keep an eye on you."

"Could you borrow a gas company vehicle, with the logo and everything?" Mason asked.

Flattop groaned. "When do you want to do this?"

"Tomorrow afternoon."

He was quiet for a minute, considering. He looked at Billy, and even though Flattop was trying to conceal it, Mason could see the longing.

"It's easy to get a truck on the weekend," Flattop said finally. "I'll do it for fifty."

"Ouch," Billy exclaimed, leaning back in his chair. "Be sensible."

"Would that fifty buy your promise never to tell anyone about it?" Mason asked.

Flattop leaned toward him and held his gaze. "The only reason I'm even considering this is that we're brothers. I know Billy is completely fearless—I've seen him walk down Sixth Street in a dress on his way here. And you—I've seen you in here before, so I know you're one of us."

"I am," Mason said, "and I love your spirit. Gay solidarity."

"Things need to change," Flattop said firmly. "We're not criminals."

Billy grinned. "Well, technically, we are."

Mason ignored him, and raised a palm, and said emphatically, "Preach."

Flattop looked mystified. "What?"

"I just mean I agree with you," Mason said, dropping his hand and feeling his face redden.

"Anyway," Flattop said, "I'll help you—and I know how to keep my mouth shut."

Mason looked at Billy.

"Fine by me," Billy said. "But you have to do what we say."

"Let's drink to that," Mason said, and clinked his bottle with them again.

"I can get the truck and the uniforms in the morning," Flattop said, his tone businesslike now. "Don't worry about shovels and all that—they're already in the truck. Where and when?"

"I have to be in Los Feliz before that," Mason said, and they talked about where to meet.

"So can I see some of that scratch now?" Flattop asked.

"Ten percent," Billy said flatly. "Balance payable on completion."

Mason pulled a wad of bills out of his pants pocket, out of view below the table. The top one was a ten, and he palmed it, then handed it to Flattop. "How about twenty percent?"

Flattop glanced at the bill once he'd moved it into his lap, and grinned broadly. "Another round, boys? I'm suddenly feeling flush."

"I have to go," Mason said. "I got up way too early. I'll see you tomorrow."

"I'll walk with you," Billy said, and to Flattop, "Don't get too tight. You need to be sharp tomorrow."

Flattop gestured widely. "For fifty clams, I'll do whatever you say, boss."

Mason remembered to take his hat when he saw the row of them on the pegs by the door. As he walked up the stairs behind Billy, they passed a man coming down.

"Have a good night, Billy," the guy said, with a louche grin.

Mason chuckled, and once they were outside in the alley, said, "He thinks you're getting lucky."

"You should come to town more often. It does wonders for a girl's reputation."

As they walked out to the street, Mason put an arm around his shoulder and gave it a squeeze.

Billy stopped on the sidewalk and faced him. "So—am I?"

"Are you what?"

"Getting lucky," he said, and playfully punched Mason's shoulder.

"Oh—wow. That's so tempting, Billy. I can't—I'm with someone, and we're exclusive. Committed, I mean."

"He's not here, though, right? He doesn't have to know."

"I can't lie to him."

Billy nodded and looked down, and they strolled toward the corner of the block. "Although you have no problem lying to strangers about a gas leak to tear up their lawn."

"See, the difference there is that nobody gets hurt. If I sleep with you, somebody gets hurt."

"How about this—come over to my place and have a nightcap. Just for an hour. We can talk, and maybe cuddle a little, but we'll keep our clothes on. That's not going to break your vows."

Mason shook his head slowly. "I can't do that. Ten

minutes alone with you, and I'd have to go all the way."

Billy sighed. "Yeah, that was kind of my plan. It's called the bait-and-switch. You really are a detective."

"It's not that I distrust you—I know how I am. You're hot, and I wouldn't be able to control myself."

"Again with the flattery."

"What about Flattop? I saw the way he was looking at you. He's totally into you."

"You think?" Billy wrinkled his nose. "I don't get that feeling."

"The only reason he agreed to help us was that you were the one asking. He's just shy—flirt with him a little. You'll see."

"I might just do that, but not tonight." He shrugged, sliding his hands into his pockets. "So where do you want me to meet you tomorrow with my truck? You mentioned Los Feliz. Are you staying up there? I can drive you tonight, if you want."

"That's where the drum is. I'm actually staying at the Baltimore." He gestured to its hulking mass, visible farther up the street.

"Of course you are," Billy said, and sighed. "I'll be out front at ten. Look for a Studebaker half-ton."

"I don't know what those look like."

"You can't miss it. It's canary yellow." He turned and walked away.

"Good night, Billy," Mason called after him, feeling a jumble of guilt, and desire, and regret.

"Good night, sweet prince," he said, half turning around but not breaking his stride.

Mason crossed the street and headed toward the Baltimore. It was so tempting, and it would be so easy to cave. If he'd had another beer or two, he just might have. But he knew it was the right thing to do, sleeping alone, despite the longing in the reptilian core of his brain.

Up in his room he hung his suit and his shirt in the closet, hoping to air out the smoke that still burned his eyes. In the mirror they looked bloodshot, probably as much from lack of sleep as from the smoke. After he brushed his teeth, he called down for a wakeup call, then collapsed into bed, sinking rapidly into deep sleep, carrying back no memory of his dream life.

Eleven

Once again the strident bell in the phone dragged Mason into consciousness. He answered groggily and then showered, sniffing suspiciously at his shirt before pulling it on. There wasn't time to look for coffee in the lobby, he decided, and when he stepped out to the street, he saw that had been a wise choice—the canary-yellow truck was already waiting at the curb. It was a cute little thing, with bulbous swooping fenders. When Mason stooped to look in the passenger's window, he found Billy behind the wheel, wearing dark-blue work clothes and a painter's cap.

"Howdy, Red," he said cheerfully, and pushed open the door for him.

Great, Mason thought—a morning person. He pulled off his hat as he climbed into the low headspace and scrabbled for his seatbelt, but there wasn't one.

"Have you had breakfast?" Billy asked. "We can stop at a diner."

"That would be perfect," he said, grateful for the suggestion.

"You're not really dressed for shovel work." Billy eyed him as he revved the engine and pulled away from the curb, one hand on the steering wheel and the other fiddling with a knob under the dashboard.

"Yeah, I know. We'll have to make it work. First, I need coffee."

He watched the unfamiliar city roll by, the massive lumbering cars visibly spewing pollution. There was so much more visual clutter—signage, advertising, wires strung everywhere. He wasn't sure how Billy was seeing the stoplights, because they were tiny, and dim, and there was only one at each corner. There were other cues, though; a little sign swung up to say STOP when the light turned red, switching to GO when it went green again. The mechanism made a loud *ding* each time it changed. That must get annoying for anyone who lived nearby, but noise abatement didn't seem to be a priority here.

"You must be from a small town," Billy said. "You're gawking at everything."

"It's all new to me. Where I live doesn't look anything like this."

But he still knew the bones of the city. The underlying streets and the curve of the hills were mostly unchanged. It felt like Billy was taking an odd route to get to Los Feliz, through Chinatown, but Mason didn't ask. He was also using an inscrutable driving technique, sometimes pumping the clutch and revving the engine before he shifted gears. Driving was hard enough where he lived, where the machines were starting to drive themselves; he couldn't imagine learning to drive the way Billy was.

Soon they pulled into a parking lot beside a little diner, and Mason followed him inside, hanging his hat on the stand by the door. The waitress behind the counter brought two cups without even asking, plunking them down and sloshing coffee into them. Billy rattled off an order of eggs and bacon and toast, explaining concisely how he wanted each of them cooked—"over-easy, crispy, and dark."

"Oatmeal, with no milk," Mason said when she eyed him. "Do you cook the hash browns in butter?"

"That's right."

"So I'll have a double order of oatmeal, and a fruit cup."

Once she'd gone, Billy asked, "Who doesn't like butter?"

"It's a whole thing," Mason said grimly. "Don't ask."

He laughed. "Drink some joe. I get the feeling you don't function too well in the morning."

The food came quickly, and after they'd started into it, Billy said, "So where are we picking up your drum?"

"It's in this guy's garage. When we meet him, let me do the talking. The drum is kind of fragile, so it can't be rolling around in the back of your truck."

"I've got rope to tie it down."

"It has to be transported upright."

Billy grinned at him, chewing on his toast. "That's fine, Mason. I know what I'm doing."

"I believe you. I guess I'm just being a control freak."

"I'd call you more of a food freak, eating oatmeal with nothing on it."

Once they'd finished, Mason paid, and they walked out to the truck.

"Do you want to drive," Billy asked, "since you know the way?"

"I know how to drive, but I don't know how to operate that throttle thingy you were using."

"It's called the choke. It's not hard to learn. But not today."

Mason directed him into the hilly part of Los Feliz. When they drove up Hawley's street, the Roadmaster wasn't in the portico, but Mason saw it parked farther up the driveway, beside the garage. From this vantage point the grill looked like baleen, the bulbous black hood curving backward like a cetacean's head.

"Give me a second," Mason said, and jumped out, approaching the front door and ringing the bell.

Dorothy answered after a minute, and told him formally, "Mr. Hawley will meet you at the garage."

Mason thanked her and climbed back in the truck. "We'll load it at the top of the driveway."

"I'll turn around here, then," Billy said. He pulled across the street and then backed through the portico, his tanned arm on the back of the bench seat, craning to see out the rear window. Engine roaring, he drove faster than Mason would have in reverse, stopping abruptly a few feet from the garage door.

Hawley was just walking up from the house as they climbed out of the truck. "Good morning," he greeted them, unperturbed by the loud vehicle and its reckless speed.

214

"This is Billy," Mason said. "He's helping me today. Billy, Augustus Hawley."

"Pleased to meet you, Billy," Hawley said, with a subtle tilt of the head, and to Mason, "Does he work for the bureau?"

"Billy's a subcontractor," Mason said.

Billy's eyebrows rose, and he grinned at Mason.

"You can back in a little closer once I've opened the garage," Hawley said, and moved to pull open the doors. The drum was still sitting in the middle of the floor on its pallet. Billy got in the truck again and revved the engine, backing up until Hawley waved at him, and stopped just a few feet from the drum. When he climbed out again, he stood with them around the drum, hands on his hips, assessing the load.

"Should we lift it with the pallet?" Mason asked.

"It'll be easier without," Billy said, and grabbed the drum, tipping it toward him.

"Careful with that," Hawley said. "It's fragile."

"Yes, sir," Billy said, and set it down again. "It should be easy enough to lift. Can it be set on its side at all?"

"Not for transportation or storage, but that's fine while you're maneuvering it."

Billy went back to the truck and reached behind the driver's seat. He threw a pair of work gloves to Mason, who caught them awkwardly against his chest, examining them for a second to figure out what they were.

Billy pulled on his own pair and said, "Hike up your skirt, Alice."

"What?" Mason asked.

"Take off your jacket and give me a hand."

"Right," Mason said, and pulled on the gloves, then tried to take his jacket off. He had to take the gloves off again first, then hung his jacket on the tool rack at one side of the garage, and pulled the gloves on again, feeling his face burning as the two of them watched his fumbling.

"All right," Mason said finally, approaching the drum. "Tell me what to do."

"I'm going to tip it," Billy said, and looking to Hawley, added, "very gently. You lift from the bottom."

Billy dropped the tailgate of the truck and hopped up, squatting and pulling the top of the drum toward him. Mason lifted his end, happy that it wasn't unmanageably heavy. Maybe he'd built up some strength moving furniture around his office. Billy heaved it upward, and Mason pushed, and soon the drum was upright in the bed of the truck. Billy took over, nimbly rolling it on its rim toward the cab.

"Now it's just a matter of securing it," he said.

"What can I do?" Mason asked him.

"It's easier if I just take care of it," he said, and grinned confidently.

Mason stepped back and stood with Hawley, pulling off the gloves, and the two of them watched Billy at work, deftly tying down the drum with rope.

"I still have reservations," Hawley said, "even though I know you're more likely to achieve this task than I am. It feels like giving up one of my children."

"I promise I'll take good care of it. I want to see it installed too."

"Do you have a time frame in mind?"

"I can't go into detail, because it's classified," Mason

said, watching Billy. "I can say that the plan I've put in motion will take at least two years."

Hawley sighed. "The man who knows the future."

Billy hopped down off the truck and closed the tailgate. "We're ready to go," he said.

Mason turned to Hawley and met his eye. "Mr. Hawley, thank you for trusting me with this. I'll do my best to keep my word."

"Good-bye, Mr. Braithwaite. Do keep in touch." He reached out and shook Mason's hand.

"It may be some time before I can contact you again."

Hawley nodded. "I understand."

Mason retrieved his jacket and climbed into the cab with Billy, who started the engine and rolled down the driveway. Mason felt a wave of sadness, knowing this was the last time he'd see Hawley, that his death was in the offing.

Billy drove carefully through the portico and onto the street, and glanced at Mason, then did a double-take.

"You're verklempt," he said. "How well do you know that guy?"

"Not very well. I just know that he's a brilliant man, and I'm sad that I won't see him again."

Billy furrowed his brow. "How can you be sure of that?"

"I guess I can't," Mason said, and wiped his eyes.

"He asked you if I worked for the bureau. Did you tell him you were a G-man?"

"In a way. I told him I worked for a fictional agency. It was the only way I could gain his trust."

"So you're stealing this fragile thing, whatever it is, from him."

"Not at all," Mason snapped. "I lied about my job to get my foot in the door. I have every intention of putting this object where it belongs—where he wants it to go—on top of a building he designed. It's going to take me a while. I'm just sad that he won't live to see it put in place."

"How do you know how long he's going to live?" Billy demanded. "Mason, what's going on here?"

Mason looked at him, saw the concern in his eyes, and thought quickly. "He told me he was ill. A terminal cancer diagnosis. He's going to leave this world well before I can get this thing mounted."

"He didn't look sick."

Mason tapped his temple. "Brain cancer. No pain with that one."

Billy turned onto the boulevard, his head swiveling as he checked for traffic and did his double-clutch shifting technique. "That is a horrible disease."

"You said it, brother."

"I want to see what's in that drum," Billy said quietly, keeping his eyes on the road.

"I'd be happy to show you. We'll pull the lid off before we bury it." He glanced at Billy. The guy was smart, and obviously knew that Mason wasn't telling the whole truth. He couldn't afford to lose Billy's trust.

Passing a bank, Mason saw the clock mounted out front. "We're right on time to meet Flattop."

"Let's hope he shows up," Billy muttered. He pulled into a side street, then into a vacant lot across the alley from the back of a row of shops. The lone vehicle in the space was a heavy panel truck, with a pointed nose and big fenders over the front wheels, and a logo on the side that read CITY GAS.

"Is that him?" Mason asked.

"That'll be him." Billy pulled around the far side of the big truck and killed the engine.

Flattop was waiting in the driver's seat, and waved them toward the back of the truck. They climbed out and walked around, and the big vehicle's back door rolled up with a loud rattle.

"Howdy, boys," Flattop said, glancing around at the alley and waving them in. He was wearing dark-green coveralls with the City Gas logo on one side of his chest, and an embroidered patch that read EUGENE on the other.

Mason took off his hat as he stepped up into the truck, and had to stoop a little to stand inside. The interior was lined with tools strapped into racks, and a low wooden locker spanned the width of the vehicle behind the front seats. Flattop rolled the back door shut. It was a small space for three men, and Mason was thankful he wasn't claustrophobic.

"I found an extra-large pair of coveralls for Combat Kelly," Flattop said, and handed them each a bundle of green fabric.

"Who?" Mason asked, unfolding the garment.

"You know, from the comics—big fellow with red hair."

"I guess we change in here, huh," Billy said.

"One at a time, though," Flattop said. "There's not much room."

Billy sat on the wooden locker, clearing some floor

space. "Mr. Braithwaite, after you."

Mason pulled off his jacket. "Should I keep the trousers?"

"That'll be very uncomfortable," Flattop said. "I'd leave them in the truck. I wouldn't wear the dress shirt either."

Loosening his necktie and dropping his trousers, Mason felt his face heating up, knowing he was being watched.

"You've already seen this performance, I'm thinking," Flattop said to Billy.

"No way, brother. I had my hopes up, but this here is a lot more man flesh than I got to see last night. Mason is chaste."

"I'm not chaste," Mason said, hanging his pants among the tools. "I just happen to have a smoking-hot man waiting at home. I'm not going to jeopardize that by humping Billy."

"Hoo-wee," Flattop said, slapping his thigh, and Billy guffawed.

"It's so strange to be in a work truck with two men's men," Flattop said. "The conversation with the guys I work with is usually, 'Did you see her boobs?'"

Mason stepped into his coveralls and zipped them up. "Your turn, Billy."

Billy changed clothes, unabashed, and Mason saw that he had a great body, muscular and toned. Flattop watched closely.

"So you're Dexter today," Mason said, reading the patch on Billy's chest.

"Sure enough, Sam," Billy said.

Mason pulled out the fabric to read the patch on

his own chest. "That seems appropriate."

"You can't really pose as a ditch digger wearing the derbies, though," Flattop said, nodding to Mason's feet.

"I thought these were oxfords."

"Close, but those are definitely derbies. How do you feel about wearing someone else's work boots?"

"It seems like I don't have much choice."

Flattop opened the wooden locker and pulled out a pair, and Mason changed into them.

"They're a little too big, but I guess that's better than too small."

"Lace them up tight," Billy said. "You'll be fine."

Mason sat on the locker to tie his boots. "So what are we going to tell the homeowners?"

"Leave that to me," Flattop said firmly. "So where is this place?"

"Not far. I'll guide you."

"I guess I'll follow with the spinach," Billy said.

"After we stop," Mason said, looking up at him, "park farther up the hill. That way whoever leaves the house won't see the drum and get suspicious."

"Roger that," Billy said, and climbed over the locker, hopping down through the driver's door.

Flattop sat behind the wheel, and Mason joined him in the passenger's seat as he started the heavy engine.

"Turn left on the boulevard," Mason said. "The layout of this place is a double garage with a little bit of driveway space in front of the doors. We'll park on the street just before the driveway, so they can see the truck and the logo from their front door. That'll also block the view of the yard from the street, so we'll have some privacy when we dig. Should I come to the door with you?"

"You should grab one of the banjos and stand near the truck, where they can see you," Flattop said. "The sales pitch works best if I'm on my own."

Mason glanced into the back, trying to remember what was there. "A banjo?"

"It means a shovel," Flattop said. "You were never in the service, huh."

"Nope."

"So what if nobody's home?"

"Damn it," Mason snapped. He hadn't even considered that. Where was his head?

"Don't worry," Flattop said. "We'll dig anyway. If they come home, it'll be harder to explain, but I can sell it."

Mason looked at him, appreciative. "I believe you can. I wish you could be that confident with Billy."

"What?" His voice rose, and he glanced quickly at Mason. "What are you talking about?"

"I just think there's romantic potential there. You should spend some time with him."

"Are you serious? You think he likes me … in that way?"

"Maybe," Mason said. "Just a hunch."

"He's so handsome, but he's all girly sometimes. At the Blue Moon, half the time he's wearing a dress."

"I don't think he's doing it because he wants to be a woman. He's doing it because it's fun. And he's not very girly the rest of the time—I saw him lift a two-hundred-pound drum this morning like it was a can of soup."

"It's hard not to think of those dresses, though."

Mason pointed out a turn, and looked back to Flattop. "My boyfriend is really into cars. I have no idea what he's talking about half the time, and honestly I don't even get why he likes them so much. I ride a bicycle everywhere, and take the meh—, uh, the streetcar. But that doesn't mean we can't share other things."

"He's not a sissy, then. Could you be with a sissy guy?"

"I like sissy guys."

Flattop frowned. "Why?"

"Well, 'sissy' implies sensitive, and a sensitive guy is much less likely to trample your heart."

Flattop was quiet, lost in thought, as they drove up into Mason's familiar neighborhood, the engine roaring with the effort of climbing the hill. It was such a weird feeling for Mason to see his own street in such different shape—trees and hedges were sparse, and some of the houses he didn't recognize, long since torn down and replaced.

"There's the garage," Mason said.

Flattop pulled to the side and killed the engine, which died with a tinny rattle.

"That's the lawn? It's tiny."

"So it'll be easier to pick a spot to dig," Mason said.

Flattop leaned over him and looked out the passenger window. "The next house is down the hill and behind a hedge, so they won't see anything."

"Good," Mason said, but more important was that the little quadrangle looked the same as it did in his time. Apart from Ned's futile attempt to grow cucumbers in the heavy shade, it had remained untouched through the decades. It was weird to see the house, and the garage too. The shapes, the outlines, were the same, but everything else had changed—the doors, the windows, paint, siding, shingles.

"Give me some cash for their stipend," Flattop said.

Mason climbed over the wooden locker and took a moment to find his pants in the dim interior, hanging with the tools, then dug in the pockets. "How much?"

"Ten clams ought to be enough."

"If you give them more, will it work better?"

"Yeah, if you've got it," Flattop said. "The more money they have to spend, the less hurry they'll be in to get home."

Mason handed him a twenty, one of the pristine ones that had cost more, and through the windshield saw the canary-yellow pickup roll by with the drum tied in the back, its engine loud. Flattop grabbed a clipboard and tucked the money under the top sheet.

"Here we go," he said, and took a deep breath.

"I'll get my banjo," Mason said, and grabbed a shovel, but it was strapped to the wall, and it took him a minute to figure out how to get it loose. He rolled up the back door and closed it again after he jumped out, then went to the front of the truck.

Flattop was standing at the house, talking to a woman inside the screen door, her arms folded. She had curly dark hair and wore a white sleeveless blouse, and even from this distance Mason could see she looked worried. He leaned on his shovel, trying to look like he did it all the time, and strained to hear their conversation.

Flattop's tone was insistent. "We have to dig for it," he was saying, "but it's dangerous, so I have to ask you to leave the area for a few hours."

"Where's the leak?" the woman demanded, her tone shrill.

Flattop gestured vaguely to the truck. "We'll be digging beside the street, but we might have to dig into your yard."

"Is it going to explode?"

"Not if I can help it. Listen, ma'am, I have to ask you to keep this on the QT. My boys made some mistakes that caused the leak, and I need to fix it quietly."

She frowned at him, unsure. "My husband is out of town."

"There's a stipend for you, so you can go get a meal, or entertain yourself. Go see a movie." He made a show of glancing furtively at the street as he pulled out the twenty. "The money is only for you. Don't mention it to your neighbors, whatever you do, or I'll be in for it."

Once the cash was visible, she quickly made her decision. She pushed open the screen and took the bill, then went back inside. "I'll just be a minute."

Flattop walked toward the truck, a grin on his face. He caught Mason's eye and winked, then went around back and returned a moment later with a shovel.

The house's screen door burst open, and two young children emerged, both boys. The younger one looked bashfully at Mason and Flattop, but neither one of them spoke. The woman hurried out after them, wearing a coat despite the warmth of the day, a purse slung over her forearm.

"Can you help me with the garage door, Eugene?" she called to them.

"Yes, ma'am," Flattop said, and set his shovel against

the truck, trotting over toward her. "Did you lock up your house?"

Her eyes grew wide. "Gosh, I forgot."

Flattop pulled open the garage door as she hurried back to the house, and then the three of them clambered into the car. It was bulky, and powder-blue, with a white top. She backed out, pausing in the driveway to roll down the window.

"I'll close up the garage for you," Flattop said.

"How will we know there's no danger when we get back?" the woman demanded.

"If we're not here, it means we've solved the problem and sealed up the line. If things get worse, there'll be a fire truck blocking the street."

"Please be careful," she said.

"We will—and I appreciate your discretion, ma'am. I can't afford to lose this job."

"When can we come back?"

"Not before six."

She looked at Mason. "You should be wearing a hat."

Mason waved as she roared out of the driveway and turned down the hill.

Flattop moved to close the garage door, a broad smile on his face.

"You're a natural-born con artist, Eugene," Mason said.

Flattop laughed. "I have to do stuff like that all the time just to do my regular job. It's always easier when there's a dame. I just make the puppy-dog eyes."

"I'm sure there are plenty of guys who'd melt for you too."

Billy strode into the driveway. "It looks like it worked."

"As slick as grease," Flattop said.

"Should we pull the pickup in?" Mason asked.

"That would look too suspicious," Billy said. "Let's dig the hole first."

Flattop took Mason's shovel. "Can you get a pickax and another shovel?"

"Grab a spade too," Billy said, looking at the lawn.

"I would," Mason said, "except I only know what one of those things looks like."

Flattop handed the shovel to him again and went to the back of the truck.

"You're a blue blood, like that guy we visited this morning, aren't you," Billy said, frowning. "A fancy lad. You know how to drive, but not how to use a choke. That means you've only driven expensive cars."

"Not even close," Mason said. "I just don't know anything about this kind of work."

"You seem out of place," Billy said, hands on his hips, his expression thoughtful. "Not so much that most people would notice, but something is off."

"You sound like that senator from Wisconsin," Mason said.

Billy laughed, to Mason's relief, and went to help Flattop carry the tools around to the yard.

Twelve

"**D**oes it matter where we dig?" Billy asked.

"Wherever it's least likely to get dug up by mistake," Mason said.

"There aren't any utilities here," Flattop said. "They're all on the other side of the garage. I saw the gas meter and the water."

Billy looked around the little yard. "I'd say put it far from the house, close to the street."

"Fine by me," Mason said.

"We want to preserve the sod," Billy said, looking at him, "so we can lay it down again when we're done. It won't look undisturbed, but if the grass is there, it's less likely that someone will dig into it." He picked up one of the shovels, shorter than the others and with a flat edge instead of a rounded one. "This is called a spade," he told Mason.

He set to work cutting into the grass, not pushing

it in very deep but making a straight line, then cutting another line parallel to it. Flattop went to work doing the same thing, seemingly knowing what to do without any instruction.

"You can roll it up while I cut," Billy said, and showed him how to do it.

It came up remarkably clean, taking an inch or so of dirt with it. Mason had seen rolls of sod before, but had no idea this was how they were made. He rolled and stacked the grass as the two of them cut it. Eventually they'd cleared a broad patch of earth, about ten feet across.

"The drum isn't nearly this big," Mason said, straightening up with the last roll.

"Right," Billy said, "but we've got to go down six feet, and you can't dig a perfectly vertical shaft by hand. It's not safe, and besides, we'll need room to work."

The two of them started digging, tossing shovelfuls of earth to one side of the yard, and Mason picked up a shovel and emulated them. Once in a while a car would roll up or down the street, and he'd pause to watch, wary, but no one paid them any attention. He was soon exhausted from shoveling, his arms aching. After a while he stopped to stretch his back and wipe the sweat off his brow.

"This is slow work."

"Funny," Flattop said. "I was thinking we're lucky the ground is so soft. It's coming up easy." He slammed his shovel into the earth and went to the side of the house, twisting the spigot and drinking from the garden hose attached to it.

Billy took a turn, and then Mason did. Water had

never tasted so good. Standing beside the house, it was strange to think that he was looking at his own bedroom window, displaced in time. He was tempted to look inside, but he couldn't, as the curtains were drawn.

They went back to digging, the hole steadily growing deeper and wider, and after what seemed like forever, Billy, standing at the bottom, stopped shoveling.

"The ground is well over my head. This is plenty deep."

"Sweet," Mason said, taking in the hole and the huge pile of displaced dirt. Billy had been right—the hole was the size of the drum at the bottom, but at the top it was more like ten feet across.

Billy reached for Flattop's hand, and he pulled him up the sloping side of the pit. "I'll get the drum," he said, and walked toward the street.

Flattop went to the hedge at the side of the yard and zipped open his coveralls, unself-consciously peeing on the shrubbery. Mason had to grin; he'd never seen anyone do that, except out in the woods. But these guys had lived through economic collapse and fought the Nazis—they didn't stand on ceremony. Billy's pickup appeared in the driveway, bouncing over the concrete walkway and backing onto the grass, stopping at the edge of the pit. Billy climbed out and quickly untied the ropes, then rocked the drum on its rim to the edge of the tailgate. Mason and Flattop helped lift it down.

"What's inside this thing?" Flattop asked. "You're going to an awful lot of trouble to hide it."

Mason was glad they wanted to know, glad they'd both asked—once they'd seen the corona, they'd realize it wasn't anything of value, except to him and Hawley, and they'd be less likely to gossip about it, or come back and dig it up.

"I'll show you, if you have two wrenches to open it up," Mason said, tapping the bolt that secured the seal.

Flattop raised his eyebrows, and wordlessly went to the City Gas truck, returning a moment later with two adjustable wrenches. He handed one to Mason, who passed it to Billy.

"I'm not very good with tools," Mason explained.

The two of them set to work and quickly had the lid off. Mason reached in and pulled out armfuls of the excelsior, dumping it on the ground. Here and there on the blond strands were flecks of rusty brown—Hawley's blood.

Flattop and Billy reached in and helped him pull out the packing material, and Billy stopped when he'd revealed the point of the longest spike, touching it tentatively.

"What is it?" Flattop asked, pulling out more excelsior.

"A sculpture. It goes on the top of a building."

"It's beautiful," Billy said, digging deeper, "at least what I can see of it."

"It's made of glass?" Flattop asked.

"A type of glass," Mason said. "I don't know the details, but it cost a lot to make, even though it's not worth anything—except to the guy who designed the building. Billy met him this morning."

"It doesn't seem like something that needs to be buried," Flattop said. "Don't you have a friend with a garage? Or the railroad—they store stuff like this for people."

Billy was still gazing into the drum. "It's not our business, Flattop. We're not getting paid to ask questions."

"Right," Flattop said, clearly losing interest in the corona. He scooped up an armful of excelsior and dumped it into the drum. Mason and Billy helped, punching it down when it was full, and soon they had the lid back on and bolted closed.

"You're tallest, Mason," Billy said. "You should go in the hole, and we'll lower the drum to you."

Mason clambered down, his boots skidding on the loose earth, and stood at the bottom. They rolled the drum into the pit, sliding it in on its side. Mason grabbed the rim as it came into reach and maneuvered it into the bottom, his boots askew as he set it in place, with just enough room to straddle it.

"Is it stable?" Billy asked.

Mason wiggled the top of the drum. "It seems to be," he said, and looked up at him.

"Then come on up," Billy said, with forced patience, as if talking to a thick child, "and we'll bury the damn thing."

The two of them pulled Mason up by his hands, and the three of them shoveled the dirt onto the drum, slowly reducing the pile of earth and filling the hole. It seemed to go a lot faster than the excavating had, although they spent a lot of time tamping down the earth with the shovels, and stamping on it with their boots to flatten it. They rolled the sod back over the dirt, and when they were finished, the three of them stood in the driveway, assessing their work. Again Billy was right: the ground had obviously been dug up, but the grass mitigated the damaged look.

"I wish we had a rake, to clean up the rest of the yard," Billy said.

"I saw one in the garage," Flattop said, and went to open the big door.

Billy climbed in his truck and pulled it out onto the street. When he came back, he took the rake from Flattop and spent some time on the lawn, exposing the grass where their dirt pile had been, and cleaning up the stray strands of excelsior. When he was done, Flattop pulled the garden hose off the side of the house and soaked the entire lawn, languorously casting the stream and letting the water run for a long time.

Mason stood in the driveway and watched him work. "It's kind of a little hill now," he said to Billy.

Billy nodded. "That'll subside with time."

"I hope the homeowners don't decide to dig it up."

"Why would they do that?" Flattop said. "There's a dangerous gas line down there."

Flattop coiled up the hose and put it back on its rack on the house, then said, "Can we leave? The dame won't be back for an hour or more, but that's no reason to hang around here."

"Let's go," Mason said, and they carried the shovels to the back of the truck, where Flattop strapped them in place.

Once Flattop was finished, Mason climbed in and changed back into his clothes. It felt wrong, as he was so sweaty and dirty. Jumping out again, he scanned the quiet street to make sure they weren't being observed, then pulled on his hat. Billy went in to change, and Flattop went to the driveway to have a final look around. While he was doing that, Mason counted out fifty dollars from the stash in his pants pocket. When Flattop returned, he handed him the bills, folded in half.

"Oh, you know what I like," he said, and quickly counted it, then looked up, frowning. "You already gave me ten."

"I know, but you worked really hard. I couldn't have done it without you."

"Thank you, Mason," he said, pocketing the cash. "You're a bit of a queer duck, but I like you."

"Back at you," Mason said, grinning at his turn of phrase.

"Can I drop you somewhere?"

"I'll take him," Billy said, hopping out of the back of the truck, wearing his work clothes again.

"Thanks," Flattop said, and cleared his throat. His cheeks visibly reddened.

Why is he blushing? Mason wondered, and realized this is what people must see in Mason all the time.

"So, uh, Billy," Flattop said. "You and I should spend some time together. Maybe we could go bowling, and drink some beer."

Billy's eyes widened in surprise. "I'd like that. Say, it's Saturday night. Why not tonight?"

Flattop broke into a huge silly grin. "All right, then. I'll get cleaned up, and meet you at that alley on Santa Monica in Hollywood?"

"It's a deal," Billy said.

Flattop climbed into the back of the truck and rolled down the door, and Billy walked up the street with Mason toward his pickup.

As they climbed in, Mason could feel his aching muscles start to relax, grateful to be sitting down after all that exertion.

"You were right," Billy said, grinning at him as he started the engine. "Flattop has taken a shine to me."

"He'd be an amazing boyfriend," Mason said. "He's smart, like you are, and he's not afraid of hard work."

Billy cackled. "I wonder if he had a little help deciding to ask me out? It wasn't Dutch courage, because he's sober as a judge. That leaves you."

"I maybe gave him a tiny little nudge," Mason admitted, "but it's still his idea."

"That reminds me of my mother. She does the same thing, only with girls."

Billy pulled into a driveway farther up and then backed out again, heading down the hill in the late-afternoon shadows. He soon caught up to the lumbering City Gas truck, and they followed it to the boulevard.

"Back to the Baltimore?" Billy asked.

"That would be great."

"I don't suppose you want to come bowling," he said, glancing at Mason.

"Good god, man, it's a date. The last thing you need is a chaperone."

Billy laughed, revving the motor to make a quick left.

"I'm going to leave town tonight," Mason said, "so I won't be seeing you again for a while."

"That's too bad," he said, serious now. "I hope you'll come back."

"It depends on the work. But I'd like to."

"Open the glovebox there," Billy said, nodding to

it, "and you'll find my business card. Call me when you get back to town."

Mason found it, and read it. "Thanks," he said, and tucked it into the pocket inside his jacket.

They rode in silence, Billy keeping his eyes on the road. Maybe he was disappointed Mason was leaving.

As they were nearing the Baltimore, Mason reached into his pants pocket, pulling out his cash. He had lots of it left, and counted out a hundred and thirty. Billy pulled up at the curb in front of the hotel and killed the engine. When Mason handed him the cash, he didn't count it, but fanned the bills apart.

"This is way too much. I would have settled for half of what Flattop wanted."

"I know. But you trusted me, Billy, and that's worth a lot."

Billy folded the bills into his shirt pocket and reached for him, and caressed the back of his neck, his eyes soft, sad. "I wish I could kiss you good-bye, at least."

Mason grinned. "You did kiss me once, remember?"

"I know you said that I did, but it was back when I was drinking too much—I can't remember."

"That doesn't seem fair. I remember it so well. I had to explain it when I got home."

"Did you wind up in the doghouse?"

Mason chuckled, and gently tilted his head back, pressing it into Billy's grasp.

"You know," Billy said, "If you kissed me now, it would be like the first time for me. You wouldn't have to confess again, because you already did."

Mason thought about it. "That actually makes perfect sense."

Billy shifted toward him, and Mason leaned in to meet his mouth, strong and insistent, yielding and probing and perfect. Eventually he pulled away, feeling dazed.

"I can't go any farther, Billy, or I'll get lost."

Billy groaned. "I have such a woody right now."

"Save it for Flattop. He's a knockout, and he likes you."

He nodded, and put his hands on the steering wheel. "I'll be seeing you," he said, with a sad smile.

"Good night, Billy," he said, and climbed out. He watched the little truck pull away, engine revving. He felt a lump in his throat, but turned away, and headed into the hotel.

Up in his room he had a shower and ate some of his fruit, then made his way downstairs, handing his key to the desk clerk and explaining, "Checking out."

Back on the street, he walked the few blocks to the Primavera Building, and pulled on the door to the lobby, but as he'd expected, being Saturday, it was locked. He walked around to the parking entrance and stood at the chain. It would be easy enough to step over and go down the ramp, but he knew the watchman would see him.

"Hello?" he called.

A man appeared from the shadows inside, gray-haired and looking tired, in a blue uniform. He was of the same demographic as the guy who had been here yesterday, but it wasn't the same man, Mason decided.

"I'm so glad you're here," Mason said as the watchman approached the chain. "I think I left my keys in the mail room."

"You work here?"

"I'm in payroll accounting, on the twelfth floor. On Friday I checked the mail on my way out, and I must have set my keys down."

The watchman's eyes flicked to Mason's shoes. "I'm sure someone would have collected them by now."

"It was late yesterday—they might still be there. Can I just run up quickly and check?"

He sighed. "I should go with you, but I can't leave my post."

"I'll be two minutes at most."

"Can't it wait until Monday? They're probably sitting in the janitor's room anyway."

"I have to try," Mason said. "I haven't been able to use my car, and I had to break into my own apartment last night."

"All right," he said. "You hurry along, now."

"Thank you, sir," Mason said, stepping over the chain and hustling toward the back of the garage.

Trotting up the stairs into the deserted lobby, his heart was pounding. This moment was critical, and if anything went wrong … but he pushed the thought aside, and forced himself to calm down. The lobby was dimly lit, abandoned for the weekend, so he was alone. Facing the mail room doorway, right where he'd fallen yesterday, he stood and closed his eyes, clearing his mind, working to get into the bleed-through mind-set. It took time, and he calmed his breathing to help make the shift. He thought about home, and going home, pushing the edges of his mind outward and using emotional imagery to amplify the state, envisioning the junky furniture in his glammy office, his bicycle, and sweet Ned.

His eyes were half open, and the room grew darker around him. Hanh materialized just in front him, and he took an involuntary step backward.

"Wrong way," she said, and scowled, waving him forward. "Come on—snap to it."

Screwing his eyes shut, he took a quick step toward her, struggling to project his inner power onto her, envisioning a beam of energy. She grabbed his forearms and yanked, and instantly he knew it had worked—he was home.

Thirteen

When Mason opened his eyes, Matt was there, standing right behind Hanh, looking sweaty and breathing hard. Hanh let go of his arms and stepped to the side, looking unperturbed now.

"Fuck me," Matt said, grinning at him. "That took a fuck-ton of focus."

"I did it," Mason mumbled, putting his palms on his belly, happy that all of him was here.

"With a little help from your friends," Hanh said flatly.

"That's right," he said, trying to focus. "How long was I gone?"

"Like, twenty seconds," Matt said. "How long were you there?"

Mason looked at him and blinked. His mind felt wooly. "A day and a half. Maybe a little longer."

"Right on," Matt said.

"Now that you're both here," Hanh said, "we need to plan another event."

The room swam a little, deepening Mason's feeling of being disoriented, like after a long airplane flight, being dehydrated, adjusting to a new city, a new climate. Closing his eyes, he focused on this place, willing himself to be completely here. He put his hand on the door frame to keep his balance.

"Are you all right?" Hanh asked.

"Fine," Mason said, blinking and focusing on her. "So, it's time for me to pay you back for helping me?"

"In a way," she said, "but you're already directly involved. Did you notice Astrid's paranormal hiccups worsen when you're around her?"

"Astrid … right," he said, frowning with the effort of conjuring the memories. "Yes, I did. She commented on it."

"So her condition is influenceable, and that means it's fixable. We'll do a séance. You can talk to her to set it up."

"OK," he said, struggling to follow. "Will we use your shop?"

"It'll be more effective if it's in this building. She's spent so much time and energy here. She obviously loves the place."

"So, my office."

"How many people will we need?" Matt asked. "Do they have to be psychics?"

"The three of us should be enough. Mason will take the lead, of course."

"Why me? I don't know what I'm doing."

"You're the one who seems to amplify the distortions

around her when you're nearby, so you're the one best suited to fixing it."

He gestured helplessly. "How?"

"It's a simple grounding technique, like an electric circuit that's energized and needs to return to the earth."

"I don't know how to do that."

"You'll do fine," Hanh said.

"You think?"

"Dude, you always manage to figure it out," Matt said. "Don't stress."

"Take tomorrow to recuperate," Hanh said, looking him in the eye, "and we'll do it Saturday night."

"And I'm doing the planning," Mason said, pushing up the brim of his fedora and rubbing his forehead.

Hanh shrugged. "I've never met Astrid. It would be weird if I called her, so it's on you. See you Saturday." With that, she walked toward the main entrance, her shoes clicking on the marble. She said a perfunctory good night to Janet at the front desk, then stepped out onto the dark street.

"I just got back," Mason said, watching her leave. "It's annoying to have a job dumped on me, especially one with a damn learning curve."

"Hanh will be there, so it'll work out the way she wants, even if you don't know what you're doing," Matt said. "I guess I have plans for Saturday night now too."

Mason sighed and sagged against the door frame, pulling off his fedora.

"Does it seem a little ominous that payback is due the moment you return?" Matt said.

"I don't think so. I knew she was going to ask for our help anyway." He closed his eyes again, but felt

Matt watching him.

"You're going to be sick as a dog soon," Matt said. "Can I give you a ride home?"

"I'd really appreciate that," Mason said, standing up straight again. "Can I throw my wheels in the back of your car?"

"I'm parked right down the block."

They rode the elevator up to Mason's floor, and pushed through the unlocked door. As he collected his phone and keys from his desk, he looked at the corner with the hidden stairwell, and envisioned the melioreum, wondering what would happen when the corona was attached to it. He had to smile; even in his current spaced-out state, he could relish the unexpected success of finding the object.

Matt held the door as he wheeled his bike into the hallway, and then Mason locked up. He said good night to Janet on the security desk, and they went out to the street.

"So tell me about 1952," Matt said, as they walked toward his car, Mason rolling the bike between them.

"Well, I accomplished what I set out to do, I think."

After they'd loaded his bike in the back of Matt's SUV, they climbed in, and Matt started the engine. On the drive home, Mason told him about what he'd done.

"So that thing is just sitting there," Matt said, "after all these years, buried in your own damn yard."

"I hope so. It's a long time ago, and someone might have found it, but I remembered that Ned once said the house and garage hadn't changed much since they were built in the 1940s. It was the safest place I could think of."

"Fucking brilliant, Mason. It's such a great idea." He turned onto Mason's street and started up the hill.

"I guess we'll see tomorrow when I dig it up. Want to help? It's a lot of shovel work."

"No way, brother. Hire one of those little excavators. Save yourself all the manual labor."

"I've seen those," Mason said. "Ned will know how to get one."

Matt pulled into the driveway and shifted into Park. "First, you're going to need a lot of sleep. Take some pain meds before you crash."

Matt helped him unload the bike, and after he said good night, Mason parked it in the garage and went into the house, closing the door behind him as gently as he could. It was dark and quiet, and he turned on the kitchen light, changing out of his suit and smelly shirt and old-timey underpants right there, and folding them all into a trash bag. He'd air out the suit later, but for now he didn't want the lingering tobacco smoke to permeate the house.

Hurrying down the hallway, in case Peggy stuck her head out and found him naked, he popped some pain-killers for the impending migraine and took a quick shower, washing away any contact filth he might have picked up from wearing such dirty clothes.

When he stepped softly into the bedroom, his heart soared at the sight of Ned, curled up under the covers. Mason climbed in and cuddled up to him. Ned didn't wake but murmured something indistinct in his sleep. This was the best place in the world, he knew, and it felt so good to be back here. He draped an arm around Ned, luxuriating in the warmth of his body, nuzzling his shoulder blade, and then felt a twinge of guilt at the memory of kissing someone else. But there was really nothing to explain; that kiss was basically just a re-creation of the first one, a blip. He could have gone much farther, done things to really shatter Ned's trust, but he hadn't.

The dream world was a jumble of jagged images, shapes racing by and then slowly dragging, everything out of sync and changing at the wrong times. It was uncomfortable, and when he swam up closer to con-sciousness, he tried to shift gears, change the narrative.

As he awoke he had the sensation there was a steel band around his head, attached with a nut and bolt, but it was way too tight, and his head was throbbing. If he could just find a wrench and reach up and loosen it. Laying there in discomfort, he gradually remembered what had happened, why he had a headache. Ned was gone, and outside the windows the sun was bright. He threw off the covers and sat up, and instantly his head throbbed, the pain more intense. It was like having a fever—he felt unnaturally cold, almost shivering. In the bathroom he took more pain meds, more than he probably should have, and went back to bed.

It was almost noon when he woke again, feeling a little better, his head numbed by the painkillers. It felt a lot like a hangover, he realized, and forced himself to get up and get dressed, then went to the kitchen to make coffee. Eating some fruit made him feel better, and the caffeine gradually started to kick in.

When he went into the office, Ned glanced up

from his computer.

"How was your psychic night out, sleepyhead?"

"Productive," Mason said, folding his arms and leaning on the door frame. "I acquired some important information. We have to dig up the yard."

Ned turned to look at him. "What are you talking about?"

"There's something buried in the yard outside our bedroom window. Do you know how to rent one of those mini excavators?"

Ned stared at him for a moment. "Mason, we're not digging up the yard."

"I know it sounds crazy, but we have to. There's a container buried three feet down, and I need to get what's inside it."

"How do you know this?" Ned demanded, his voice rising.

"Research."

"You mean psychic research."

"That doesn't make it spurious," Mason said, struggling to keep his voice even. "I know it's there. Besides, a little digging won't hurt anything. Your cucumbers died out well before Labor Day, and the grass dried up during the drought."

Ned closed his eyes and took a breath. "Serenity," he said quietly.

Mason waited for him to open them again. "Part of the serenity thing is accepting things you can't change, right? This is one of those things. It's happening."

Ned stared at him for a moment and then cracked a smile, his chest heaving with mirth. Reclining, he laced his fingers behind his head.

Mason was surprised at the shift in his demeanor; he'd expected more pushback.

"What is it that you think is buried out there?" Ned asked.

"It's the last piece of the light fixture we found in Owen's building. I'll show you once we retrieve it."

"How did it get under our yard?"

"That part is a little complicated."

"Of course it is. It always is, Mason—complicated and impossible to believe."

Mason suppressed the instinct to react, to say something snippy about being small-minded. At least Ned was being calm.

"I'll explain it all later. Right now, though, we need a mini excavator. Didn't your friend Gustavo go to excavator school?"

"That was forklift school. But I bet he knows how to get hold of one."

"Do you have his number?"

Ned sighed. "Oh, Mason ... you're going to do this no matter what I say, aren't you."

"I'm afraid so, sweets."

"I'll call Gustavo."

"Thank you," Mason said emphatically. "And do we have a shovel or a spade?"

"Isn't that the same thing?"

"To the layman, perhaps."

He laughed. "I didn't realize you had insider knowledge about that kind of work. There's a thing that I would call a shovel hanging on the wall in the garage. But please don't start digging. I'll call Gustavo right now."

"Cool. I'm just going to go out and look."

That had gone pretty well, he thought, walking out to the garage. He found the shovel—it was a shovel, not a spade—and decided to leave it there, overcoming his instinct to rush. It would feel so good to tear into the soil, to find what was down there. But the drum had waited for decades; he could wait a little longer. Seeing him shoveling dirt in the yard would only make it seem crazier to Ned.

Walking across the driveway into the little yard, it looked the same as the day they had dug it up, yesterday, so long ago, although the hedge at the back was different, and the turf was gone, replaced by dirt and crabgrass and sparse mowed weeds. In one corner Ned's failed cucumber patch was just a stretch of tilled earth.

Mason stood directly over the spot he and Billy and Flattop had dug up. It didn't look like anything was buried there. Closing his eyes, he tried to sense the corona, feel its presence with his mind through the earth and the steel and the excelsior. It took a few minutes, but it was there, he decided—it hadn't been moved. Waiting patiently, ready to be uncovered, like the fossils in the tar pits.

Ned stepped out the front door. "Thank you for not starting your dig."

"You know I wanted to," Mason said.

"Gustavo's going to bring an excavator around in a couple of hours. He's working at a place that has one. It's already on the truck."

"Today? That's excellent. Thank you, darlin'." He went over to embrace Ned, and kissed him on the neck, pulling him into a lingering hug.

"Somebody's randy," Ned said. "Does the thought of construction machinery wind you up?"

Mason chuckled, releasing his grip. "It's all about Ned—take-charge, get-things-done Ned. It's hot."

"You will have to pay Gustavo."

"Do I get to operate the machine?"

"I asked—I wanted to too. It's only for people who've done the training. Gustavo will do it. It wasn't forklift school, either. It's called heavy equipment school."

"Thanks for helping with this," Mason said.

Ned reached up and ruffled Mason's hair, looking him in the eye. "I hope you know what you're doing."

"I do," Mason said, nodding confidently.

"No matter what you find down there, you have to put the dirt back the way it was."

"Deal," Mason said, and followed him into the house.

Ned went back to his office, and Mason took a notepad out onto the balcony, getting comfortable in one of the chaises longues. He spent a few hours making copious notes about the last few days, his meeting with Hawley and learning why he'd built the melioreum, and enlisting Billy and Flattop to bury the corona.

Gustavo had arrived, he knew, when he heard the distinctive vibrato of a diesel engine idling on the street. He went back inside and out the front door, followed by Ned. A flatbed truck was parked in the driveway, and perched on it was the excavator, a cute little machine that by volume was mostly the operator's cab and the scoop-shaped bucket. It had two caterpillar tracks, and the folding arm with the bucket, but overall it was small enough that it could be driven down the hallway of his office building with room to spare.

Gustavo was a high school friend of Ned's, from the same neighborhood, and had the same complexion and dense black hair. He was shorter than Ned, and thick, and as he climbed out of the truck, Mason saw that he was dressed decidedly blue-collar today, in worn jeans and a grease-stained hoodie.

After they'd greeted him, Gustavo asked, "So where are we working?"

Mason led him over to the side of the little yard. "It's right about here. Three feet down. It's an oil drum, buried upright."

Gustavo frowned. "Does it have oil in it?"

"It's a glass sculpture, packed in wood shavings. It's very fragile."

"Sounds easy enough," he said. "Let me check on the utilities, and I'll get unloaded."

Ned spent a minute pointing out the water and gas lines on the other side of the garage, and once Gustavo was satisfied he wasn't inadvertently going to damage any infrastructure, he went to the back of the flatbed and pulled out the ramp for the excavator. Ned and Mason watched as he unchained the machine and started it up, then drove slowly down into the yard, the treads clanking on the steel ramp. On the side of the cab, Mason saw, stenciled in swirly white script, was LITTLE LOU.

With Little Lou on level ground, Gustavo, sitting in the cab, was right at eye level. He and Little Lou crawled over to the site Mason had pointed out, and without even a pause, started digging, scooping up dirt and dropping it daintily to one side. The volume of earth in one scoopful would have taken Mason ten minutes' sweaty work with a shovel, and he watched in awe at the effortlessness of it.

Ned stood with his arms crossed, watching. "I'm glad my cucumbers didn't take hold."

"Yeah, me too." If they had, Mason thought, he would have buried the drum closer to the house.

"I have to get back to work," Ned said finally. "Call me if anything crazy happens." Walking toward the house, he turned back and corrected himself: "I should say, anything crazier."

Mason watched the excavation, happening so fast, even though the excavator moved relatively slowly, methodically, elegantly. Doubt flickered in his mind as the hole got deeper and the pile of displaced soil grew. Maybe it wasn't really there. Maybe he'd gone to some other 1952 version of Los Angeles, splintered off on a divergent path, and the drum had never even been here. The soil looked browner, drier than it had yesterday. Maybe someone had dug it up.

But then the bucket hit something, its teeth striking metal with a hollow thud. Gustavo pulled up, then delicately lowered the bucket again, scraping the dirt away with the teeth. Mason was amazed at the precision he could achieve. He stepped closer and looked into the hole. That was it—the round top of the drum, and the bolt on the hoop enclosure poking out of the dirt.

"Yeah," he shouted, and gave Gustavo an enthusiastic thumbs up.

Gustavo grinned in acknowledgment, and Little Lou dug around the drum, gradually revealing it. He even dug two steps into the earth to make it easier to access, and stopped when most of the drum was visible.

Opening the cab, he called to Mason, "We should be able to pull it out now, yeah?"

"Absolutely," Mason said. "Let me get a pair of gloves."

He hustled over to the garage and found a pair of cotton gardening gloves, then rejoined Gustavo, who had climbed down onto the neat earthen platform he'd carved out beside the drum. They grabbed the top on either side and moved it back and forth, gradually loosening the base.

Ned appeared at the top of the pit, hands on his hips. "I'll be damned. How did you know about this?"

"Psychic power, baby," Mason said, grinning at him.

"Do you need a hand?"

"It'll definitely be easier to move it with three," Gustavo said.

"I'll be right back," Ned said, and returned a minute later, wearing a pair of black gloves.

The three of them heaved on the drum, pulling it out of the soil and up each of the dirt steps, eventually lifting it onto the surface.

Gustavo wiped his brow, and Ned examined the top of the drum, brushing dirt off the closure.

"That nut is rusted solid," he said.

"No surprise," Mason said. "It's been buried for decades."

"You'll never get it open with a wrench," Gustavo said. "You'll have to cut through it. So there's a sculpture packed inside? Why was it buried?"

"Long story," Mason said. "Let's fill in the hole, and

worry about opening it later."

"An excellent idea," Ned said.

Gustavo climbed into Little Lou and started moving the pile of dirt back into the hole. Mason examined the drum, running his hands over its surface. It was dirty, and rougher than the last time he'd seen it, the paint and the FRAGILE stencil either gone or covered in grime. The bolt was red with rust, but there were no dents or damage that he could see. He couldn't help but smile, and finally sat on the ground with his back against it, leaning into it, feeling its cold hard ribs—it was real.

He watched Gustavo and Little Lou for a minute, but then closed his eyes, and thought of Billy and Flattop. The day they'd buried it, working so hard with the shovels and spades, saving the sod and rolling it up. It was like he was there again, smelling the freshly tilled earth, sweating, the sound of a shovel biting into earth.

Catching himself, he opened his eyes and took a breath, forcing himself to focus on Little Lou again. His heart was pounding. It was like he'd started to bleed through to that day. It had been a lot of work to get there, and maybe some strands of his mind were still sticking to that place, like the rusty spots in the swirls of excelsior. No way did he want to inadvertently drift back there.

When the ground was level again, Gustavo idled the excavator and stepped out of the cab, and Mason rose, walking over to him.

"How does it look?" Gustavo asked.

"I'm fine with it," Mason said, scanning the yard, "but let's ask the boss. What do I owe you?"

Gustavo quoted a figure that seemed incredibly reasonable, considering how much shovel work it had saved him. Mason went inside and stuck his head into Ned's office.

"Gustavo's wrapping up. Can you make sure the yard looks OK?"

In the bedroom, Mason found the stack of cash he kept at the back of his sock drawer and counted out the bills, adding a hundred more than Gustavo had asked for. When he returned to the yard, Gustavo was driving the excavator up the ramp onto the truck. After he'd chained it down, Mason handed him the cash.

"Thanks, guys," he said, beaming. "I'm glad Little Lou was available to help out today."

"I'm glad you were too," Ned said, and they watched him drive away.

"Do you think someone would steal this if we left it here?" Mason said, turning to the drum.

"It's made of metal, so yeah, a scavenger might go after it to sell for scrap."

"Can you help me move it into the garage?"

"Nothing would give me greater pleasure," Ned said, meeting his eye.

They put on gloves again to manipulate the drum, rolling it on its rim and lifting it over the concrete walkway, until it was just inside the garage door. Ned pushed the button to roll the door down and hopped over the sensor into the driveway.

"I'm going to make eggplant parm for dinner," he said, pulling off his gloves.

"I'd love that," Mason said, and put a hand on his shoulder as they walked back to the house.

"You seem so tired today. Almost like you're hung over from your séance. Eggplant parm is a good hangover-day meal."

Mason glanced at him, surprised that he'd picked up on that, even using the word that had come to his own mind. He was lucky that Ned was so tuned in to him, cared for him that much, even though he disbelieved how Mason did what he did.

Flopping down on the bed, he closed his eyes for a minute. He was exhausted, still headachy, but there was so much to do. Pulling out his phone, he texted Owen:

Home tonight? I have news.

Owen replied soon after:

Come on up.

He'd rest, he told himself, just for a minute, and the next moment Ned was beside him, waking him for dinner.

Ned was right—the oily cashew-cheese mess was good for his psychic hangover. It wasn't clear to him why there was even eggplant in it, as it kind of melted into the substrate, with the other ingredients providing the flavors.

"Where's Peggy?" Mason asked, waving his fork, suddenly realizing it was well after work hours.

"With Matt tonight, I think," Ned said. "I told her what I was making, and she said she'd enjoy the leftovers."

When they'd finished eating, Ned carefully set down his fork and leaned back in his chair. "So how did part of a downtown office building—the one that happens to have your office in it—wind up buried in our yard?"

Mason twirled his knife on the tabletop and nodded thoughtfully. He'd known this was coming. "Last night I was able to have some influence on where it was buried."

"Retroactively? How is that possible?"

"Even your science people think our notion of time is just a construct. So once you're able to work around that," Mason said, and shrugged.

"With psychic power."

"That is correct."

Ned leaned forward and took his hand. "Sweetie, I love you, but I worry about your sanity."

"I know," Mason said, folding his other hand into Ned's. "I'm OK with that. It doesn't really impact what's between us, right?"

"Not us. Only the lawn."

Mason grinned. "It hasn't been a lawn since we've lived here. It's just a patch of dirt where cucumbers refuse to grow."

Riding down the hill later, the feeble headlight on his bicycle straining to illuminate the arching bougainvillea at the bottom of the street, he still felt a little woozy, but the cold air in his face sharpened his focus. After he locked up his bicycle at the station, he took the train downtown, and greeted the security guard in the lobby of his building on the way in. He rode the elevator up to 12 and knocked on Owen and Sweet Marie's door.

Owen pulled it open, a bright-red popsicle in one hand, half eaten. He was wearing sweatpants and a white T-shirt, and his hair was loose in an unkempt mass. "Come on in."

"Aren't you supposed to eat those in summer?" Mason asked, following him into the vast apartment.

"We get these dinners delivered, and this was part of it," he said. "Do you know that pop star Artémise? She set up a vegan catering business. The food's great."

"So you're going vegan?"

"We're going to try. We figured you seem healthy enough, and Ned's buff, so it can't be that difficult."

"Good for you. You'll never regret it."

Far across the floor, Sweet Marie rose from a sofa in front of a giant television, the image frozen, paused in the middle of a game show. It looked like a glitzy version of hangman, with some letters blank and some filled in. As he walked over, he called to Mason, "Hey, man."

"You look like you're in another time zone over there," Mason said.

Owen led him to a different set of sofas and worked on his popsicle as Sweet Marie padded over. Barefoot and wearing jeans, Sweet Marie's mousy brown hair was splayed out on one side, as if he hadn't touched it since he rolled out of bed.

When he finally got to them, Sweet Marie asked, "Do you want a drink?"

He frowned. "You're not old enough to drink."

"I meant water or something, you big lush. Not every drink is a margarita."

Mason laughed. "I'm fine. Listen, I figured out what the column is."

"Seriously?" Owen said, sinking onto the sofa. "How?"

Sweet Marie tucked a foot under as he sat with Owen.

Mason sat across from them and leaned forward. "Augustus Hawley left his papers to Live Oak College."

"That's out in the Valley, correct?" Sweet Marie said.

"Right. I went to look through the collection."

"It's like his artwork and his floor plans?" Owen asked, munching on the last of his popsicle.

"Also his letters. People used to keep paper copies of everything they wrote and received. He kept journals too."

"So what is it?" Owen asked.

"He called it the melioreum," Mason said, and spelled it. "His plan was to bring metaphysical solar energy into every floor of the building."

"That explains why it sticks through the roof," Sweet Marie said. "But why not just use regular windows? That staircase has two outside walls."

"It's for more than just light. The crystals in the glass column somehow transmute the sun's energy."

"That's what the knockouts were for," Owen said. "So the light could get into the offices."

"Right. The building's owners got a look at the stairwell during construction, and they made him hide it. It was already built, so they didn't tear it out, but showing the melioreum through doors and windows was just too unconventional for an insurance company."

"What did he mean by metaphysical energy?" Owen said.

"Hawley compared it to drinking coffee. He believed it would improve everyone's lives by energizing them." Mason explained Hawley's interest in crystals, and Hermetic transmutation, and the symbols he'd incorporated into this building and the water building in Chicago.

"What a creative guy," Owen said.

Sweet Marie murmured agreement. "I wish I could have met him."

"I wonder how much metaphysical energy the melioreum could emit, though?" Owen waved a hand. "It doesn't do a very good job of transmitting visible light. It barely illuminates the stairwell."

"That's because there's a part missing," Mason said. "It's called the corona, and it's supposed to go on the roof to gather sunlight and solar vibes, and transmit them down through the column."

"I wonder if that part was ever built?" Owen said.

Mason grinned. "It's sitting in my garage."

Sweet Marie's eyes grew wide. "Where did you find it?"

"It was buried in a drum in someone's backyard. Hawley's papers led me to it. I dug it up this afternoon."

"Whose yard?" Sweet Marie said.

"That falls into the same category as your German banking windfall. I'd rather not get into detail."

"I get it," Sweet Marie said, holding up a palm. "Enough said." And to Owen, "We have to put it up there."

"Absolutely you do," Mason said.

"Have you told Astrid any of this?" Owen asked.

"Not yet. I thought we could invite her to watch when you do it. You'll finally be crowning the building in the way it was designed. She'll love it."

"Great idea," Owen said. "We should do it this weekend, when I'm not in school."

"Sunday afternoon?" Sweet Marie said.

"That works for me." Mason nodded. "I'll call Astrid. Before that, though, we need to transport it here, and get it unpacked. Can your building staff do that?"

"If not, they can hire people," Sweet Marie said. "How big is it?"

"It's in an oil drum, and it's made of glass, so it's fragile."

"What's an oil drum?" he asked, his brow furrowing, and after Mason had explained the size and shape, he nodded. "I'll have them call you to set it up. I can't wait to see it."

"I can't wait to see what effect it has," Owen said.

"How would you feel about inviting Teresa from 920?" Mason said. "She's the one who turned me on to the mystery. I know Miss Cassie is curious about the missing space in her office too."

"Sure," Sweet Marie said. "There's lots of room on the roof."

"Bring Peggy and your hot boyfriend too," Owen said.

"It's fine if you just call him my boyfriend," Mason said flatly. "I might ask this freemason friend of mine as well. Buildings are kind of their thing, and they're on the same wavelength about personal transformation."

Sweet Marie nodded. "So how many is that total?"

Owen counted on his fingers. "If they all come, that's eight."

"If Peggy brings her boyfriend, nine," Mason said, and moved to stand up, rising slowly, as his back was still stiff from all the shovel work, and the pain meds he'd taken were wearing off. "Also, I might ask Hanh, the woman who helped me acquire the Corona, so ten."

"This is becoming an event," Owen said. "We should ask the office staff, and the parking people, which means we're closer to twenty."

"Too much?" Mason asked.

"For the crowning ceremony of this glamorous building?" Owen said. "An event that's almost a century overdue? I think it's appropriate to go all out."

"We'll plan some nibbles," Sweet Marie said, waving his hand.

Riding home on the train, Mason left voice messages for Miss Cassie and Teresa.

"I found out what the missing space is in our offices," he explained. "Come up to the roof on Sunday and see for yourself. The building's owners are hosting a small gathering."

After he'd left a longer message for Yoshida, he dialed Astrid.

"*Hola,* psychic Mason," she answered.

"I have a mentor in the psychic world," he said, "named Hanh. She has a plan to relieve you of your paranormal visitors."

"Why are you gossiping about my personal life?" she demanded. "I told you that it wasn't fixable."

"Hanh thinks it is. She's quite adept at this stuff.

We'd do a séance and see if we can shake it loose."

"A séance, like sitting around a table in the dark?"

"Exactly."

"That sounds a little crazy," she said, her tone hesitant.

"Just like seeing a guy with a black hat who causes car accidents just by walking past."

The line was quiet for a moment before Astrid spoke. "Who will be doing it?"

"Just four of us—you and me and Hanh, and Matt—he's Peggy's boyfriend. You met Peggy."

"I remember," she said.

"It can't hurt to try, right? The three of us are psychics, so we all understand what you're going through. We could do it tomorrow night. Can you come to my office?"

"I'm single, so Saturday night isn't reserved. I'll be there."

At home, Ned was sprawled on the sofa, nose in a book. Mason sat with him and told him about the plan for Sunday.

"Do you want to come? You can see the sealed stairwell and the corona."

"I definitely want to see that," Ned said, "especially since I watched Gustavo dig it out of my yard."

"Maybe don't mention that to Owen and Sweet Marie. I didn't tell them exactly how I obtained it. It seemed too bizarre."

Ned scoffed. "That actually makes it easier—I won't have to talk about it."

Climbing into bed later, Mason noticed Ned was watching him.

"What?" he demanded.

"You seem so up," Ned said. "I take it this whole thing has turned out the way you wanted."

Mason kissed him, and moved closer. "It has been a resounding success."

"I know I tend to react."

"More precisely, you tend to freak out."

"Sometimes, yeah. But I see the success, and I'm proud of you."

"That's all I need to hear," Mason said, and moved closer.

Ned responded by meeting his mouth and twisting his knee over Mason's, initiating sex. Despite his aching muscles, Mason didn't hesitate to dive into it.

Fourteen

Alone in bed when the alarm sounded, Mason slapped it off and dragged himself up, swinging his feet to the floor and rubbing his eyes. It was cold, leaving the warmth of the covers, but he forced himself to stand, and got dressed. Ned was having breakfast at the counter in the kitchen.

"You're up early," he said, glancing at him in surprise.

"I've got stuff to do," Mason said irritably.

"I'll make you some coffee."

Mason sat on a stool and ate some fruit, sipping gratefully at the steaming mug of espresso Ned brought over.

"What's so pressing that it forced you out of bed at this extreme hour?" he asked.

"I have to get more furniture for my office. I hope Ruben is available."

"Is that the guy who hauled your desk downtown?"

"He's also strong as an ox. He practically carried the desk by himself."

Ruben was available, Mason learned, after he'd imbibed enough caffeine to be able to phone him and talk sense. They arranged to meet in a couple of hours at the giant thrift store. Mason changed into a black polo shirt—he had a séance later, after all—and cycled to the metro. Riding the train to Lincoln Heights, his phone rang.

"Hey, Mr. Yoshida," he said, picking up.

"It sounds like you've been busy," Yoshida said.

Mason explained about the melioreum, and the corona, not outlining how he'd obtained it, but inviting him to the crowning tomorrow. Yoshida didn't seem all that surprised at the story.

"Do you think you could tell people about the significance of completing the building?" Mason asked. "That's kind of what freemasons do, isn't it?"

"I'd be happy to say a few words," Yoshida said.

At the thrift store it took a bit of time to find the right table, as it had to be round, but eventually he found one that was a reasonable size and had sturdy legs. He paid for it and had the clerk put a SOLD sticker on it, but Ruben wasn't here yet, so he wandered through the furniture, stopping to check out a low sofa, upholstered in solid cobalt blue.

Ruben appeared at his elbow, his bushy mustache starting to show some gray, his little belly protruding above his belt. He studied the sofa with Mason. "It's long enough even you could sleep on it."

"It's kind of perfect, don't you think? It could go

against the far wall, if I moved one of the bookcases."

"You'd have to get it cleaned."

"Easy," Mason said. "Let me pay for it, and we can load it on your truck."

A store staffer helped get the sofa and the table, and the chairs that went with it, loaded into Ruben's truck. Mason watched him tie everything down, and climbed into the cab for the ride downtown. The two of them carried everything into the freight elevator and then down the hall to his office. Ruben knew well how to manipulate furniture, and gave him clear instructions, which made it seem easy. He helped Mason position the pieces, placing the new round table in the void of open floor that had so concerned Peggy. Before he left, Mason paid him for his work.

His arms ached and he felt sweaty, but he didn't have time to stretch out on the lengthy new sofa, despite how inviting it looked. Instead he walked up the street to the library and spent the afternoon reading about psychic grounding.

It seemed to be more about inducing equilibrium than about what Hanh had described, de-energizing. Some of the sources outlined psychic grounding techniques, and by the time he'd read through several more, he was satisfied that he could pull it off.

Walking out to the street through the library's little yard, the sun was gone, replaced by the twilight of the streetlamps. He stopped at a drugstore to buy tea-light candles and a lighter, then grabbed an espresso at his building, happy to find the place still open, and went up to his office. He slammed the coffee and set the tea lights in the middle of the new table, then stretched out on the new cobalt sofa. Ruben was right—it smelled gamey, and needed cleaning, but it was comfy.

Waking, he felt disoriented, wondering if he'd heard a knock or if that had been in the dream world. But the knock came again, and he rose, checking the time on his phone. It was too early for the séance. When he opened the door, however, there stood Astrid.

"I didn't know what to wear for a séance, so I wore this," she said, lifting her arms. It was a black body suit with a billowy black cape attached. A black sequined turban covered her hair.

"You look amazing," Mason said. "Come on in."

She looked around as she walked into the space. "You need better furniture. This junk makes my work feel sad."

"Lucky for me, you're not the boss of my furniture. I need comfort, not style. Designers always pick uncomfortable stuff. If I tried to sit on one of those Barcelona chairs at your house, it would collapse under me like doll furniture."

Astrid scoffed, and sat on the sofa by the window. "Beauty requires sacrifice."

The moment Mason sat in the adjacent chair, there was a loud clatter on the glass.

"What the hell?" he said, and went to the window the sound had come from. There was no mark on the glass, and nothing outside but empty air.

"It's just my visitors," Astrid said, waving languidly.

"On the tenth floor?"

"Think about it, Mason. They're not real, so they're

not limited by gravity."

He sighed and sat down again. "I wanted to tell you that I found out some more about the stairwell. Can you come back tomorrow afternoon?"

She grinned at him. "I think you like having me around here. What did you find?"

"You should come and see it. A visual is better than any words I could use."

"I don't know what more I could learn. I spent a lot of time in that space."

"I found a missing piece."

She leaned forward. "What are you talking about? A piece of what?"

"Come tomorrow and see for yourself. I don't want to bias your experience with my explanation."

"Can we go look at it now?"

"It's not here yet. It's being delivered in the morning."

Astrid scowled. "Such a mystery."

A blue orb floated past the window, seemingly just a few feet outside, moving quickly, followed by another. Mason watched them intently, feeling the hair rising on his neck, but didn't bother to point them out to Astrid. As eerie as it was, she'd made it clear this was routine for her.

He rose when there was a knock on the door, opening it for Hanh and Matt. After he introduced everyone, Hanh rubbed her hands together.

"Let's get started, shall we?" she said, walking toward the round table. "You thought of fire—excellent."

Mason took the lighter and started lighting the tea lights. Astrid and Hanh sat, scooting their chairs closer to the table, and Matt stood with his hands on the back of a chair, waiting for Mason.

"So you all know about my condition?" Astrid asked.

Matt and Hanh both said they did, and Astrid glared at Mason.

"Gossip," she said.

Mason could only shrug as he finished lighting the candles, and went to douse the room lights.

"Aren't we supposed to hold hands?" Astrid said, dubious. "Your table is too big for that."

"As long as we're all touching the table, it'll work," Matt said, and pulled out the chair adjacent to her to sit. "We don't have to be touching each other."

Mason joined them, sitting opposite Astrid. The flickering light of the candles illuminated their faces, but little else—they were all wearing black, Mason realized.

"Mason will guide us into the correct mind-set," Hanh said.

"Uh, sure," he said. "Put your hands flat on the table." He spread his fingers on the tabletop, palms down, and waited while the others did so.

"Where we want to be," he continued, "is calm and clear-headed. Let's close our eyes." He paused, and then spoke in a softer voice. "Clear your mind, and focus on your breathing. Feel how regular it is." Another pause. "Focus on bringing Astrid down to earth. Help her keep her feet on the ground."

"No matter what happens," Hanh added, "keep your hands on the table."

"Right," Mason said. "Stay grounded. I'm envisioning Astrid completely grounded."

They sat in silence for a while, the only sound

the rumble of traffic outside. Mason opened his eyes a crack, and beyond the candlelight glinting on the sequins of Astrid's turban, a few feet behind her head, was a glowing orange pinwheel, a spiral, like an illustration of distant galaxy, but alive, rotating slowly, the yawning black emptiness at the center obscuring the windows beyond. He quickly closed his eyes again, heart pounding, and envisioned closing that gap, pushing the void away.

Astrid moaned softly, as if she had a migraine, and suddenly the table jumped a few inches, landing with a *bang,* the candle flames bouncing and flickering.

"Fuck me," Matt exclaimed.

Opening his eyes, Mason saw that their hands were all still on the table, and Astrid still had her eyes closed. All around her head now was a glowing aura, distorting the windows behind, tinged with rainbow colors at the edges, pulsating.

"Maintain your focus," Hanh said quietly. "Just a little longer."

Mason screwed his eyes shut again, trying to clear his thoughts, and envisioned Astrid, wearing her funky black cape, barefoot on the sand, somewhere out in the desert, her form perfectly symmetrical and balanced, connected to the earth. He held the image until Hanh spoke.

"That's it," she said.

Mason saw that Hanh had pulled her hands off the table, and she was grinning—noteworthy because it happened so rarely.

"I didn't really feel anything, except the table jumping," Astrid said.

"You released a lot of energy," Hanh said, holding her gaze. "I think things should improve now."

"You could see it?" she asked her.

"And feel it."

"I think I saw it too," Mason said. "Rainbow colors."

"I saw that—vibrating all around her." Matt made a swirling gesture with his palm.

"Being in this building helped," Hanh said, and eyed her. "Astrid is emotionally connected to it." She turned to Mason. "It's no coincidence that you spent so much time here, and took an office in the building, and found the melioreum. You're attracted to this kind of thing."

"Yeah, I think maybe I am. Subconsciously, at least."

"What's the melioreum?" Astrid said.

"Mason can explain it." Hanh rose from her chair. "It was nice to meet you, but I'm out of time."

"Out of sequence, you mean," Mason said, and watched her leave.

After the door closed, Astrid looked to Mason. "What was she talking about?"

"The glass column. It's called the melioreum," he said, and explained what he'd learned about it. He'd hoped to save this for tomorrow, but Hanh had let it slip, making it inevitable that he describe it for Astrid.

"It makes so much sense," she said, leaning back in her chair. "I know Augustus Hawley was a freemason."

"More than that, he was interested in transmutation," Mason said, and they talked about it for a while, Astrid explaining more aspects of alchemy, which she knew about in surprising detail, and Matt chiming in sometimes with ideas about how it overlapped the scientific approach.

It was late when Mason locked up his office and rode down in the elevator with them. Matt gallantly offered to wait with Astrid until her ride-share arrived, and Mason bade them good night on the street corner, and went to catch the metro.

He was too exhausted even to shower, and climbed into bed beside Ned's sleeping form. Sinking quickly into the hypnagogic state, he started awake again with a feeling of dread. What if it was cracked, or broken? It had spent so many years in the ground, decades inside that dark drum, weathering countless earthquakes. It would be impossible to recreate—only Hawley knew how to make the glass, knew its crystal components and properties. He couldn't do anything about it now, he knew, and pushed himself back into sleep.

Mason woke to his phone ringing, and picked it up, squinting to find the answer button and mumbling "Braithwaite."

"It's *ha-bee* from the Primavera Building," a man's voice said.

Ha-bee, Mason thought, his mind still half asleep, trying to parse the word. Harvey? No, he decided, it was Javi, short for Javier.

"How's it going?" he mumbled.

"I'm picking up a package from you today," Javi said. "Where is it at?"

"It's actually an oil drum, and it's very fragile." Mason rattled off his address.

"I'll be there in half an hour," Javi said, and ended the call.

Mason rolled out of bed and went to the kitchen. No one was around, and he started the espresso machine, and dumped some muesli into a bowl, drowning it in soy milk. By the time he'd drained his second mug of coffee, he heard voices out front.

Ned had pulled the Crown Vic into the driveway, with buckets and rags lined up for his ritual loving grooming of the old beast. A guy in the familiar blue jumpsuit of the Primavera Building's staff stood chatting with Ned—this, presumably, was Javi. A little white van was parked in front of the Crown Vic.

Mason walked up and greeted them.

"You're 1020, right?" Javi said. "I think I've seen you at the building. I was admiring your boyfriend's wheels."

"They don't make them like that anymore," Mason said, raising his eyebrows. He knew it was inane, but it always got a positive response from classic car people, like a magic phrase to open a locked door.

"That's exactly what I'm saying," Javi said, waving at the Crown Vic.

Ned caught Mason's eye and shot him a grin.

"Let me show you the drum," Mason said. "It's in the garage."

Javi followed him inside and sized it up, folding his arms.

"This bolt is how you open it," Mason explained.

"It's completely rusted out," Javi said, feeling it with his fingers. "Do you care about keeping the drum itself?"

"All that matters is the contents."

"Maybe I'll cut into it, then, right about here." He drew a line with his finger, a few inches below the hoop closure.

"That'll work. The bulk of the object is farther down, under a lot of packing material. It's made of glass, and it's very fragile."

"As you mentioned earlier," Javi said. "I'll be careful."

With Ned's help, they loaded the drum into the empty van, where Javi threw a moving blanket over it and then lashed it to the wall with bungee cords.

Javi was soon on his way, waving as he pulled the van into the street and headed down the hill.

"How did he know you were my boyfriend?" Ned asked.

"I suppose Owen and Sweet Marie told him. Owen calls you my 'hot boyfriend.'"

Ned laughed heartily. "That's quite a compliment, coming from a teenager."

After lunch, when they were getting ready to leave, Mason checked on his suit, still folded up in the trash bag in the bottom of his closet. Miraculously it didn't smell like he'd been sweating in it for several days, and only held the faintest whiff of tobacco smoke. It bore nary a wrinkle either; the futuristic fabric never seemed to need ironing or cleaning. As he got dressed, pulling on the jacket, he decided to forgo the fedora.

Ned came into the bedroom and stopped short. "You're getting dressed up? That means I have to."

"You could wear your gym clothes, and you'd still look better dressed than me," Mason said.

"You do look great in that suit," Ned said, giving him the once-over. "Maybe I'll just do a tie but skip the jacket."

Mason sat on the chair at the foot of the bed and watched Ned change. He pulled on a pair of black trousers and a royal-blue shirt, then added a leopard-print necktie. It didn't matter what he wore, Mason knew, he always looked sharp.

"We'll take the Barracuda, I think," Ned said, checking himself in the floor mirror.

"With that necktie, it's the only sensible option."

Ned backed the car out of the garage, its throaty engine rumbling, and Mason climbed in. Despite the Barracuda's potential for speed, Ned's driving was calm and confident. When he pulled into the garage of the Primavera Building, they climbed out, and Ned handed the keys to the valet.

"I'm in 1020," Mason told him, and they took the elevator to the top floor.

"Hey, guys," Owen called to them as they stepped out. He was over by the stairs to the roof, wearing a sport coat and jeans, and had tamed his hair by tying it back. "That thing is crazy-looking."

"The corona?" Mason said. "Where is it?"

"The guys opened the can in the basement and took it up to the roof," Owen said. "Before we go, though, let me pay you for all your work."

"I'll be around during the week," Mason said.

"It'll just take a second. Come on in."

Ned and Mason followed him into the penthouse, where a long table had been set up in the wide space between the door and the first grouping of furniture.

Two uniformed waiters were arranging trays of food around a dramatic floral centerpiece. There was enough food on display for twice as many people as they'd decided to invite. At the end of the table closest to the entrance was an oversize card with CATERED BY ARTÉMISE written on it in formal bold script.

"Wow," Ned said, stopping beside the table. "Artémise only does vegan food—this whole spread is vegan?"

"We're both eating vegan these days," Owen said.

"Right on," Ned said. "Is that a bar?"

Mason saw it now, farther inside, another table with a woman in a black vest and a bow tie setting out glasses.

"I wasn't sure if we should do that, considering the time of day, or just have soft drinks," Owen said.

"I can see at least six bottles of Veuve Clicquot," Ned said.

"Artémise thought we should play it safe. It's a celebration, after all. It's Sunday, so mimosas, right?"

"I wouldn't waste good champagne on a mimosa," Ned said. "Use the cheap stuff."

"Good to know," Owen said, raising his eyebrows. "I'm not really into booze."

Ned clapped him on the shoulder. "In my experience, it's a waste of your time."

Owen led them to the kitchen space, one of the few walled-off parts of the penthouse, although there was no door, just a wide entryway. When he opened a cupboard, tall enough that it was probably intended to store mops and brooms, Mason saw there was a safe—a modern one, not like the door into the stairwell—on the floor, filling the bottom third. Owen squatted and typed a four-digit number into the keypad. The lock beeped and he pulled it open, then took out a grocery-store cardboard box and set it on the floor. It was half full of bundled cash.

"Whoa," Ned said.

"I know, it should be in a bank," Owen said, squatting beside the box. "But a lot of people want to get paid in cash." He looked up at Mason. "How many days am I paying you for?"

"Let's see," Mason said, and thought about it, counting in his head. "Eight, if that's not unreasonable."

"That sounds fine," Owen said, and counted out eight bundled stacks. They were twenties, and each bundle bore a purple band marked $2000. He rose and offered them to Mason with both hands.

"I thought I told you I charged five hundred a day," Mason said, not reaching for them.

Owen looked confused. "OK, so how many of these?"

"Just two," Ned said.

Owen nodded, and handed over two stacks, dropping the others back in the box, and then locking them in the safe.

"Thanks," Mason said. "Do you need a receipt or anything?"

"Nah," Owen said.

"You're not going to run through all this money in a year or two, are you?" Ned asked, putting his hands on his hips.

Owen grinned at him. "I'm sure it seems like I'm flaky about it, but we have an accountant, and a woman who handles investments, and all that. Let's go upstairs."

Mason tucked the bundles into his jacket pockets, but they were too bulky. In the elevator lobby, he told Owen, "I need to stop in my office for a second. I'll catch up."

Ned came with him, trotting down the stairs behind Mason.

"I love this," Ned said, admiring Mason's name on the office door. "The yellow really pops."

"Loud and proud, toots," Mason said, unlocking the door and pushing his way inside.

Breaking the band on one of the bundles of cash, he stuffed a sheaf of them in his pocket, then put the rest in the back of his desk drawer.

"At least Owen had his locked up," Ned said, watching him.

"I don't think anyone looking at my furniture would assume there's anything of value hidden in here, do you?"

Ned looked around the office. "Good point. It is kind of thrift-store chic. You got the conference table yesterday? It really completes the room. Now you can have conferences."

Mason chuckled. "Let's go."

They went to the main stairwell and climbed up to the penthouse lobby, where the crash door to the roof stairs was propped open. An easel with a signboard on it bore a large arrow pointing up, with the words CROWNING RECEPTION.

"Those boys could do party planning," Ned said. "They thought of everything."

As he headed up the stairs, Mason said, "Sweet Marie does drag. Drag queens do not mess around when it comes to stuff like this."

When they got to the top, they found a small group standing near the platform that covered the top of the melioreum—Owen, Sweet Marie, Astrid, and a woman he recognized from the management office. As they approached, Mason saw that they were gathered around the corona, perched on a furniture dolly with big casters. The four of them were captivated by it, and Mason stared at it in awe along with them—this was his first look at the whole thing. In real life it was so much more dramatic than Hawley's drawings. He hadn't expected the glass to be so dark. In the bright sunlight it was a deep translucent shade of sea green.

"That's what was in the drum?" Ned asked quietly as they walked over.

"That's it," Mason said.

Sweet Marie looked up as they approached. His strong nose looked narrower in the daylight, perhaps because he was wearing subtle makeup, along with a light jacket in sparkly flowing lamé. "Can you believe this thing? It looks like someone dropped a rock in a pond, and the water froze in mid-splash."

Stepping around it to get a better look, Ned said, "Or an artichoke frozen halfway through exploding."

Mason nodded. "Or a melted pineapple."

Astrid was wearing a simple red dress, and beaming as she admired the corona. "We talked about this," she said to Mason. "Behold an *objet* that gives you a glimpse of the true nature of reality."

"Does it?" Mason said, inspecting the corona more closely and stepping around it. No cracks were visible, and nothing seemed to be broken off—that was a relief. But a glimpse of the true nature of reality—of that, he wasn't convinced. The more he looked into the glass, though, the more he thought he might be getting a sense of what she meant. Gazing at the surface of the spiky mass was like looking into the sea in the tropics.

The domed skylight was gone, Mason saw, once he'd stopped ogling the corona, revealing a flat surface atop the box with the ventilation grate. It had been built as a platform meant to support the corona. He stepped closer and looked at the top of the column, protruding through a ring of black sealant. Only the outer part of the column was glass, he saw. The core looked like some kind of fibrous material, maybe wood. The column was perfectly round but the shape of the core was ovoid, and positioned off-center in the glass, closer to the street side of the column, so that the thicker part of the glass faced into the building. Hawley would have designed it that way.

"Does the corona look like it'll fit?" Mason asked.

"Javi said it will," Sweet Marie said, gesturing broadly, his shiny jacket billowing. "He measured. But it's hard to believe it'll make the column brighter."

"I have no doubt about it, dear boy," Astrid said. She seemed to be wearing a permanent smile today. That was understandable, Mason thought, given that they'd figured out for certain what the melioreum was, a mystery she'd lived with for years.

Teresa from 920 appeared at the top of the stairs, wearing a sports top and black leggings, her dark hair pulled into a tight bun. She made a beeline for Mason. He was probably the only person here that she knew, he realized.

"What's going on?" she asked him.

Mason briefly explained that the void in their offices was a stairwell, and what the corona was for.

"How did you find all this?" she asked, gaping at the corona, its bizarre form demanding attention.

"Too big a story for today," Mason said. "This is Ned, my boyfriend."

Before long they were chatting about dog couture, and Mason saw Yoshida come up the stairs, and went to greet him. He was wearing a sweater-vest, like Hawley had, and clip-on sunglasses. Mason introduced him to Owen and Sweet Marie.

"You've acquired a real gem, gentlemen," Yoshida said, seemingly unfazed that the owners of the building were teenagers.

When Miss Cassie arrived, Mason introduced her to Ned.

"It's nice to put a face to the name," she said, beaming at him.

"The face of all Mason's angst?" Ned asked, raising his eyebrows.

She laughed. "Hardly."

Mason repeated his explanation of the melioreum for her, and Miss Cassie went over to examine the corona, like everyone else unable to keep her eyes off it.

Peggy and Matt appeared, and Peggy said to Ned, "I heard you've been doing some gardening."

Ned chuckled. "The yard got caught up in Mason's whirl of perpetual confusion."

Peggy went to gaze at the corona, then came back to speak quietly to Mason. "Matt told me about your excursion. Isn't it weird to think that thing has been buried there all the time we've lived in that house?"

"Extremely weird," Mason agreed. "I was thinking it was like the fossils in the tar pits. They're just kind of waiting there until someone digs them up."

"A fitting analogy," she said, "except the people who dig up the fossils didn't put them there."

More people were arriving, many of them faces he didn't recognize, and it was getting noisy, like a party. Javi and two other guys in the building's uniform came up and stood at the edge of the crowd. Owen stepped up on the platform that contained the stub of the melioreum and spoke loudly.

"People—quiet please."

He smiled at them, playing the benevolent host, reveling in the attention. *Such a teenager,* Mason thought.

"Thanks for being here," he continued. "Today we're adding the missing piece to the melioreum, which you'll all get to see afterward in our apartment. We wouldn't have this dramatic crowning piece, or even know the name of it, without Mason's hard work. So, thanks to LA's premier gay vegan psychic detective."

Everyone clapped. Mason held up a hand in acknowledgment and turned bright red.

"Thanks to Teresa, here," Mason said, gesturing to her, "for pointing out the missing space in our offices. Without her, we never would have got started."

After another round of clapping, Owen spoke again. "Mr. Yoshida is going to tell us a little about the significance of what we're doing."

"Owen is like a middle-age PR guy in a teenager's body," Ned said quietly.

"He's taking a speech class this term," Peggy said, leaning toward him. "I guess that actually works."

Yoshida didn't climb up on the platform, but spoke loudly, his voice booming, which was surprising given his slight frame.

"When we lay the cornerstone of a building," Yoshida began, "we symbolically make sure that the stone is properly set so that it will support the entire structure, both physically and intangibly. When we're certain it's right, we say that the craftspeople have done their duty. Today it's almost the opposite: we're placing an element that's not fundamental to the structure of the building, and in fact the building has stood for nearly a century without it. But in the architect's plan, this corona, as he called it, is fundamental to the building's metaphysical structure, and today I can say that Owen and Sweet Marie, the new proprietors, are doing their duty, and fulfilling this building's true potential by making it whole and complete. The company that commissioned this structure rejected Augustus Hawley's vision in 1929, and Astrid Luna, who's here with us today, managed to preserve it during her renovations just a few years ago. Today I think the world is ready."

They all clapped again, and Yoshida waved to Javi, saying, "Gentlemen, if you will."

Ned leaned toward Mason. "It's interesting how he managed to say all that without once saying that he's a freemason."

Mason nodded. "I guess they know how to be discreet."

Javi and the guys with him picked up the corona,

maneuvering it carefully, with so many eyes on them, and moved it up onto the platform, then lowered it slowly over the column.

"It fits perfectly," Javi announced finally, to a smattering of applause.

"It's directional," Mason called out.

Javi looked toward him. "What?"

Mason was standing at the back, as he usually did, because he was so tall, but now he stepped toward the platform. "The longest spike should be pointing due south."

"We can rotate it before I tighten the set screws," Javi said. "Where's south?"

"This whole part of the city is on the Spanish colonial grid system," Astrid said. "The Spanish thought every house should get equal access to sunlight. This wall faces exactly southwest, and this one southeast. So this corner of the building points due south."

"I bet Hawley planned that," Mason said. "I bet that's why he put the melioreum in this corner—it's closest to the sun."

"It's also the only corner not adjacent to other construction—just the streets below," Astrid said.

Javi squatted, and with both hands rotated the corona. "Tell me when it looks right."

With everyone watching, bright light suddenly appeared in a ring at the base of the corona, like someone had flicked on a switch.

"Stop," Astrid cried. "That's it."

Javi tightened the screws with a little wrench, and then stepped off the platform.

"It looks so perfect," Mason said.

Ned put his arm around his waist and gave him a squeeze.

"Let's go see what the stairwell looks like now," Sweet Marie said, loud enough for everyone to hear. In a stage whisper to Owen, he said, "Tell them about the food."

"You're all invited for snacks and refreshments in our pad," Owen said. "It's where we have to go anyway to see the melioreum."

They all trooped down the stairs, momentarily ignoring the table laden with Artémise's snacks and bypassing the waiters, and marched into the closet. As he approached, Mason could see bright light streaming out the safe door, swung wide open.

Peggy was ahead of him, and when she stepped into the stairwell, he heard her exclaim, "It's so much brighter now."

Other people expressed amazement too, and when Mason stepped in, he was rapt at the now vibrantly glowing column.

"How is it possible that thing is transferring so much light?" Ned said.

"I've no idea." Mason grasped the railing and gazed down along the now brilliantly lit shaft. "Hawley was a genius."

Astrid, a few steps below, enthralled by the melioreum, reached out and touched the glass surface. She had no effect on the light, unlike when she'd touched it before—her fingers had become inert. There had been zero paranormal activity around her today, Mason realized. The grounding séance must have worked. He reached out to touch the surface himself, and found it still cool despite its luminance.

"We've got to start breaking through those knock-outs," Sweet Marie said.

"Yes," Astrid said emphatically. "Put frosted glass doors and windows. That's what I wanted to do."

"Sign me up," Teresa called down to them.

"Me too," Mason said. "I'd love to have this kind of light coming in."

Gradually they wandered back into the penthouse, Mason feeling a little dazed from standing next to the bright light. He loaded up a little plate at the food table.

"How did you get this set up so quickly?" Ned asked Owen, standing at the table. "Mason said you just planned for this on Friday."

"It's the weekend," Owen said, "so they were catering half a dozen parties last night. It was easy to add our small event."

"Isn't this stuff amazing?" Javi said, his mouth half full.

Ned nibbled at a canapé. "For mass-produced food, it's not bad."

"I can tell they used mostly good-quality ingredients, at least," Peggy said.

"Of course they did." Javi eyed them as if they were both a little slow. "It's Artémise."

Peggy's eyebrows shot up in mock surprise. "The pop star? I adore her."

She didn't, Mason knew, and he had to grin. She and Ned could be excused for being food snobs. They'd earned the right, being so good at it themselves.

Hanh walked into the penthouse, and waved at Mason.

"You missed the coronation," he said, stepping over to her.

"I was just up there," she said. "It's a beautiful piece. It looks like it's exactly where it's supposed to be. Not languishing in the designer's garage."

"You know all about what I did, huh."

She grinned. "You told me yourself."

"Just not yet, in my sequence," Mason said, and bit into a canapé from his plate.

"I'm glad you liberated that object. It has such gravity, far beyond the physical world."

"It kind of feels that way, doesn't it?" Mason said. "Is that why you helped me retrieve it?"

"You've demonstrated that I can trust your instincts."

Mason eyed her appreciatively. From Hanh, that was high praise. He waved Owen and Sweet Marie over and introduced them, adding, "Hanh is a colleague in the psychic world."

Hanh shrugged. "I run a nail salon."

"I understand you helped Mason find the melioreum," Owen said.

"Indirectly, yes. It certainly improves the energy of your building."

Mason left them chatting about the melioreum, then loaded his plate with skewers of pineapple chunks in the shape of little ducks. Looking around, he saw that Peggy and Matt and Ned were out on the patio in the sunshine. Just the sight of them made him feel warm and content. He wondered if Astrid had left already, and walked back through the closet to the stairwell. Javi was standing in the doorway with a champagne flute in hand, and greeted him with "Hey."

Walking down a flight, Mason got lost again in the brilliant energy of the column, then found Astrid, sitting cross-legged on a landing.

"Pineapple duck?" he offered, holding up a skewer.

Astrid smiled. "No, thanks. I'm just appreciating the beauty of this object. Thank you for finding the corona."

Mason sat on a step. "I'm surprised how much brighter it is."

"Augustus knew what he was doing." She pulled her eyes away from the column and met Mason's. "I'm curious—I spent a lot of time going through Hawley's notes and drawings, and I never found anything explaining the melioreum. Not even a mention of it. How did you find it?"

"Psychic insight."

She grinned, and looked away. "So vague. But I guess that's what it says on your business card. It seems like a very tangible result for an intangible skill."

"There's more to the world than what we see," he said. "I know you know that, talking about glimpsing the shards of the true nature of reality."

"That's about art, not about finding lost architectural pieces."

Mason munched on his pineapple. "I get the feeling it's the same thing."

Also from Dagmar Miura

The Mason Braithwaite Paranormal Mystery Series

No one is ever quite sure whether psychic investigator Mason gets results with actual psychic power or his more mundane flatfooting, but the disheveled redhead manages to resolve some intractable mysteries.

mason.dagmarmiura.com

Penstock Canyon

While helping out a friend suffering from late-night visitations, psychic investigator Mason is confronted with aliens on the roof and other liminal beings that have him questioning the very nature of reality.

mason.dagmarmiura.com

The Slater Ibáñez Books

Don't mess with the hothead, or he might just mess with you. The first book in the series sees the insurance investigator running surveillance on an injured tech worker and tangling with blackmailers, party girls, late-night hookups with a gamut of guys, and a lot of bourbon.

slater.dagmarmiura.com

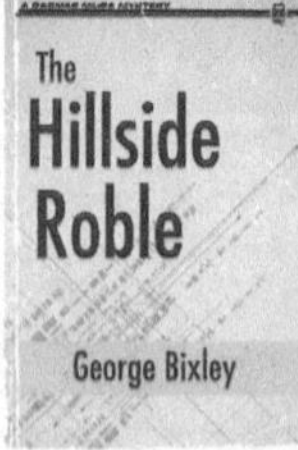

The Hillside Roble

Investigating a million-dollar heist at a gallery in the Arts District, Slater can't get a face-to-face with the owner, Eli, until he applies a little pressure. Eli turns out to be a minor celebrity, physically flawless but obsessed with his own image, and flaky in that uniquely LA way.

slater.dagmarmiura.com

Truman and Celeste

Sometimes all a woman needs is a decent man—even if she's not sleeping with him. Join Truman and Celeste as they troll the gritty underbelly of Los Angeles, never hesitating to slam that cocktail, hit on guys, or ask the next relevant question.

truman.dagmarmiura.com

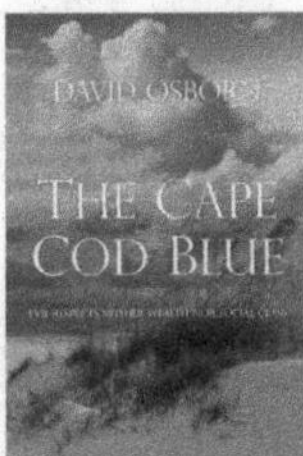

The Cape Cod Blue

The glittering, exalted world of art auctioning hides love, hate, and parricidal murder in a wealthy and socially prominent family when forgery of an anonymous Cape Cod painting is used to steal a world-famous portrait that's worth a fortune.

capecod.dagmarmiura.com

The Bone Bridge

Yarrott Benz, the 2016 Ippy Award winner for memoir, is forced to deal with extraordinary self-sacrifice in this harrowing account of teenage brothers, as different as night and day, trapped together in a dramatic medical dilemma.

bonebridge.dagmarmiura.com

The Psychic Vegan Cookbook

It has never been easier to cook vegan, and you don't even need to be psychic to do it. Whether your motivation is eating healthier or the welfare of other sentient creatures, Henrietta Flores guides you through plant-based versions of familiar dishes.

cookbook.dagmarmiura.com

www.ingramcontent.com/pod-product-compliance
Lightning Source LLC
Chambersburg PA
CBHW010347170726
48284CB00011B/2823